LESSONS IN LOSING IT

A Study Abroad Novel

JESSICA PETERSON

ALSO BY JESSICA PETERSON

THE STUDY ABROAD SERIES

Studying Abroad Just Got a Whole Lot Sexier.

A Series of Sexy Interconnected Standalone Romances

Lessons in Love (Study Abroad #1)

Lessons in Gravity (Study Abroad #2)

Lessons in Letting Go (Study Abroad #3)

Lessons in Losing It (Study Abroad #4)

FOLLOW ME, Y'ALL!

- Join my Facebook reader group, The City Girls, and hang out in one of the coolest spots on the internet. I'm biased, but I'm also pretty thrilled by how awesome the people in my group are.
- Follow my not-so-glamorous life as a romance author on Instagram @JessicaPAuthor
- Follow me on Goodreads
- Follow me on Bookbub
- Like my Facebook Author Page

Published by Peterson Paperbacks, LLC
Copyright 2016, Peterson Paperbacks, LLC
Cover by Najla Qamber of Qamber Designs

All characters in this book are fiction and figments of the author's imagination. Although the author very much wishes Fred's abs and general adorableness were real.

Editor: Kristin Anders

www.jessicapeterson.com

❋ Created with Vellum

Chapter One

FRED

Madrid, Spain
December

It's just after midnight, and the celebration is in full swing. Our squad captain's swanky flat is bursting with people, noise, and cigar smoke. The floor throbs in time to a catchy pop song as girls dance on a nearby table. One of them keeps looking at me.

Well, checking me out, really. Her eyes devour me from my legs to my chest, but they stop there. She doesn't bother to look any higher than my neck.

I slip out of the hall and make a beeline for the (relative) safety of the kitchen. The euphoria of tonight's win over our rival, Barcelona, is beginning to fade, and my knee is sore as fuck from the hit I took late in the match.

Being ogled like just another footballer piece of meat is not doing wonders for my very real desire to get the hell out of here and read *Harry Potter* in bed. I recently picked up the series, and while it's taken me a bit to get through the books

—football keeps me quite busy these days—I bloody love that little wizard and his mates.

I use the bottle opener on my key ring to pop the top off one of the beers I brought with me. I take a long, hard swig, wondering if it's too early to pull a Houdini.

I felt great on the pitch tonight. I helped the squad cinch a huge victory. I was on cloud nine, like I usually am when I'm playing footy.

But now? Now I'm tired and sore as hell, and after a half dozen post-match interviews, my capacity for small talk is nonexistent.

As a solid introvert, I prefer to recuperate alone after the craziness of a match day. Football is the only thing that energizes me—it's the only thing I've ever been good at—so I've practically lived and breathed the sport since I was fifteen.

It's not a bad gig. Not in the slightest. I may feel a bit out of place at these parties. I don't have to be here, but showing up keeps our captain, the flashiest Frenchman to ever walk this earth, happy, and it does boost morale to have the whole squad here. Overall, though, I love my job, and I'm fucking good at it. I get paid an obscene amount of money. Not that football's ever been about the money for me, but it's definitely a nice perk.

Another girl wanders into the kitchen. She offers me a smirk before her eyes latch onto my crotch.

"You are very big boy, yes?" she asks in heavily accented English. "Big feet. Big hands. I bet you have the big everything."

"Uh . . ." I scratch the back of my head. "Thanks, I guess?"

I mean, how the hell am I supposed to respond to that? As the only son of a single mother, I have a lot of respect for women. I'd never talk to a girl like this. Like she's nothing more than a pretty hole I can stick it in whenever I feel like it.

I suppose I'd like to be treated with a bit of respect myself.

Sometimes I wonder if I'm ever going to find the sort of girl I'm looking for—the sort who's genuinely interested in me and not my money or my body or my career. I'm looking for a girl who wants the same things I do.

A girl who wants to get serious, maybe have a family someday. Not anytime soon, of course, but I like the idea of being in a relationship with forever potential. I know Mum would love to see me with someone. She worries about me being so far from my family back in Germany. But I can't get excited about being with a girl like "big hands" Betty here.

I murmur an apology to her and duck out of the kitchen. I head toward the living room, which just so happens to be one room closer to the nearest exit. I've been at this party for a couple hours already and paid my dues. Time to go home.

I hang out in the corner of the room and quickly drain the rest of my beer. I'm digging my keys out of my pocket when Rhys Maddox, one of my few friends on the squad and our resident golden-haired heartthrob, claps me on the shoulder. He nods at a group of girls, all of them pretty and smiling, across the room. "Ready to go say hello? Laura's friends are lovely girls."

Laura is Rhys's American girlfriend. She's funny, she's nice, and she's really great for Rhys (even though he may not know it yet). Basically, she's one of my favorite people.

I've seen these girls before. They're her American friends she's studying abroad with in Madrid. I told Rhys earlier tonight that I'd introduce myself. Now I'm really regretting that decision. Hermione and Ron are calling my name, and my knee is killing me.

3

Shit.

"They're pretty," I say, feigning anxiety when really, I'm just impatient to *get the fuck out of here already*. "Really pretty. Forget it. I changed my mind. I can't go talk to them, not right now."

I'm about to turn for the door, but Rhys tightens his grip on my shoulder, turning me back toward the girls.

"Listen, mate," he says, "if you can't talk to girls after winning our most epic match yet, there's something seriously wrong with you. C'mon."

With a sigh, I let Rhys steer me toward the girls. I only have to play nice for two minutes. Two minutes, and then I can go home.

"Hi," Laura says, smiling at us.

Rhys smiles back, a big, dorky thing I've never seen on him before. "Feeling all right?"

"Yes." She turns to me. "Fred! I'm so glad you came over. The girls have been dying to meet you. This is my friend Vivian, and this"—she loops arms with a very pretty, dark-haired girl— "is Rachel, she really loves, uh, sports . . ."

Meeting my eyes, Rachel smiles and holds out her hand. I'm struck by the friendliness of her smile. It's a high-wattage, Julia-Roberts smile, but it's somehow sincere too. She meets my eyes as she takes my hand.

"Hi, Fred," she says. Her American accent dips a little, curls at the edges. "Nice to meet you. You looked really great out there tonight."

She gives my hand mine a firm, warm squeeze. My eyes flick down her body, back up again. She's petite—I practically tower over her—with a hot little figure. If I were looking to take someone home tonight, she'd be just my type.

Rachel drops my hand. I blink, mentally chastising myself for ogling *her* like a piece of meat. I don't like being looked at that way, and I doubt Rachel does either.

4

"Thanks," I say. "I hope you enjoyed yourself."

"We froze our asses off, but it was worth it," she says. "The energy in that stadium is ridiculous! It was so loud my ears are still ringing a little. Is it that loud on the field—the pitch, I mean?"

"Oh, God, yes," I say. "So loud you feel it in your chest. Other squads say it's the toughest place to play when you're on the road."

"You were really feeling some pain after that hit you took," she says. "Let me guess—patellar dislocation?"

I blink. How in the world would she guess that?

"Yeah," I say, slowly. "How'd you know?"

"I was close enough to the field to see the physio perform the reduction."

I raise a brow at that word.

She grins. "Means moving the knee cap back into place. Bet that hurt like hell."

"It wasn't that bad," I lie.

"Hence the dramatic grimace and screaming," she says, her grin deepening. She looks bloody pleased with herself for knowing just how much fucking pain I was in.

Smart girl.

I shove my hands in my pockets and bite back a smile. "You really know your medicine."

"Well. Trying to know, anyway." She shrugs. "I've done some work with the women's teams back at Meryton University—soccer, basketball. I saw a couple patellar dislocations last year on the court. If you don't mind me asking, how is the physio going to rehab yours? I'm thinking RICE . . ."

Her eyes, dark and intelligent, are on the hip in question.

"RICE?" I ask.

"Rest, ice, compression, elevation."

"Oh. Yeah—lots of that," I say. I'm still a bit bewildered. I've never met a girl who knew so much about sports and sports medicine. I sort of adore it. "The physio also recommended a knee brace for the next couple months."

Rachel nods. "Makes sense. Once you experience a patellar dislocation, the chances of it happening again get higher. A brace will stabilize your knee and hopefully keep everything in place. Anything else she recommended?"

"Just rest, like you said," I reply. "Some ibuprofen to help with the swelling. That's about it."

"Oh." Her shoulders slump. "I was hoping she had some cool new rehab trick—something I hadn't heard of. The sports medicine dork in me loves learning new stuff."

I shift my weight back onto my good knee. "Trust me, I was hoping for a cool trick too. I wanted to keep playing."

"Right? Nothing worse than being sidelined."

"It's bloody awful," I say. My pulse is thumping, and I'm not quite sure why. "You play any football?"

"Tennis, mostly, but I played a little bit of everything in high school—basketball, volleyball, soccer—sorry, *football*. I don't play much anymore. But I love to watch, you know, as a spectator, and I've gotten really interested in the medical side of sports in the last couple years."

"Do you have a favorite?" I ask. "Sport, I mean."

"To play or to watch?"

I'm grinning now too. "Brilliant distinction. Both."

"Well, American football is definitely my favorite to watch," she says. "But to play? I mean, if we're considering all sports, real and imaginary, my favorite would obviously be Quidditch. I'd make a mean keeper, although I'd settle for being a chaser too. If I had Nimbus 2000—oooh, or even a 2001, I'd gladly sell my soul to He Who Shall Not Be Named for one—I'm confident I could play any position, really."

I try not to stare at her. I cut a glance at the room instead, looking for Rhys. Am I being punked? Rachel is hitting on all my favorite things—wizards, sports, wizards *in* sports. I've got to be dreaming. This girl—this conversation—is almost too good to be true.

"Wow," Rachel is saying. "I'm being a huge nerd, aren't I? Sorry—"

"Seeker," I blurt. "I'd be a seeker."

She pulls back. "Whoa. A seeker? Really? Someone's a little full of themselves. I mean, do you really think you could beat out *the* Harry Potter for the position?"

I straighten my collar. "I do indeed, Rachel. And I wouldn't need the Nimbus 2001 to do it either."

"Just as long as you had your knee brace," she says.

"Exactly," I say, laughing. "No time for reductions on the Quidditch field, I'm afraid."

"Definitely not," Rachel says, and now she's laughing too.

The sound floods my ribcage with warmth. It's not forced, her laugh, or fake. I'd know, I'm an expert at coaxing belly laughs from my niece Lilli (pro tip: the peek-a-boo game goes a long way with a nine-month-old).

I have no idea what the fuck is going on, but I suddenly want to stay at this party more than I want to dive back into *The Prisoner of Azkaban*.

I'm suddenly having more fun with a real person than I would with fictional ones.

This is usually the point in the conversation when I'd excuse myself, pleading one of three vague, but believable, excuses—I'm fucking exhausted, I've got to go to [insert football-related activity here], or so sorry, but my mum and/or sister is calling me. My life is predictable enough that one of the three is usually true at any given time.

But right now, I actually want to stick around. See what else Rachel has to say about . . . well, *anything*.

I notice that sometime in the past few minutes, Rhys and Laura disappeared. Rachel's other friends are gone too. Can't say I'm not glad to have her all to myself.

"You know your sports medicine, and you know your Potter," I say. I don't know how it happened, but Rachel and I are suddenly standing close to each other. Very close.

"I do," she replies, tucking her long, shiny hair behind her ear. "I love anything with witches and vampires and forces of evil in it. *Harry Potter*, *Lord of the Rings*, *Tournament of Kings*. I love them all."

"Yeah. Potter's been big in Germany for a while now."

"That's right, you're German. Where in Germany are you from?"

"The south. A town called Weilheim in Oberbyern. It's in Bavaria. Best beer in the world there. I actually brought some bottles with me—want to grab one?" I ask, nodding my head toward the kitchen.

Rachel looks at me. She appears as startled by the invitation as I am. I'm never this cool or forward with girls. With *people*. But it's not every day I meet someone who's as into sports and fantasy fiction as I am.

"Yeah," she says after a beat. "Yeah, I'd like that. Everyone here is drinking this fancy champagne—someone said it was the most expensive in the world—but I'm more of a beer girl myself."

Jesus Christ, Rhys really must be punking me. Not only does Rachel like football and Quidditch—she likes beer too? I mean, seriously, what the hell is going on tonight? I feel like I'm in the twilight zone.

"Yeah, that's our captain, Olivier Seydoux, for you. Only the best of the best for that bloke." I glance back at her as we head for the kitchen. "So, you really like beer, huh?"

"I do. My dad's from Milwaukee, and my grandmother worked at one of the big breweries there. Needless to say, my beer education started at a young age. My high school friends thought it was so cool that my dad would let me have a beer with him when we watched college football—American football—on Saturdays." She rolls her eyes. "I was so badass back then."

I reach inside the cabinet where I hid my stash and grab the last two beers. "You're not badass anymore?"

"Meh," Rachel says with a shrug. She watches as I grab the key ring from my pocket and use the opener to pop the tops off the bottles. Her eyes linger on my hands. "Do you always carry a bottle opener with you?"

I spear her with a look. "You don't?"

"I don't. But!" She rummages around in her purse, and pulls out a pair of these little foam sleeve things. "I *do* always have a couple of koozies on me."

"Koozies? What the hell are those?"

"Watch and be amazed." She slips the first foam sleeve onto one beer—it's printed with white letters that read BATCAVE SPRING FORMAL 2016, MERYTON U—and then the second, emblazoned with a donkey's ass and nothing else, onto the other beer.

"You see," she says, handing me the one with the donkey ass, "it keeps the beer cold. Although we're not drinking it cold, so I guess it would just keep the beer from getting too warm from our hands?" She scrunches her nose. "I don't know. I guess it makes sense koozies wouldn't be a thing in Europe. Still, the beer's gotta be better than the champagne, right?"

"Abso-fucking-lutely," I say, and I mean it. I've never been one for the flash and excess my squad mates have embraced. That includes the champagne and thousand-euro-a-bottle cognac they like to drink. I've stuck to plain old beer, and I have no plans to change that.

Appears Rachel doesn't either. I bloody love her down-to-earth attitude. There's nothing fake or forced about it—a world away from the painted-on smiles of those other girls.

"At the very least, these koozie things keep you from

getting your bottle mixed up with someone else's, yeah?" I offer.

She laughs, crossing one leg over the other. Her body tilts toward mine, just a little, and suddenly the temperature in the room goes up a notch.

"Yeah," she says. "I'll take it, mostly because I got to show off my koozie collection." She holds out her beer. "Cheers, Fred. Congratulations on your win. And on your amazing theatrical performance, considering that patellar dislocation apparently didn't hurt."

"Thanks. I worked quite hard to get my performance just right tonight," I say, and now I'm laughing too. Genuinely laughing. I give her a little bow, my fingers brushing hers as our bottles tap on my way up. A ribbon of heat unfurls inside my hand, moving up my arm.

We hold our bottles like that for a beat too long. My gaze latches onto Rachel's and doesn't let go. She's feeling it too—this energy, this attraction between us.

"You're staring," she says with a smile.

"Can't help it," I say. "Sorry."

"Why are you sorry?"

"Because I hate when people look at *me* like . . . like I'm a piece of meat, I guess."

"I don't feel like a piece of meat right now."

"No? Good. What do you feel like?"

"Like . . . I don't know." She gives a little shrug. "Like I'm having fun with a really tall, really cute dude at an otherwise lame party."

I grin. "It is quite lame, isn't it? And here I believed I was the only one who thought that."

"Of *course* it's lame. I mean, it's amazing, but also lame. It all seems kinda fake, I guess—the schmoozing, the fancy champagne." Rachel shrugs again. "I'm having more fun with you than I would be mingling with everyone else, that's for sure."

This girl—it's like she's reading my bloody mind.

I close my eyes, take a deep breath.

"You okay there, killer?" Rachel asks.

"Yes," I grunt.

She laughs. "That's the least convincing 'yes' I've ever heard."

I open my eyes and look at her. Jesus, she's pretty. Lit up.

It's weird, but something about her laugh reminds me of home. There's always laughter in my mum's house. My ribs ache for days after I spend a holiday at home with my sister and cousins and Mum. I miss that.

We sip our beers. Rachel smacks her lips and lets out a sigh of satisfaction. "That's delicious."

"You like it?" I meet her eyes. Her irises are so dark they almost fade into the pupils. Almost, but not quite.

"I love it. It's different—tastes like a wheat beer, probably my favorite."

"I'm glad. These Bavarian beers can be a bit of an acquired taste." I take another sip. "So, the sports thing—are you planning to go into sports medicine?"

"I hope to," she says, setting her beer on the counter. "Maybe physical therapy or something like that. As a matter of fact, I had a phone interview for an internship at the Meryton University athletic department right before the match."

"That's brilliant," I say, and I mean it. "How did it go?"

She shrugs again. "I'm trying not to get my hopes up. But it'd be really awesome if I got that internship. My ultimate goal would be to work for a female sports team, but interning at the athletic department is a great way to get my foot in the door. The women's basketball team at Meryton is ranked first in the nation, and our soccer and field hockey programs are also pretty stellar."

"You know," I say, my heart skipping a beat, "if you want a tour of our team's training facility, all you have to do is ask."

"Yeah, right, I'll just ask for a tour of the training facility that belongs to the world's most valuable sports franchise. The facility that's more closely guarded than the Pentagon. No big deal," she says.

"Rachel, it's really not a big deal." She meets my eyes when I use her name. "If you want a tour, I can make it happen. Easy. I'll ask the club medical staff to show you the ropes. Might give you a better sense of what you're looking for. The club just built a new medical facility that is bonkers, and we've got a couple doctors on staff, plus fitness coaches, physios, even a sports psychologist. A bit of everything, really."

She blinks a couple of times. Looks away. Looks back up at me, her hair falling into her face. "Seriously? You'd do that?"

"Of course. You're in Madrid, for Christ's sake, so you might as well do it while you're here."

"Wow," she says, pulling her hair back. "I don't know what to say. Thank you. This is huge for a lot of reasons—I'm heading back to the States in, like, less than a month, and if I hadn't talked to you tonight . . . just. Wow. I'm the luckiest freaking person on the planet. Thank you."

I grin, even as my pulse slows, just a bit, at the knowledge she's leaving Spain so soon. Of course I'm hitting it off with a girl I can't fucking have. "Not sure if you saw how great I looked on the pitch tonight—"

"Now you're just bragging," she says, rolling her eyes.

"I am. But the squad really, really likes me at the moment, and they'll do pretty much anything to keep me happy. I'd love an excuse to exercise some of that muscle, especially on behalf of a mate's friend. The tour would be asking a small favor, nothing more."

"Small favor? Fred, I can't tell you how many sports medicine internships I've secretly applied to without ever hearing a peep back."

"Secretly?" Now I'm intrigued.

Rachel waves me away. Her eyes change. They're sad, I think. Sad or hurt. "Long story."

"How does Wednesday sound? I'll arrange everything, and I can send my driver round to pick you up."

She blinks. "You have a driver?"

"I do. I usually drive myself around, but it's always nice to have someone on call."

"Uh. Wow. Sorry, sorry, I know I keep saying *wow*, but this whole thing is just—I mean. Wow! I'm speechless. Wednesday works for me."

I smile. So does she. Bloody hell, that smile. "Great," I say.

"Great," she says.

I try to tamp down on the pulse of warmth low in my belly, between my legs. I really like this girl. She's different in the best way. I want to take her home, but I can't.

Don't get me wrong, it's not like I haven't fooled around with girls casually before. I'm not a monk. But every time I'd get physical with a girl without any intention of seeing her again, I'd end up feeling empty. Lonelier than before. Used, even as I felt like *I* was using *her*. It felt disrespectful on both ends.

I'm done with that shit. I've been done with it for a while now. Rachel may not have said outright she doesn't want to get serious with a guy, but she's moving thousands of miles away in a month's time. There's no way she's looking for forever with someone in Spain.

I am. Which may explain why I'm twenty-two years old

and still haven't swiped my V-card. Yeah, I'm not proud of the fact I'm still a virgin, but I suppose I'm an old-fashioned bloke. I want to fall in love before I have sex, fall for someone who will stick around for the long haul. I want to respect the woman I have sex with, and I want her to respect me too.

At this point, I've waited a long time to lose my virginity. Why not lose it to someone special? Someone who really means something to me? I think sex is sacred. It's important I get it right.

So . . . yeah. As attracted as am I to Rachel, as lovely as she is, I'm not interested in a casual hookup with her.

With a sigh, I tug a hand through my hair. I've been here before. I've been attracted to girls who clearly weren't my forever, and I managed to keep it in my pants then. I can do it again. The attraction fades. It always does.

But damn if that smile of hers doesn't make me feel fucking awake and alive and, yeah, more than a little turned on.

Chapter Two

RACHEL

Wednesday

I'm so excited for my tour of Fred's training facility I can hardly pay attention in my one and only class of the day. But I have some work to do—exams are coming up—and the driver isn't picking me up until later this afternoon. So after class, I run a few errands, then head to the Reina Sofía Museum. I'm writing a paper on a gorgeous Herman Anglada Camarasa painting that hangs in a gallery there.

I study the painting for a bit before sitting down to write in the museum café. It takes me way longer than it should to get started on the paper. Now I'm not only thinking about my tour, but I'm thinking about the cute, charming guy who made it happen—Fred Ohr, soccer star and all around stud.

Athletes are my type, and not just because I'm an Exercise and Health Sciences major. Fred is a big guy, with thick shoulders that taper into a slender but still well muscled torso (I may or may not have googled shirtless pictures of him when I got home from the party). I felt like a pixie next to him.

I liked it. Him. I liked him a lot. His unabashed love of

Harry Potter. His laugh. The way his blue-green eyes got all squinty when he smiled.

I noticed him even before we were introduced. He was standing off to the side, alone, nursing a beer. I wouldn't say he looked sad or anything. I mean, the guy was getting plenty of attention from girls at that party. But I definitely picked up on some loneliness there. I've felt lost at parties too—the old cliché of being in a room full of people but feeling lonelier than ever—so I could sympathize. Plus, I really liked the fact that he didn't seem interested in the flash and glamour his teammates so readily showed off.

I'd like to think Fred felt a little less lonely after our chat. I sure as hell did. I haven't stopped thinking about how much fun I had, talking to him.

How goddamn hot *he* was.

My memory of how Fred looked is crystal clear. He's handsome, but in a way that's totally different from the rest of the guys on his team. Guys like Rhys Maddox, who, with their smoldering gazes and cheekbones and ridiculous Euro haircuts, could easily be underwear models.

Fred is less classically good-looking, more square and masculine. His blond hair is cropped close to his head, and he had it combed in a hipster schoolboy swoop to one side. He's got a hockey player nose: a little too big for his face, a little crooked too, like he's broken it a couple times in epic fist-fights with the losers who threw him into the boards. I loved how imperfect his nose was. He was dressed in jeans and a blue sweater he wore over a white button-up. Simple, nothing fussy, but still sexy. I remember how freaking handsome he looked.

I liked that he was different. The other footballers were too much for me. Too pretty, almost. Too fake and perfect. Weirdly enough, they reminded me of Mom and her unap-proachable, impeccably put together, all-around-douchey plastic surgeon colleagues with their perfect fake teeth and fake faces and yes, fake noses too. Fred, with his crooked nose and adoration of Quidditch, is the complete opposite of that. By owning his dorkiness, by just unapologetically being himself, he made his flashy teammates—and Mom's colleagues—look like insecure idiots in comparison.

I'm so distracted by the memory of his enthusiasm for beer and the zing of warmth it sent through me that eventually I give up on my paper and check my email instead.

My heart skips a beat when I see a note in my inbox from the athletic director at Meryton.

The internship I've applied to—the one in sports medicine I really want—there's news.

My fingers shake as I guide the mouse across the screen. I open the email, my eyes moving over the words faster than my brain can process them.

You've made it to the final round of candidates . . . you will receive a call for one final phone interview . . . please provide proof you are able to find housing in the Durham area this summer . . .

"Holy shit!" I say, loud enough to make the old Spanish dude beside me look up from his newspaper.

I sheepishly offer him my apologies, then reread the email. Oh my God, oh my God, oh my *God*. The internship is prestigious and highly competitive. I've been waging a secret war for the past three years to get it. Ever since I left home for college—ever since I escaped Mom's ever-vigilant gaze—I've worked my ass off to put together the perfect sports medicine résumé: tons of biology, chemistry, and physiology classes, hours spent bugging the physical therapists who treat the women's teams, nights spent pouring over anatomy textbooks.

The sports program at Meryton is a big deal. In fact, it's one of the reasons I decided to go there. As a Division I school, we're home to one of the best basketball programs in the country—last year, the men *and* women brought home national titles. Our soccer and tennis teams also slay it on the regular, and our women's golf team is currently ranked number one in the nation. It's a sports lover's paradise, and it'd be a dream come true to intern there.

I've applied to dozens of other sports medicine internships, but this one is at the top of my list. Not only is the program amazing, they award scholarships for graduate school to interns who put in a solid performance too. That'd be huge for me. Plus, I'll be able to network with all the coaches, administrators, athletes, and physiologists in the hopes of landing a full-time position when I'm done with grad school. They make a habit of hiring former interns, which would be awesome.

Never mind the incredible education I'm sure to get while interning at Meryton. We have amazing sports programs, which means we have an amazing staff too. I'll be shadowing and learning from some of the best physical therapists and doctors in the world. Plus I'll get to travel with some of the teams, which would be awesome.

I fall back from my computer. Wow. Now that this sports medicine thing might really happen, I recognize how badly I want the internship. The thought of getting it and working at the athletic department all summer long makes me so excited I can hardly sit still. I want this. I really, really want this to work out.

Sports medicine combines two of my favorite things: sports (obviously) and science. Mom wants me to channel my interest in science into a career being a superwoman plastic surgeon like she is, but over the years, I've seen how her job absolutely consumes her life. How stressed she always is. How stuck-up and self-important she can be, along with the other surgeons in her practice.

I'd like a career that offers less . . . I don't know, superficiality, and more balance. I want to work to live, as cheesy as that overused byline is, and not the other way around. I want enough room in my life for things like travel. Books. Kids— lots of kids—and fun. I've talked to several people—doctors, physical therapists, trainers—and from what I can tell, I have a much better chance of finding that balance in sports medicine than I do in plastic surgery.

But I know how disappointed Mom will be if I don't go the surgeon route. And if there's one thing I really hate, it's letting her and Dad down. They've been so good to me. They've worked so hard to make my dream of going to Meryton University come true.

Probably why I haven't told them anything about my undercover mission to pursue sports medicine. Just the thought of having that call with Mom makes my stomach hurt.

I blink when an IM pops up at the bottom of my screen.

It's Mom. Of course. My heart falls. I don't know why I'm surprised, she's always had an eerie sixth sense of when to appear so she can convince me to stay on track.

I left you a voicemail this morning, she types. *I've been waiting for you to call back—I heard from Dr. Roby, the head of the anesthesiology team. Said he may be able to get you in for some shadowing this summer.*

I stare at the screen. I've shadowed doctors in Mom's hospital before, and I pretty much hated it every time. I can't imagine having to do that again instead of working at the athletic department.

I also can't imagine telling Mom I'm passing up anesthesiology for sports medicine.

Ugh.

Something must be up with my phone—I didn't get any voicemails today. Weird.

That's a lie; lately I've been avoiding Mom's calls. I need a break from her constant barrage of questions and suggestions and thinly veiled threats. Talking to her is exhausting.

Maybe you should get it checked out? It would be a catastrophe if you missed a call about an internship opportunity.

I roll my eyes. Of course Mom would use the word *catastrophe*. Like my phone dropping a call is on scale with a category-five hurricane.

I'll see what I can do, I type.

You need to make a decision soon. Have you applied to the research group I told you about? They are doing some great work with new rhinoplasty techniques. This summer is huge for you. That's when I interned at the Beverly Hills practice, remember? And I met Dr. Zhu, who got me into Yale.

Yes, I remember. You tell me that story every time we talk. Couldn't forget it if I tried.

You don't need to get so snippy, you know, she says. *I'm only trying to help. You have to do something with yourself this summer, and it'd better be amazing. I'm not paying sixty grand a year for Meryton for you to end up working at a gym. You can do so much better than that.*

I'm working my ass off trying to figure it out, trust me, I reply.

But even as I type the words, a well-worn feeling—something like panic—makes me short of breath. Two minutes ago, I was pretty sure about what I wanted. I wanted to get my dream sports medicine internship. I was so excited about checking out the training facility of the best soccer team in the world.

Now I'm not so sure. I'm not excited.

I'm stressed.

A familiar set of memories moves through my head like the slides on a projector. Mom's grinding frustration over not getting the promotion she wanted turning into a howl of joy the day I got into Meryton (her top pick for me). How the stress she wore like this heavy overcoat every day would disappear if I came home with all As on my report card. How I distracted her from another fight with Dad by telling her I'd take up violin, even though I *so* wasn't into music or instruments or the creepy lady who taught orchestra. She, however, was thrilled, mostly because she'd read somewhere that playing music helps increase your standardized test scores.

My mother is not the happiest person in the world. I recognize that. But when I make her happy—when I can make her proud—it's the best feeling ever.

I want to see Mom happy more often. I mean, duh, I love my mom. She's *my mom*. But her bouts of happiness never seem to last, which leaves me scrambling for another accomplishment, another achievement to wave in front of her. I keep thinking that maybe *this* will be the thing that tips the balance. This semester's GPA or this exam score or this internship will be the thing that finally *keeps* her happy.

Doing this internship at the Meryton athletic department is definitely not that thing. As great as it feels to make Mom smile, I can only imagine how awful it's going to be if I piss her off or, worse, disappoint her.

I don't want her life. I can't stand the superficiality of her world. The stress.

But I also want her to be happy.

I mean, maybe I should be more worried about ending up at a gym, the work-life balance I'm looking for be damned—although, honestly, what's wrong with working at a gym? A gym filled with athletes is my happy place.

Then again, maybe I should be shadowing anesthesiologists. It would look great on my résumé. Maybe I am wasting Mom's hard earned money by not working harder. I'm really lucky I don't have to worry about paying for college, and I definitely don't want to be the kid who freeloads off her parents' generosity.

But it's not like I haven't been working hard. I've just

been working toward sports medicine, not surgery. I've invested a ton of time in making this dream come true. I'd like to honor that.

I've just been really busy getting ready for exams, I type. *I'll get on my summer plans once they're over.*

All easy As, she replies. *At least this semester won't be a total waste for you—those grades will help your GPA, and medical schools will love that.*

Right, I say. *That's exactly why I came to Spain. To boost my GPA.*

That's my girl, Mom types, clearly not picking up on my sarcasm. *I can't wait for you to come home. We can work on the essays for your applications together. I already have some good ideas for the Yale essay—you know the one about rising to meet a challenge? I figure you can talk about the research you did at the oncology center.*

I fall back into my seat with a heavy sigh. When I think about pursuing Mom's route, I feel this surge of satisfaction at how thrilled and proud she'll be of me if I do pursue plastic surgery. But at the same time, my gut ties itself in knots. It knows it's not the path for me. It tells me in no uncertain terms I'm not going to be happy.

Mom will be though. Maybe her happiness will be big enough and bright enough to keep me happy too. I don't know.

I *do* know if I have to talk to Mom for another second, I am going to fling myself down the nearest elevator shaft.

Gotta run, I type. *Call you later.*

Good luck studying. Can't wait to see those grades!

I slam my laptop shut. Shut my eyes too against the sudden sting behind my lids. I swallow hard, and take a deep breath.

Today is a really great day. I'm not going to let Mom ruin it for me. How often do I get to rub elbows with some of the best physical therapy professionals on the planet? I'll worry about my summer plans—and my future—later.

I decided when I arrived in Spain this would be my semester of hashtag-YOLO. And so far, I've done a pretty great job of living in the moment.

This tour will be no exception. I'm going to enjoy the hell out of it. After that—who knows? Maybe I'll get lucky and enjoy the hell out of Fred too.

My heart is pounding as the driver—Fred sent a guy in a ridiculous black Mercedes to pick me up from school—glides through security at the gate to the football club's training facility. I wasn't kidding when I said the place is guarded like the Pentagon: fences and cameras everywhere, a guardhouse, even a couple security officers patrol the perimeter. I knew Fred's team was a big deal in Spain, but it's hitting me just *how* huge this whole operation is.

And how famous. A couple minutes ago, we turned off the highway and took an unmarked, one-lane road that wound through a mile or two of arid countryside before the giant training facility came into view like a spaceship that landed in the middle of nowhere. My driver explained that the facility "must remain hidden" so fans and the media, and even rival football clubs, can't get a glimpse of the players as they train. It's like their tactics are a closely guarded national secret or something.

I shiver. This is wild—the fact that I'm here.

Wild, and really exciting.

The driver makes his way through an orderly parking lot packed with brand new Range Rovers and sports cars with blacked out windows. It looks like the parking garage at Mom's practice, just with fewer Bentleys.

I wonder which car is Fred's. I don't know him, not well, but I get the feeling he wouldn't drive anything quite so flashy. Just doesn't feel like Fred—he's more understated than that.

I smile. I like how Fred doesn't seem to give two shits about what other people think of him. I mean, the guy was drinking beer and cracking Harry Potter jokes with me at a super swanky footballer party. Everyone else was busy getting drunk off fancy champagne and ogling all the hot girls there. Not Fred, though. I dig that about him.

Maybe that's why I'm so damn attracted to the guy.

Finally, the driver pulls up to the medical facility, all glass and gleaming angles, and hurries to open my door.

Thanking him, I make my way to the entrance. I catch a glimpse of one of several practice pitches just off to the side of the building. It's a cold day, a little before three o'clock; the sky is clear but already darkening, the blue tinged with purple. A couple guys are out on the field, running some pretty brutal looking drills. I can faintly make out shouts, a bark of laughter. I look for Fred's tall, well-muscled figure, but I don't see him.

My heart falls. He didn't say if he'd be here or not today, but I'd secretly hoped he would be.

I hope he's here. I really do. He still has my koozie, for one thing, and for another, I'd like to thank him—with dinner, maybe a drink—for putting this whole thing together. He doesn't know me, and he didn't have to help me out. But he did, and I want to show my appreciation.

I'd also like to make out with him, pretty badly. It could be totally one-sided, but the attraction I felt between us practically sizzled. I'm getting tingles just thinking about it.

I head inside the training facility, and I'm immediately greeted by a cute woman, forty, maybe forty-five, in a snazzy Madrid tracksuit. Her name is Valentina, and she is the first team physiotherapist—meaning she works with the best players on the team to prevent and rehabilitate injuries.

Valentina doesn't speak great English, so I get to practice my Spanish as she gives me a tour. She's warm, friendly, and has a great, self-deprecating sense of humor; she answers all my idiot questions patiently. I have a lot of them. Like, a *lot*. Probably because I'm so enthralled by everything I see and everything she says I can hardly stand it.

We start in the training facility's main building, a gargantuan complex that is as big as a mall. Maybe even bigger. It's *sick*. Not only is there an Olympic-sized pool, there are actual treadmills and stationary bikes in the water. We pass through an enormous gym, an indoor running track, two weight rooms, massage therapy rooms, saunas and steam rooms, and a mod, chic-looking cafeteria. Everything is new and clean and state of the art.

My head is on a swivel.

Players greet Valentina as they pass us. She asks one guy about his knee, promises to help another with his hamstrings. She turns to me, eyes lit up, and for the next twenty minutes tells me all about hamstrings and how to rehabilitate them and how to keep from hurting them and how they work. Her delight is infectious. Her smile grows and so does mine, even though I don't understand half of what she's saying.

How different she is from my self-important, status-obsessed mother, who throws her nose in the air as charges down the halls of her fancy high-rise office (lest anyone think she is not super important, she practically sprints from one appointment to the next in her Jimmy Choo stilettos).

After my tour, Valentina and I pore over her schedule in her office—she's filling me in on what her typical day looks like. It seems she's got a pretty great work-life balance and has time for both work and play. She says with two kids and a husband who also works it's not easy, and some days are absolute hell. But for the most part, she enjoys her time at the facility and at home. Her job is interesting and challenging. She knows she is part of something bigger, something important.

I don't know Valentina well, but I can tell she's a happy person. It radiates from her. She is patient and kind and down to earth. She lights up when she talks about her kids, her work, her husband.

This—finding this kind of life—this is what I want. My own version of this kind of contentment. Of *balance*.

If I could just find the courage to go after it, instead of toeing the line and doing what Mom wants me to do.

I'm asking Valentina about her post-graduate path when a familiar voice sounds at the door.

"Enjoying yourselves, ladies?"

I start, my pulse leaping as I look up. *Fred.*

He fills the doorway, leaning a hip against the jamb. He's still in his practice clothes—black compression tights underneath shorts, a sweatshirt, gloves, cleats covered in grass—sweaty and huge and smiling.

It's like a bullet straight to the chest. I grab onto the edge of Valentina's desk, hoping my legs don't buckle as I meet his eyes. I can smell him from here. Soap, something simple but clean, cut with an edge of sandalwood.

Heaven help me.

I think it's safe to say I am attracted to Fred. Very, very attracted.

"Hello, Fred," Valentina says in heavily accented English before switching to Spanish: *I am having fun showing Rachel around. I can tell she likes it here.*

"Hey," I manage.

"You came," he says, his eyes getting all squinty with pleasure.

"This place—it's pretty incredible, Fred," I say. "Thank you. Seriously. I can't thank you enough."

"My pleasure." I love his weird little accent, his words flavored with German, a bit of British too. I guess it makes sense that he'd have a British accent since he does play with a bunch of guys from England.

He glances at Valentina. "Are you done with Rachel yet? I don't want to rush you . . ."

"She is very much yours now, yes," Valentina says with a knowing grin. She kisses my cheeks.

Come back anytime, Rachel, she says in Spanish. *If you're interested, we have a formal internship program you can apply to for the spring. It is very competitive, but also a fantastic opportunity. You are always welcome here. Mostly because I've never seen Fred smile like that.*

Color creeps into Fred's face as he laughs. Man, he's cute. Hot. Huge. He is all those things, and it is all I can do not to stare.

He tilts his head. "Come on, then, Rachel. There's something I'd like to show you."

Chapter Three

RACHEL

Fred helps me into my jacket—as if being super hot wasn't enough, he's also a gentleman, *I am dying*—and I follow him out of the building. Our breaths billow around us in a thin cloud as we head toward one of the practice pitches. The sun is setting, igniting the sky with one final blast of colors: oranges that burn to reds, pinks that fade to violet. I pull my hand out of my pocket and hold it up against the searing light to get a better look at the pitch, the cold air filling my lungs.

A goalie is still working inside the net with a coach, launching himself again and again after balls the coach kicks his way. The guy moves with lethal speed, his footwork immaculate, his athleticism apparent in the way he jumps, runs, anticipates the ball. It's like watching a dance.

"That's Alexsandr Fernandez," Fred says as he leads me onto the pitch. "He's probably the best goalie in the world right now. Brilliant, isn't he?"

"He's amazing," I breathe. The turf swishes underneath our feet. Fred's cleats catch in it, making this short, raggedy sound. The field is giant—much bigger than I thought it'd be. "You sure I'm allowed to be out here?"

Fred looks at me. The sun catches in his hair and on his pale eyelashes. "You're with me," he says. "Of course you're allowed out here."

The possessive way he says that—you're with *me*—has my pulse doing this funny thing where it throbs and skips all at once, hyperaware of the way Fred moves beside me. He's at home on the pitch, that much is clear, and his stride is enormous and confident as we keep moving.

He owns this place.

I kinda sorta want him to own me too.

Again, it could be totally one-sided, but I think the space between our bodies sparks with energy. Want too. God, I bet this guy would be an unbelievable lay. He's so big, and the confident way he moves on the pitch, and those giant hands of his . . .

Alexsandr raises his hand, waving us over. "So she *does* exist!" he calls, a smile lighting up his face. "Come on, then, I've got to meet this girl."

"Oh, Jesus," Fred mutters, running a hand up the back of his head. "Rachel, I swear I didn't say anything—"

"Well, aren't you just lovely," Alexsandr says. His accent is British, thicker than Fred's. He drops the ball and pulls me into a hug. "Sorry, love, I'm a bit sweaty, but I'm just so bloody happy Fred's brought a girl round I can't help it. I've heard great things about you—Rachel, is it?"

"Um. Uh. Yeah?" I manage, my words muffled by Alexsandr's bright orange singlet.

"Olivier's been running his mouth again, has he?" Fred sighs and runs a hand up the back of his head.

"Indeed he has. Said he saw you chatting it up with a lovely dark-haired lady at the party the other night, and it wasn't long before we uncovered her identity." Alexsandr pulls back, holding me by the shoulders. "So when's the wedding?"

"Oh," I say, my body prickling with heat from head to toe. "Oh, well, Fred and I—we're not—I'm just—medical staff?"

"Adorable," Alexsandr says, and plants a kiss on my forehead. "Welcome to the family, love. We're glad to have you."

"Rachel and I are—uh—just acquaintances," Fred grinds out, untangling me from his teammate's grasp. "For God's sake, Alex, you're suffocating her. Don't you have somewhere to be?"

"I don't." Alexsandr grins down at me. He's hot in a very footballer way—dark hair that's cropped in a slick Euro-hipster syle, a thick, well-trimmed beard I'd call conquistador-chic. I can see why he's a favorite of the girls here in Spain, but I for one prefer Fred's unique, effortless handsomeness. "Have you got any friends, love? Seems Fred's passed on his dry spell to me, and I could use a bit of company going into the holidays—"

"Goodbye, Alex," Fred says. He grabs my hand and tugs me across the pitch.

"Lovely meeting you, Rachel," Alex calls after us. "I'll be on the lookout for an invitation to the wedding!"

I stumble after Fred, laughing. "What's up with that guy? He's hilarious."

"If by *hilarious* you mean *hilariously awful*, yes, I agree."

"He's your friend, then?"

"I don't many have friends on the squad, so no. I'm sorry if he offended you. I swear I didn't say anything about us—you—to the lads."

I meet his eyes. He looks at me squarely, his gaze open, honest.

It hits me that I've been waiting for the other shoe to drop. Back home in Dallas, everyone has an agenda. Everyone puts on a mask and pretends. It's all an act, all fake. The same is true for a good chunk of the status-obsessed student body at Meryton. I guess I've been waiting for Fred to quit the cutesy Harry Potter act and show his superficial true colors. You know, he'd use the Quidditch angle to get me into bed or something, or he'd brag to his footballer friends about getting laid by an American chick. I'm so jaded it's not even funny.

But Fred keeps being honest and so damn *real*. It's taking me off guard.

"Are you usually so discreet?" I ask, casually tossing the question between us.

"Always," he says. "I like to keep my private life private."

My heart skips a beat. I admire that about him—he doesn't kiss and tell. Maybe chivalry isn't dead, after all.

Still, I'm more curious than I should be. I'm just . . . gah, I love how *real* he is. How genuinely at home he is in his own skin. He couldn't care less about impressing anyone, or flashing his talent or his wealth in people's faces.

I'm also loving the fact that Fred is so sweaty right now. Alexsandr was sweaty too, but Fred takes the I-just-spilled-my-blood-sweat-and-tears-on-the-pitch thing to a whole other level. There's almost something medieval about it, like he's some powerful, sexy blond warlord just returned from slaying his enemies in battle.

I blink. Since when have I had such an, er, *active* imagination?

I think I need to make out with this guy, pronto.

"This was a really awesome thing you did for me today. The driver, Valentina, the tour—now this." I nod at the field. "Thank you. I can't tell you how much I appreciate it. I owe you, big time."

He turns his head to look at me. The light, searing and bright, catches on the mussed whorls of his hair. His eyes get all squinty again when he grins at me. "You don't owe me anything, Rachel. I promise it wasn't much work at all to put this together. You're a friend of my mate's girlfriend—I was happy to do it."

We're on another practice pitch now. This one is bigger than the others with bleachers off to one side and huge billboards for Madrid's sponsors hugging the edges of the pitch.

I'm fighting a serious case of *who the hell am I?* I mean, I'm in Madrid, walking across the field where the best soccer team in the world practices.

I'm with Fred Ohr, a super-hot, super talented defender. Probably the most talented in the entire Spanish football league.

Probably the hottest, handsomest, most gentlemanly guy I'll ever have the pleasure of meeting.

I'm gonna hit on this guy. If it works, who knows what sexual awesomeness the next three weeks can hold? If it doesn't work, I have nothing to lose. I'm leaving the country, for God's sake. I'll never see him again.

I did ask my friend Laura—she's one of the Madrileñas, a group of girls I'm studying abroad with—about Fred. While she didn't know much about him, she said he doesn't really date much. Which could be perfect. Maybe he's looking for some honest, no-strings-attached fun, just like I am.

"What do you think of Spain so far?" he asks.

I grin. "I'm head over heels in love with it. I wish I could stay for another semester—"

"Why can't you?"

"Lots of reasons," I say with a shrug. "Mostly because I signed up to take the MCAT in June—"

"MCAT?"

"It's this big standardized test you have to take to get into medical school back in the States. It's eight hours long or something ridiculous like that. Totally brutal. I am *so* not looking forward to it, but my mom wants me to take it, so . . . yeah, I guess I'm doing it. But I'm enjoying Madrid in the meantime. I really loved Salamanca. One of our classes is this study abroad experience class—our program takes us to places all around Spain. We've done Barcelona, Granada, and a bunch of other cities. But Salamanca was my favorite."

He shakes his head. "I've never been. I hear great things, though."

"You've never been?" I tease, elbowing him. "What gives? Why haven't you been to Salamanca yet? It's amazing. Is there not a football team there?"

"Not since I've been in Spain." It's his turn to shrug. "And I suppose I've been busy here in Madrid with the squad. We travel a good bit, but I don't get to really experience the places we go. I also don't get a lot of time off, and when I do, I usually go home to Germany. But one day I'd like to explore Spain a bit more."

My heart thumps. This is my chance—I can ask Fred out now, or forever hold my peace. I'm not imagining this connection between us. The beer, the Harry Potter stuff, the honest, searching way he looks at me . . .

"So, let's go," I blurt before I can lose my nerve. "Let's go to Salamanca. It's an hour and a half train ride, so we can do it in a day. It's an easy trip. I'll be your tour guide so I can—um —you know, repay this favor."

"I told you, you don't owe me anything," he says, his grin fading.

"Whether or not that's true, you need to see Salamanca. Trust me, Fred, it's awesome. Please, *please* let me take you. I think we'll have fun together."

He slows his stride. His grin is completely gone now. I think I've turned him off—damn it, I didn't mean to be pushy!

He turns and faces me. Now he's *looking* at me, really looking, the two of us standing in the middle of the field. He's close again and I can make out the freckles that dot his nose and cheeks. I don't know what to make of his expression. He looks . . . uncomfortable, I guess.

Shit.

"Rachel," he says quietly, "are you asking me out on a date?"

I swallow. "Uh. Maybe? Yes?"

Keeping his eyes locked on mine, he takes a deep breath, lets it out through his nose. He tugs a hand through his hair, still wet with sweat.

"Listen, you're a really great girl, and I appreciate the invitation—"

"Oh," I say, letting out an embarrassed laugh because I don't know what else to do. Also, I want to die. His honesty was such a turn-on before, but now it's just uncomfortable. "Oh, God, this is awkward. Sorry. I'm so sorry, Fred, I thought—I misread—"

"I like you," he says. My pulse skips a beat. "A lot."

"Well. Um. Thank you, I guess?"

"And I'm attracted to you." His gaze moves down my body. I feel it as a physical caress and have to close my eyes. "I don't know if you felt it at the party . . ."

"Yeah. I did, kinda." God, did I. I'm feeling it now.

"I felt it too. Any girl who can carry on a conversation about Quidditch . . . Christ, Rachel, suffice it to say girls like you are few and far between. But as much as I want to—I can't."

I open my eyes, confused. "You can't? Do you, like, have a girlfriend or something?"

He shakes his head. "I don't mean to be presumptuous, yeah? But I know you're heading home soon, which means you probably aren't looking for something serious right now."

"I mean, yeah, I am leaving," I say. "So, starting something serious really isn't on my radar. It can't be."

"Figured as much." Fred spears a hand through his hair again. "But I am looking for something serious. Some*one* serious, I mean. I suppose I'm just a relationship sort of bloke. Which means—"

"Right." I look down at my feet, grinning tightly. "Means you're not interested in a casual date. Casual is pretty much all I can offer at the moment."

He lets out a breath. "Exactly. I hate to be lame—"

"You're not being lame. You're being cute. And honest. Not to sound like a total asshole—or make soccer players sound like assholes, I mean—but I never would've guessed someone like you would be so committed about *being* committed. I'm jealous you know what you want. I sure as hell don't."

I'm jealous of that someone he'll eventually find and get serious with. Fred seems like a really freaking great guy. A genuine guy. And yeah, I still think he'd be an even better lay. Not that I'll ever find out.

Disappointment presses down like a thumb on the center of my breastbone. Not only is this embarrassing. It's a total bummer.

Then again, what did I expect? Fred is famous, for God's sake. He's hot. He knows what he wants, and I have no doubt he'll find it with some very pretty, very lovely girl here in Spain who also happens to like beer and sports.

I am not that girl. Fred and I—we're clearly not mean to be.

I just wish he was less . . . deliciously ripped. Talented. Genuine. Maybe then I wouldn't be so disappointed.

"I appreciate that," he says, and the depth in his eyes lets me know he's telling the truth. "I was raised by a single mother, and she taught me to respect women. I just can't . . . you know. Use someone. It feels wrong."

I grin. This guy is honest—he's real—to a fault.

"I get it," I say.

"Do you hate me?" he asks.

"Of course not. I mean, I may crawl under a rock and die when I get home tonight, but besides that . . ."

He grins. "I'd still like to go to Salamanca, though. If you're interested in going as friends, I'd love to."

"Really?"

"Of course. I have a few days off coming up, which doesn't happen often. We're playing Galicia at home on Saturday, and then we don't have another match until the following weekend. I have Sunday and Monday off—would either of those days work?"

I look at him. I'm picking up on it again—that loneliness I saw in him at that party. Does he really have nothing else to do on his rare days off than visit Salamanca with someone he just met at a party? He said he doesn't have many friends on the team. Now I'm wondering if he doesn't have many friends, period. I didn't really think about this before, but I imagine it is difficult to meet people—good, genuine people you want to be friends with—when you're famous and living in a foreign country on top of that.

I feel for him. I want to help with his loneliness.

Only I wish I didn't also want to screw his brains out.

Ugh.

"Yeah," I say. "Sunday is perfect."

He runs a hand up the back of his head again, mussing his hair. It's an adorably shy gesture that somehow manages to be sexy at the same time. "Great. I'm looking forward to it."

"Me too," I say, turning away from him. The way he's looking at me now—it's too much. He's too real. Too sexy.

"Wait just a moment." He reaches out and puts his hand on my arm, looking up at the sky. "The thing that I wanted to show you—it's about to happen."

I look up, sucking in a breath at the charge of electricity that moves through me from his touch. The sky is a blank slate of purple now, darkening with each passing heartbeat.

We're breathing in synch, Fred and I, long, unsteady inhales and exhales that cloud above our heads.

I hear a *pop*, then another, and another and another, and I blink as the beehive-like field lights come on, illuminating everything. The grass and the bright white chalk lines. The massive goals. The stands and the training facility in the background. The enormous breadth and width of the field itself.

It's like I've been plopped on the pitch in the middle of a night match. The sky above might as well not exist. It's all about the field, what dramas happen here, what tragedies and triumphs are about to go down. Forget up close and personal, I'm actually *inside* this world now. The world of professional football.

Fred's world.

My heart's in my throat. "Oh, wow," I breathe. "Fred, this is . . . it's incredible."

"Still gets me every time." I look down to see him pulling up his sleeve. He holds up his forearm—his thickly muscled forearm, the skin crisscrossed by veins and ridges of sinew—to show me the goosebumps there.

I tug at the sleeve of my jacket. "I have them too!"

"Brilliant, isn't it?" he asks.

"Brilliant," I say, trying on a very bad British accent. "That's exactly how I'd describe it. Totally random thought—but d'you think you could play Quidditch at night?"

He blinks, like he's surprised by the question.

"Hm," he says. "Never really thought about it before. But I don't think you could. The rules let you fly—"

"—as high as you want," I finish, biting back a grin. "Which is pretty damn high with that Nimbus 2001 I was talking about."

He's grinning too. "God, you're a nerd."

"Pot," I gesture to him, then to me, "meet kettle."

"You really want to know what I think about playing Quidditch at night? Because now that I'm mulling it over, I've got some opinions . . ."

I laugh. How fun is this, indulging our inner Harry Potter fans together?

"Of course you do," I say.

He smiles down at me. Our faces got really close all the sudden. When did that happen?

For a second I think . . . I don't know what I think. My eyes flick to his lips. They're perfect and I imagine they'd be deliciously kissable. My own lips feel heavy, tingly.

This can't happen. Fred just told me that this can't happen.

I meet his eyes. They look hungry. A little scared. He makes no attempt to hide what he's feeling. And that, more than anything else, is what's turning me on right now.

I fall back. Look down, rolling my lips between my teeth. *Stop.* We're just friends. *Friends*, not future fuck buddies.

"I should get going," I blurt. "It's late, and . . . I, uh, have homework?"

He looks away. "Right. Of course. Sorry to keep you."

"Don't worry about it. Thanks again for today. Not a lot of people get to experience this."

"Don't think anything of it." He clears his throat. "I told the driver to wait for you out front. I'd drive you home myself, but I've got to stay for an appointment with the masseuse. Before you go, though, can I, um, possibly get your mobile number? That way we can make the arrangements for Sunday—"

"Yeah," I say. We've been communicating through Rhys and Laura up to this point, and the thought of having Fred's number in my cell phone makes my pulse hiccup. Seriously, I need to stop. "Of course. Sure."

All the way back to my dorm, I ride a tidal wave of—of

every good feeling that exists, I guess. The skin on my cheeks still tingles with the memory of the kisses Fred left there before I got in the car to go. As a matter of fact, my entire *body* is tingling. I can hardly sit still.

This doesn't bode well for the let's-just-be-friends thing Fred and I talked about. These tingles are definitely not the friendly kind.

He's not interested in me—he just told me he's looking to settle down with someone, someone who wants a serious relationship, like him. I am *not that someone*. Which means I need to wrangle my attraction into submission and move the hell on. There will be other guys. Guys who are as chill and as honest as Fred.

So, yeah. In the meantime, I'll just keep my hands to myself. I'm not stupid enough to fall for a guy I can't have. I can control my attraction to guy, no problem. Fred is no different from all the other guys I've wanted but haven't touched.

I've kept it in my pants before. I can definitely do it again.

Definitely.

Chapter Four

FRED

Later That Night

I sit down on the edge of my bed and suck in a breath. My knee is on the mend, thanks to a brace and lots of icing, but it's still sore. Valentina is doing a brilliant job with my rehab. Still, I wonder what Rachel would do.

I wonder how her hands would feel on my skin as she examined me. Her touch would be gentle, confident, and she'd be wearing this tight black dress underneath her lab coat—

I blink at a sudden rush of heat to my groin. Jesus Christ, fantasizing about Rachel playing doctor on me is the last thing I need to do right now. I just told her I only wanted to be friends, for fuck's sake.

But I can't stop thinking about her. About our conversation. About the way she looked at me.

And now I'm starting to want her.

I grit my teeth, trying to get my body under control. Bloody hell, I'm attracted to this girl in a way I haven't been attracted to someone in a long time. It was all I could do not to kiss her right there on the practice pitch. The way she looked at me after the lights came on—they way she joked about Quidditch—I bloody loved it. It made me feel . . . I don't know.

I suppose it made me feel like I was finally at home on that pitch. I've been with the squad for two years now, but I still fight a nagging sense of being lost in Madrid. I haven't really "found my people," so to speak. The lads are nice enough, but there's something superficial about their obsession with showing off their money. Hot cars, hot girls, hot parties—they can't brag enough about their exploits. And here I am, a virgin who loves wizards and cheap beer.

Needless to say, our interests don't quite mesh. I've tried to make friends. But no one likes beer and books quite like I do, and I can't get excited about dropping six figures on a bloody car. Coming from such a big, close family back in Germany, it's been an adjustment feeling so out of place. I miss being around people I know—people who know me.

I haven't felt known, not once, since I've been in Spain.

But I felt known tonight with Rachel. I felt like she could see inside my skin, like she understood what made my pieces and parts come together.

And I was tempted to kiss her, because I want to understand her too. Because she might be one of my people.

If that makes any bloody sense at all.

I tug a hand through my hair. Of course I want to know the girl I can't have. The girl who is leaving the country in a month's time.

I glance at my phone. I set my alarm—eight A.M. like always. Then I pull up my contacts.

My thumb hovers over Rachel's number. I shouldn't, but I hit the text icon anyway.

You awake? I text. *Knee's bugging me. Thought you might have some advice.*

She texts back right away. *I heard beer helps,* she says.

Bavarian beer, in particular. Something about the hops they use being an analgesic. Science!

I smile. What I wouldn't give to have a pint with her now. But that'd be crossing a line. Friends don't get pints together on random Wednesday nights. Do they?

Looking forward to Sunday, I say.

Me too, she types back. *I'll be sure to bring my koozies.*

Saturday Night

Slinging my bag over my shoulder, I walk out of the locker room. Bloody hell, I'm knackered. Tonight's match was one of the most physical I've ever played.

I hit the button at the bottom of my phone, and the screen blinks to life. I've got the usual texts and missed calls —mum, my sister, my agent.

And then Rachel's name pops up at the top of the screen. I ignore everyone—everything—and open her text so quickly my phone freezes for a moment.

OMG! she texted at 9:37 P.M. *That call was bullshit! The guy clearly had it out for you. I watched the replay and he def tried to bite your finger off after the whistle blew. Totally deserved a red card AND a punch to the face. Hope your finger is ok?*

My exhaustion disappears. I grin, even as I shake my head. Part of me still feels like I'm being punked. Rachel cracks jokes about Quidditch, about Bavarian beer. And now she wants to talk football penalties?

Seriously, how the hell do I *not* want this girl?

They had to remove the nail and one knuckle. Lost a lot of blood, but I'll live.

Major blood loss never hurt anybody, she replies. *Also . . . you're joking, right?*

I am. Finger is fine, I reply, biting the inside of my cheek.

God, I wish I could call her. I'd love to chat right now, maybe help me get rid of this second wave of adrenaline that's suddenly hit me. *Did you watch the whole match?*

Always do. All the girls in my dorm freaked out when you took your shirt off, BTW.

I rarely take my shirt off after a match—especially when we tie. But I took it off tonight because I had a feeling Rachel would be watching. It was shameless of me, I know. No use egging the poor girl on.

I did it anyway. Maybe because she's got me all hot and bothered, and I want her to feel some of my pain.

What about you? I type. *Did you freak out?*

I freaked out when I thought you lost your finger to an overpaid striker with a mullet, she replies, ignoring my question.

Christ, she's a smart one. Not rising to my provocation is the right move. It's totally wrong of me, I know, to wish she'd flirt back.

You think Cruz is overpaid?

Hell yeah I do, she says. *He hasn't put up a goal in five of the last six matches. Big contract, big disappointment. Also, he tried to eat you, so obviously I am not a fan.*

Didn't know you kept up with the league, I type.

I've been in Spain for four months. I know my football stats backward and forward.

"Of course you do," I mutter out loud, shaking my head again. Talking with her like this—it's so damn easy. It's *fun*. So much easier and so much more fun than trying to chat it up with the lads in the locker room.

"You've gone and lost your mind now, haven't you? Who do you think you're talking to?"

My head snaps up at the sound of Alexsandr's voice. He's half a step behind me, reading my texts over my shoulder.

"No one," I say, shoving the phone in my pocket. "Just, uh, texting. Yeah. Texting with my mum."

"Then why are you smiling like a bloody idiot?"

"Because . . . um . . . my mum. She's funny?"

Alexsandr blows out a breath. "How's Rachel, then? Are the two of you married yet?"

I scoff. "Rachel? I wasn't texting with Rachel."

"I saw her name on your phone, you wanker. Why are the two of you chatting it up? Going to meet her later?"

"No," I say. I sound defensive. Fuck. Why *am* I chatting it up with Rachel? I have no explanation. No excuse. "Rachel and I—we're just friends."

He claps me on the shoulder. "Keep telling yourself that, mate."

"That's my plan," I grind out.

A plan I've got to stick to.

Sunday Morning

I pull up to the nondescript grey building fifteen minutes early and manage to steal a parking spot right up front from a bloke on a moped. He flicks me off, honking his tiny clown horn at me.

I hold up my hands in apology, but I don't move. Hey, it's cold out, and I don't want Rachel to freeze while walking to my car from her dorm.

Rachel. My body leaps at the prospect of seeing her. I sent my last text to her just after midnight and woke up with a raging hard-on after falling asleep thinking about her.

I took care of the hard-on in the shower, telling myself this would be the last time I'd fantasize about Rachel naked and panting in my bed. Fucking hell, I want to touch her. I want to get to know her better, be around her.

But as much as I want all that to happen, I want the real deal more. I want to be in a relationship with someone, to fall in love with her, to have sex that doesn't leave me feeling lonely or used.

I'd also like to lose my virginity. I didn't set out to keep it this long. Mum raised me to respect women. Having random sex with strangers doesn't strike me as very respectful on the part of either party. I was scrawny as a teenager anyway, and girls weren't that interested in what I had to offer.

But then I went to play at the academy in Munich, and a few years later, Madrid drafted me. The girls were interested then, but not for the right reasons. They wanted to sleep with me because I was going to be a famous footballer, not because they enjoyed my sense of humor, or fit in with my family, or liked me for me. They had no respect for who I was or what I wanted. I was just an object to them, something to be won, conquered, used. So, I passed on their advances. I still do.

Yeah, Rachel may be different from these girls. But she's still not relationship material. She's leaving Spain in less than a month. I don't want to lose my virginity to someone who won't—who can't—stick around for the long haul.

I'm a bit sad, to be honest, that she *can't* be the forever girl I'm looking for. As far as I'm concerned, she's perfect. She respects me. She likes the same things I do. She's ambitious and smart and down to earth.

But she's heading home. She has big things happening back in the States—I wonder if she got that internship she was telling me about. She has no reason to stay in Spain, and I have no reason to leave. My contract is up for extension, and my agent is already negotiating with the football club here, the numbers are looking good so far. Really good.

So, yeah. Rachel and I will just have to enjoy our friendship in the meantime. When it's time for her to go, we'll say goodbye, and that will be that.

I just wish I wasn't so bloody into her. In my head, I know

I need to keep my distance. My body though—it keeps betraying me.

I run a hand across my face. Fuck me, I need to get a grip. This is not my first rodeo. I know how to do this. I know how to control the desire I feel for Rachel. The attraction. I've always been a mind-over-matter chap.

Only it's never been so difficult before. It's never happened so damn quickly—the attraction. The connection.

I sigh, tug at my jeans. Double check in the rearview mirror that I don't have anything in my teeth. Run my hand across my face again.

I spent longer than I usually do at the sink earlier, shaving my face to within an inch of its life. I spent even longer getting dressed, settling on a nice version of my off-duty uniform: dark jeans, button-down (I went over it again with an iron, because I'm a wanker), sweater, watch, suede boots, jacket. Nothing fancy, but I wanted to look good.

I haven't had a lot of time to travel outside of football, so I'm excited about seeing Salamanca. Rachel and I texted a bit more last night to get the details in place. I offered to drive instead of taking the train—more privacy this way—and Rachel agreed.

I turn on the passenger seat heater. She'll probably be cold, right? Or maybe she'll be warm from getting out of the shower? I don't know. I also can't think about her in the shower. She'd be naked, wet, her skin lathered up in soap . . .

God *damn* it.

I decide to leave the seat heater on.

I check my watch. Eight fifty-one. Jesus, is it just me, or are the minutes crawling by? I glance at the dorm building's glass doors, glowing with the yellowy haze of fluorescent lights. Rachel can't be here soon enough.

I nearly eject out of my seat when my phone starts to vibrate. My first thought is *no*—no, no, no, it's Rachel, and she's canceling on me. I didn't realize just how excited I was about this trip until now.

I dig it out of my pocket, then sigh with relief when I see it's my sister calling. I pick it up.

Hello, Sophie, I say in German. *I can't really talk right now.*

You don't usually have stuff going on during your days off, she replies. I can hear her nine-month-old baby, Lilli, making cute baby noises in the background. *Lilli says hello Uncle Fredrik!*

Tell Lilli Uncle Fred says hello back, I say, smiling. I miss that baby. *And I, uh, have a thing today.*

Oh my God, Sophie replies. *You have a thing with a girl, don't you?*

I sigh. Again. I can't hide anything from Sophie.

Maybe, I say. *But she's just a friend. It's nothing serious.*

Tell me everything, she replies.

Her name is Rachel, and that is all I'm going to tell you. Because we're just friends, Sophie.

Fred! I'm so happy for you.

I squeeze my temples between my thumb and first two fingers and close my eyes. *Sophie, seriously, she's just a friend. I barely know her. Please don't tell Mama that I'm getting married or something. Because I'm not.*

Mama would be thrilled, my sister says.

Like I don't know my mom would lose her mind if she knew I met someone. It's all Mum ever wanted for me—to settle down in our lovely hometown with a nice girl in a nice house to start a nice little family of my own. I think she's still mystified, how many years later, that I decided to leave all that behind—leave *her* behind—in pursuit of playing professional football. Mystified, and more than a little hurt. Sure, I still want to find the nice girl, but that doesn't make up for the fact that I left home at fourteen and have no plans of going back for good anytime soon.

Dropping my hand, I glance out the window. My heart leaps.

There she is. Rachel. She's standing just outside the door, hiking her bag higher onto her shoulder as she checks her phone.

She looks gorgeous. Her hair, long and silky, hangs in loose waves over one shoulder. She's wearing a black wool coat over black jeans.

Her lips are red, redder than I remember. She's a bit done up, but she still looks like herself. She's not covering anything up, only enhancing what she's got in the best, the *best*, way.

Hello? Sophie is saying in my ear. *Are you there? Fred? FRED!*

Sorry, Em, I have to go, I say absently, my eyes never leaving Rachel. It's like I'm scared she'll disappear if I look away even for half a second. *Give Lilli a kiss for me, okay?*

Have fun with Rachel, Sophie replies. *I expect a full report tonight!*

I tell Sophie goodbye and hang up. Immediately I scroll to Rachel's contact and hit the "call" icon.

It rings.

Rachel is still looking at her phone, but all of the sudden this giant, genuine smile breaks out on her face as my call comes through.

This girl is killing me. Seeing her so genuinely lit up makes me feel like I could fly.

Seeing her also makes my chest hurt, just a little—just inside my breastbone. It's not bad, this hurt, but it's new. Strange.

In the back of my mind, a voice says that maybe this wasn't such a great idea. I haven't even spoken to Rachel yet, and already I'm losing my grip on the very good reasons why I can't be into her. Why I can't touch her.

She swipes her thumb across the screen and brings the phone to her ear.

"Hello?" I can even *hear* the smile in her voice. It's that giant. That real.

"You look fucking beautiful," I blurt. Christ, I'm a tit.

She looks up. Glances around. "Thank you. Where are you?"

"I'm in the grey car over by the steps." I wave. "Do you see me?"

Rachel keeps glancing around until her eyes lock onto mine. She waves back.

"I'll be right there."

"Okay," I say. "Bye. Or hello, I suppose."

"Hello, Fred." She's hurrying toward me, and her voice is breathless now.

I lean my elbow against the window and watch her approach. Even the way she moves turns me on. Everything, *everything* about this girl turns me on. "Hello, Rachel. How did you sleep?"

"Well. How's the finger feeling? Still attached to your hand, I hope?"

I pause at the unexpected flush of warmth that moves through me. "Still attached, though a bit worse for the wear. That bastard has sharp teeth."

"That guy is such a piece of shit. They should cut his ass already and make that trade for Rudolfo—did you see his hat trick the other night in Milan?" Rachel is at the passenger side door now.

Not even ten seconds into our conversation, and already we're talking hat tricks—when a player scores three goals in one match.

I run a hand across my face. Why does the girl who's leaving Madrid make it so fucking easy to like her?

"Have I seen it? Rachel, I've only watched the replay of

49

that match about a thousand bleeding times this week. My manager is obsessed with it."

"How insufficient did it make you feel?"

"Quite. Hat tricks are not my specialty."

"Well, yeah, obviously not, because your specialty is Bavarian beer."

I bite the inside of my cheek to keep from wincing at the desire that grips my heart and squeezes.

"You know me too well," I say.

A blast of cold air invades the car as she climbs inside. The door shuts behind her. Her perfume—something feminine and clean—fills my head.

Still holding the phone to her ear, she grins up at me. "Can we hang up now?"

"Yes," I say, dropping my phone onto the dash. She tucks hers into the front pocket of her bag.

"Hi," she says.

I'm struggling not to stare at her. She's even prettier than I remember. Her eyes dance as they meet mine.

"Hi."

I lean forward and press quick kisses into her cheeks, the smell of her perfume, of her fucking *skin,* making me see double. Her breath hitches and in the glare of the bright winter sun, I can make out the thump of her pulse just below her ear.

Her heart is pounding.

Jesus Christ. She's not faking her attraction. She's not forcing it.

She's also not fighting it.

And that's driving me bloody crazy, because I want to stop fighting it too.

I pull back, giving my jeans a discreet tug. "So. Thanks again for letting me drive. Much easier for me this way."

She runs a hand through her hair, making it fall into her face. "No problem.

Do people usually bother you when you're out? Because, you know, you're this super stud footballer who's super famous in Spain?"

I shrug, glancing in the rearview mirror. "I don't know if it's because I'm tall or I'm blond—"

"Or you're really, really famous for being really, really great at your job."

"Or that," I say, grinning. "But people do tend to recognize me. A hat sometimes helps, but you never know when someone will stop me in the street. I apologize if they do."

Rachel waves away my apology. "Don't sweat it."

I put the car in gear and nudge out into traffic.

"I like your car," she says. "An Audi—how very Christian Grey of you."

"Christian Grey?" I ask, shifting gears.

"You know, Christian Grey? The billionaire guy from the book *Fifty Shades of Grey*?"

Huh? Am I supposed to know who that is?

"Sorry," I say. "I haven't a clue what you're talking about."

"Really? *Fifty Shades of Grey* is, like, this giant cultural phenomenon. It's sold a gazillion copies worldwide. They're even making it into movies. I can't believe you haven't heard of it. The aliens living on Mars have heard about the red room of pain, for God's sake."

I feel Rachel looking at me.

I thrust the car into third. "Football keeps me pretty busy. Very busy. I don't have a lot of time for extracurriculars."

She scoffs. "Extracurriculars? Is that what you'd call reading a book? Going to the movies? Talking shit with your friends?"

Truth be told, I can't remember the last time I read a

book (other than *Harry Potter*, obviously) or went to the cinema. I've been so focused on my career, so bloody obsessed with making it work and being the best football player I can be, I haven't thought about stuff outside it. Honestly, I enjoy being out on the pitch more than I enjoy really anything else.

"I'll have to pick up a copy," I offer, lamely, in reply.

"Maybe I'll pick it up for you. Could be very useful for, uh, future extracurricular activities." Rachel says, settling into the seat. "Oooh, this feels nice. Is the seat heater on?"

"It is," I say. I look at her. "I thought you might be cold, so . . . yeah."

She smiles. "You're so nice."

You're unbelievably gorgeous, I think.

An image flashes across my thoughts—Rachel standing in my bedroom, undressing for me slowly, *slowly*, as I reach between her legs. I'd take her bare shoulder in my mouth. She'd be wet. Ready. So soft—

I blink, refocusing my gaze on the road. I have to get it the fuck together.

Rachel

Despite the awkward *Fifty Shades of Grey* bit, I meant it when I said I liked Fred's car. It's exactly what I imagined him driving: a sleek yet understated sports sedan, a car that shows he takes himself seriously but not *too* seriously. He uses it to get from point A to B, not to impress the guys on his team or show off how much money he has.

I can't stand loud, flashy cars. I think there's some truth to the rumor that guys who buy them are compensating for a small you-know-what. Fancy cars are just another layer of the douche cake. The crowd Mom associates with in Dallas are a perfect example of that. Everyone in our neighborhood back home makes sure to park their Jaguar or Mercedes in the driveway, so people can see just how fancy, or really how insecure, they are.

The thing I like most about Fred's car is the way the inside smells—like your run-of-the-mill boy body wash cut with a hint of sultry sandalwood. I'm guessing that the sandalwood is Fred's aftershave; I smelled it when he kissed my cheeks.

I seriously almost fainted it was so delicious.

Fred looks amazing, as always. The guy could wear a shower curtain and make it look good. He's casual but put together in a green jacket and jeans, and it allows me to glimpse just enough of his tall, powerful physique to have me squirming in my heated seat. Still a little wet from the shower, his pale hair is combed back, giving his whole look a slightly hipster vibe.

I dig it. I really, really dig it.

But that's as far as I let myself go. As much as I want to maul Fred right now, as much as I want to discover whether Fred's enthusiasm for sports extends to the bedroom, we're just friends. He told me point-blank he's not interested in anything casual. I've got to keep my pants on today.

I stayed up way too late working on my résumé, so of course I slept through my alarm this morning. I tried to throw myself together in the twenty minutes I had before Fred was supposed to pick me up. I managed to brush my teeth, put on some mascara and lipstick (bright red—a gamble), and change my shirt three times before settling on a white sweater. I kept telling myself I was being silly—today isn't a date, so it doesn't matter what I wear—but Fred is freaking hot, and I wanted to feel hot too.

Judging by the look on Fred's face when he saw me, I suspect the lipstick gamble was one worth taking.

We make small talk as we move through the congested tangle of Madrid into the arid, wide-open Spanish countryside. The contrast is night and day. Madrid's drab suburbs give way to bare, jagged hills, burnished yellow by the ardent morning sunshine. The hills dip into shadowy valleys, the few trees grey and still. It's so remote and so untouched it looks like a colorful moonscape.

"Look," Fred says, pointing out his window. There, high on top of a hill in the middle of literally nowhere, are the ruins of a storybook castle, complete with crumbling turrets and a high, circular tower. Its single window—more like an arrow slit—stares back at us as we pass. "How cool is that?"

"Amazing." I shake my head. "Not to like, hate on America, but you never see stuff like that in Dallas. Where I live, everything—everyone—it's all so . . . polished, I guess. Perfect. Too perfect."

He looks at me from the corner of his eye. "Have you been homesick much?"

"Honestly? No. Sure, I have my moments when I get frustrated with my Spanish, or I'm craving my dad's fried chicken. But other than that, I'm enjoying being away from all the bullshit."

"Bullshit?"

I shrug. "Where I come from—it's an interesting place. I love my parents, don't get me wrong. But the people they hang out with can be really superficial. You know, really into their money, and their fancy careers, and the fancy boarding schools they send their kids to. I never felt like I fit in, I guess, because I wasn't into those things."

"No," Fred says, grinning. "You're into college football and patellar dislocations instead."

"Exactly," I say. I grin too, hoping it will keep the sudden swell of feeling inside my chest from showing up on my face.

I don't want him to know how he's affecting me right now. I mean, I met Fred less than a week ago.

Why is he paying such attention to what I like—what *I'm* like—when he told me, point-blank, he wants to keep me at arm's length?

"I can relate," he says. "I feel like I don't fit in either, especially since I came to Madrid. The lads, they're nice enough. But they're into watches. Models. Parties on yachts, that sort of thing."

"But *you're* into Harry Potter," I say.

"I am," he says. "And I make no apologies."

I look at him, the morning sun catching on the slightly irregular slope of his nose, the fullness of his lips. A deep, almost painful pulse of longing moves through me. If I weren't leaving Spain in a month, right about now I'd be thinking how Fred could potentially be *the* guy.

The guy who cracks my world open. I've met a lot of guys, and dated a few of them. But none of them have piqued my interest the way Fred has. None of them gave me this gut feeling that something big is happening between us.

He turns his head and looks at me looking at him. His grin fades as his eyes meet mine. For half a heartbeat, I think he gets it—he's thinking it too, that I could be *the* girl.

His eyes flick to my mouth. They darken as a flare of heat passes across them.

After half a heartbeat, he looks away.

A muscle along his clean-shaven jaw tics.

I clear my throat. "What about you? Do you miss Germany?"

"I do." He nods. "I have a big family back home. I miss being around all the commotion—every meal was like this giant party, always heaps and heaps of food around, always extra friends and relatives squeezing in at the table. It's a lot of fun."

"Sounds like it, having so much family around," I say, tucking my hair behind my ear. "I'm an only child, and I always wished I had a big family. I begged my parents for siblings, but they were always busy working, so yeah, it's just me."

"What do they do?"

"They're both doctors," I say.

"Wow. That's quite impressive."

I grin, a rueful thing. "My mom never lets you forget just how impressive it is."

The drive goes by quickly—too quickly—the two of us talking and taking in the scenery. Then we clear a hill and Salamanca appears, the rounded gothic spires of its old city reflected in the still water of the nearby Tormes River.

"Christ, it's lovely here," Fred says, ducking to get a better look at the old Roman bridge as we cross the river into the city.

Watching Fred take it all in, my pulse hiccups. He's into it. Like *really* into it. As into it as I am.

I smile. This is my semester of living in the moment. Of losing myself in travel and experience and fun.

Losing myself alongside someone who's also lost in the beauty of the moment—it's indescribably sweet.

"What?" he asks, smiling back.

"Nothing." I shake my head. "I'm just excited about our day in Salamanca. There's so much I want to show you."

By some miracle, he finds a parking spot in a narrow side street. Grabbing a black baseball hat out of the back seat—I recognize the "TR" logo that belongs to the Spanish tennis superstar Tomás Rincón—Fred climbs out of the car and scurries to my door, ducking into the hat just before he holds the door open for me.

"So you're a gentleman *and* a tennis fan," I say, stepping onto the sidewalk. "I like it."

I point in the direction I want to head, and I shove my hands inside my pockets as we begin to walk. The sidewalk is narrow and uneven, forcing us to move more closely than is polite. I move away, putting some decidedly friendly distance between us. I don't trust myself when I'm so close to him.

"Thought you might like the hat," he says.

"I do."

I actually *love* the hat. I dig it when guys wear baseball hats. They're like my kryptonite.

Fred catches my admiring gaze with his. His eyes, sea green in the shade put off by the bill of his hat, sharpen, like he knows just how much I'm enjoying the view. He looks away, one side of his mouth quirking upward.

I curl my hands into fists inside my coat pockets. It's not even noon, and already my will is fraying. God help me.

I clear my throat. "I love Rincón. Such a classy guy. Although Gutierrez is probably my favorite Spanish player—she's wicked on the court. Her backhand has to be the best in tennis right now."

"I love watching her," he says. *I* love the way his face lights up when we talk sports together. "The drama is insane, isn't it, when she's playing? I actually got to see her at Wimbledon last year."

"How cool!"

"It was. One of my favorite sporting events I've ever been to."

"Although it was not Gutierrez's best showing. She had, like, a total meltdown during the second set, remember? It was tough to watch. But I'm jealous you got to Wimbledon. It's at the top of my bucket list. I'd love to make it to all the grand slams before I die."

"Of course I remember. She threw her racquet and hit the ball boy in the bollocks. Poor kid." Fred shakes his head. He turns his head to look at me from underneath the brim of his hat. "You really are crazy about sports. I have a feeling sports medicine is going to be a good fit for you."

"We'll see," I say, trying to rein in the rush of pleasure that his words have caused to bloom inside my chest. "So how about we hit up the cathedral first? Then maybe walk around a bit, grab some tapas or something for lunch—sound good?"

"Sounds perfect," he says, flashing me a smile so big and so bright, it makes all the soft parts in my chest contract.

You're perfect, I want to say.

I don't though.

I can't.

Chapter Five

FRED

Two hours into Rachel's tour, and I already adore Salamanca. Granted, she could give me a tour of my dentist's office and I'd think it was the greatest thing ever, but still—there's something magical about this city.

Could have something to do with my ridiculously gorgeous tour guide. Rachel is killing me with her patience and her passion and that red fucking lipstick. She has an answer for every question I ask, and fills me in on Salamanca's incredible, and often violent, history (home to the Moors, the oldest university in Spain, and the headquarters of fascist dictator Francisco Franco during the Spanish Civil War). I've discovered I'm a history buff, if only because Rachel's genuine interest in the subject is so damn infectious.

I'm comfortable with her. At home. More at home than I am with anyone else I've met in Spain, that's for certain. I get excited when I think about telling Sophie how brilliantly Rachel and I get on.

But then I remember we're just friends, Rachel and I, and that no matter how much fun we have together, or how well our interests line up, Rachel is bloody *leaving*. Why get Sophie's hopes up for a girl who can't stick around?

I won't be talking about Rachel with Sophie. That'd just be cruel for all parties involved. But I'm determined to enjoy the time I have with her anyway. Already there doesn't seem to be enough of it, even though we have the whole afternoon ahead of us.

It doesn't hurt that we picked the perfect day. It's just warm enough to enjoy walking around outside, especially in the sun. It gets a bit chilly when we pass into the enormous shadow put off by the cathedral, but I think Rachel is too busy telling me about its history to really notice.

As luck has it, we walk in on a mass in what Rachel calls the "old" cathedral, meaning the part that was built close to a thousand (!) years ago. We crane our necks to stare at the soaring arches of the nave as the voices of the choir rise and fall around us. The sun slants through enormous panes of stained glass, painting the pews cobalt, bright red, and green. We even manage to grab a selfie in a particularly pretty puddle of purple—the congregation's opinion of us be damned—but one of the stewards catches us and promptly kicks our stupid tourist asses out of the cathedral.

Rachel bursts out laughing when we are back outside. The honest, gut-busting sound of her laugh—bloody hell, it fills me to the point I can hardly breathe.

"What are you laughing about?" I tease, discreetly resting a hand against a flying buttress in the hopes it'll help with the woozy feeling inside my chest. "We're going to burn in hell for that, you know."

"I'll save you a seat. But look! Damning our eternal souls was totally worth it—check out the picture." She holds up her phone to show me a blurry screen, nothing more than blobs of tan where our faces should be.

I take the phone from her to get a better look and laugh. "I've always been rubbish at selfies."

"Me too," she says. "Let's take more of them. I love how terrible ours are."

I love how she can give less of a shit about how she looks in pictures. The girls the lads bring about are always so careful about posing for photos at parties. They're always so serious about how their duck lips look in a close-up.

But Rachel—Rachel only wants to have fun and enjoy the moment. I fucking love enjoying it with her. It's just so easy.

It's too easy. I can't resist.

So we walk around and take more terrible selfies, the sights of Salamanca in the background as we make faces, or laugh so hard we can't hold the phone still, making the pictures progressively blurrier. We have someone take a picture of us jumping in the air, pretending to fly our Nimbus 2001s (well, Nimbus 2000 for me) in front of a section of the cathedral that barely resembles the inner courtyard of Hogwarts. It's bloody ridiculous, and so much fun.

Luckily, I'm only spotted twice, both times by fans of the squad. I sign the backs of their shirts while Rachel bonds with them over their shared belief that Ignacio Cruz (the guy who tried to relieve me of a finger last night) is a closet cannibal.

Hearing her laugh with my fans—seeing the respect she has for my game—it has me feeling short of breath again. For a moment, I worry I might be suffering a bout of cardiac arrest. But then a beat, small at first, unsteady, comes alive in the center of my chest.

I want.

I want this girl.

I've known her all of a week, but I already want her more badly than I've wanted something in a long time.

I want.

But I can't have her.

Rachel catches me looking at her. I can't read the expression in her eyes. They are wet. Vulnerable, almost.

They look as vulnerable as I feel in that moment.

"See?" she says, trying on a shaky smile. "I knew Cruz liked to eat other people. Those guys just confirmed it."

I can't think of a witty response to that, other than *I want to eat* you. Bloody hell. I'm worried my voice might betray my lust, though I suspect Rachel knows exactly what's going on inside my head—my chest and my pants too—right then.

So I nod at an important looking building ahead and start walking, head down, hands shoved in the pockets of my jacket. My heartbeat throbs.

I want.

We make our way to a cobblestone lane beside the river, eavesdropping on the Spanish couple in front of us, when I hear Rachel's stomach grumble.

"Sounds serious," I say. My voice is gruff. Rachel's shoulders stiffen. "How about some lunch?"

"Are you hungry?"

"I'm always hungry."

"Fred! Why didn't you say something?" She looks at me. Just when I'm starting to get my shit together, the warmth in her eyes makes me feel unsettled all over again. It makes me feel welcomed. Invited. But I can't go there. I can't go in.

I shrug. I should look away, but I don't.

"I didn't want to interrupt the tour," I say. "I'm very much enjoying it."

"Thank you." She grins, squinting against the sun. Selfishly, I'm glad she forgot her sunglasses. I love being able to see her eyes. "So, for lunch, I know just the place. Only I don't exactly know how to get there from here, so bear with me."

After a few wrong turns and a detour through a lovely

little park, we pass under a colonnaded gallery and end up in a giant open square surrounded on all sides by imposing stone buildings. In the warm afternoon sun, they look like they're coated in honey. Plane tracks crisscross the blue square of sky above us, scratches on an otherwise pristine canvas.

"This is Salamanca's Plaza Mayor," Rachel explains as we head toward a small scattering of tables across the square. "Reminds you of Madrid's main square, right?"

"Very similar. I think I like Salamanca's more though."

She grins at me. "Oh? And why is that?"

Because I get to see it with you. "Because I have a feeling we'll take our worst selfie yet in this square."

"Let's do it," Rachel says. "But first, lunch?"

"Of course." I hold out my arm. "After you."

We grab a table outside in the sun, its vinyl checkered tablecloth fluttering in a soft breeze. A waiter emerges from the nearby restaurant a moment later. His gaze stays on me a beat too long—I think he recognizes me—but when I think he's about to ask me for a photo, or maybe an autograph, he asks for our drink order instead.

Rachel looks at me. "Beer? I'm thirsty."

I drop my menu. Of course she's thirsty for a beer.

Jesus Christ.

"Hey . . . hey, are you okay?" she asks. She looks concerned. A little unsure.

I manage a tight grin. "Never been better."

She grins. "Great. How does some tapas sound? The shrimp is really good, and the charred peppers are *ridiculous*."

We order our drinks in Spanish—Rachel's is much better than mine—and then she orders half a dozen tapas, or the small plates of food that Spaniards love to snack on, with breezy confidence.

She crosses her arms on the table and leans into them, her dark eyes latched playfully onto mine.

She leans toward me. I smell her perfume.

I fight the impulse to reach across the table and tuck a stray strand of hair behind her ear.

She's so bloody beautiful.

I'm struggling to get past how beautiful this girl is.

I'm struggling against the very real feeling that I'm in over my head here. I can't get a grip on this beat inside my chest— the one that wants her. Likes her.

I'm trying, but I can't.

At this point, I don't even know if I *want* to get a grip anymore. I'm forgetting why I can't touch her. I'm forgetting the promise I made myself. I'm having too much fun, laughing too damn hard, to think about those things.

"The fact that day drinking is socially acceptable is one of my favorite things about Spain," she says.

"I do love the concept of a post-day drink siesta." I lean back to let the waiter set our glasses and bottles of beer on the table. Rachel waves him off when he tries to open the bottles.

That's okay, she says in Spanish, nodding at me. *He's got it.*

I scoff, hanging my head. I grin. "The opener on my key ring. You remembered."

"Hell yeah, I remembered," she says. "It's not every day I meet a guy who can open a bottle of beer anywhere, anytime. So c'mon. Show me what you got."

My eyes never leaving hers, I dig my keys out of my pocket and pop the caps off the beers, one at a time. Rachel catches a cap as it rolls toward her, slapping it flat on the table before she reaches for her bag.

I cock a brow. "Did you remember the koozies?"

Rachel holds them up in reply. "And look! We actually need them—the beers are cold."

I let her put the koozies on the beers. Then we sit back

and drink. Spanish beer doesn't compare to the good German stuff, but—

"It's decent," Rachel says after she takes a long pull, finishing the thought for me. I mean, seriously? "Not nearly as delicious as your Bavarian beer though."

Not nearly delicious as you, I want to say.

Fucking hell, since when have I become such a cheeseball?

"Nothing quite is," I say instead.

She settles into her chair. "Tell me, Fred—how did a stud footballer become such a Harry Potter nerd? It doesn't add up."

I take a deep breath. I'm dying here, but I don't want her to know that.

"I was always a nerd," I say. "Growing up, I had it all— braces, pimples, an ant farm. I was chubby too. Those were not my best years."

"An ant farm? Amazing." Rachel laughs. "And how did this chubby little nerd become a world-class athlete?"

"I hit a growth spurt early, around fourteen. Football was really the only thing I was good at, and I loved to play. Once that growth spurt happened, I got better on the pitch. A year later, I was recruited by the academy in Munich, and after that . . ."

"After that, you dominated."

I bite back a grin. "Well, yeah."

"You're fucking ridiculous," she says.

"You don't seem to mind."

Rachel takes a sip of beer. "I don't."

Her eyes latch onto mine. A beat passes, then another. The space between us vibrates. Tightens. With the sun warm on my shoulders and the taste of the beer on my tongue and Rachel's eyes on my eyes, I feel a contentment so wide and so deep it scares the shit out of me.

I'm in over my head with this girl. I know it. I *feel* it.

I don't know what to do. I want this girl so badly it hurts. She's leaving, she isn't the forever girl I'm looking for, but none of that seems to matter when she smiles at me while we're talking football stats, or she looks at me with such honesty and such warmth I feel like I finally found one of my people.

I feel like I finally found my person. *The* person. And I did it just by being myself. My dorky, beer-obsessed self.

Fuck fuck *fuck*.

I try to calm down by focusing on the food. It smells delicious. The gambas al ajillo—shrimp with garlic sauce—sizzles in its small clay pot, and the freshly shaved jamón ibérico is so paper-thin it looks like it will literally melt in your mouth. There's some charred octopus too, and a plate of tiny blackened peppers, along with wedges of manchego cheese.

"So," Rachel says, focusing her gaze on her beer. She's worrying the top edge of her koozie with her thumbnail, her movements jerky, unsteady, like her fingers are shaking.

Holy shit, did our little staring contest overwhelm her too? Is she feeling this connection we have as much as I am? "This big family of yours—do they all live in Germany?"

I wipe my mouth, swallowing a pepper before I respond. Her eyes flick unevenly between my face and her plate, like she's uncertain. Afraid.

That makes two of us.

I clear my throat. "They do. In the same town, as a matter of fact. No one ever really leaves—they like to be close to one another."

She nods. "They must miss you."

"They do. But I try my best to stay in touch—I talk to my sister a couple times a week, and I call my mum a good bit too. They're really lovely people."

"Sounds like you guys are close. Like things are easy, if

66

that makes sense, between you. It's awesome that you guys have such a great relationship."

I shrug, offering Rachel the plate of manchego. She grins and takes a slice.

I almost drop the plate and take her face in my hands and kiss her right then.

I am so beyond fucked.

"Didn't used to be," I say. "We went through a rough patch—a really rough patch—for a couple years there."

"Really?" She looks at me. "I would never guess that. You just seem so . . . nice, I guess."

"I was—what's the expression—on my family's shit list since I was fourteen."

"That sounds intense. What happened, if you don't mind me asking?"

I wash down some jamón with a gulp of beer. My heart is pounding, and I can't get it to stop. "My family always wanted me to stay in the town where I grew up. My mum hoped I would work for my aunt's accounting firm. But I wanted to play football. I worked hard at it. Really fucking hard. And when the national German training club came knocking when I hit that growth spurt, I couldn't pass up the opportunity. I moved to Munich to train, and I haven't lived at home since. It took a while for everyone—my mum and my brothers and sister—to forgive me for that. They were so disappointed."

Rachel's staring at me now. Her eyes bore into mine. I feel like I've struck a nerve. "But they did forgive you."

"Yes." I finish my wine. "We get on well enough now. They know I'm happy, and that things are better for me this way."

"That takes balls," she says, "to go after what you want, even if it crushed your mom."

I look back at her. Her eyes are darker now—thoughtful. "But then I would've been crushed if I didn't go after my dream. It was selfish, yeah, but I think you have to be, especially when it comes to the big stuff. If I'd gone the accountant route, I'd be miserable. And I know my mum never wanted me to be miserable, no matter how much they would've loved having me at home."

"Wow," she says, gaze flicking to her plate. She smiles, but it's this sad, tight thing, not at all what I'm used to seeing on her. "Wow, that's—that's amazing, Fred. I admire you for being so brave. I wish . . ."

I wait for her to finish her thought, but she doesn't.

I wish, more than anything, I knew what was going on inside her head. As fun and as funny and spontaneous as she can be, there's this heaviness about her—a heaviness she carries around. I've caught glimpses of it, and I suspect it has something to do with her mother.

The fact that I so badly want her to let me in is terrifying. Thrilling.

"Hey," I say, softly. "Rachel, are you all right?"

She shakes her head, even as she says, "Yeah. Yes. Sorry. I've just had a lot on my mind lately."

"Like?"

"Like being damned to hell, *Tournament of Kings*-style. I wonder if I'll be turned into a vampire after I die."

It's a shameless attempt to change the subject, and we both know it. I want to know what's bothering her, but she clearly doesn't want to talk about it. I mean, who the hell am I to push her on it?

"*Tournament of Kings*?" Yet another pop-culture reference I don't get. Being with Rachel is making me feel like I've lived under a bloody rock my whole life. "Can't say I've seen it."

That gets her attention. She looks up at me in disbelief. "Okay, I kind of get how you don't know who Christian Grey is, because you're a guy or whatever. But you haven't seen *Tournament*?"

"Well, I've heard of it—some of the lads on the squad are always talking about this show where a king murders his wife, you know, the queen, and then he runs off to sleep with, like, all her sisters or something—or was it nuns? Maybe witches? I don't know. And then the queen comes back from the dead as a vampire and drowns him in his own shit or something? That sound right?"

"It was gargoyle shit, but yeah, that's the show," she replies, laughing. "It's so good. You should definitely check it out."

She's grinning again. I want to keep that grin there, make it bigger.

The idea pops into my head, fully formed, in the space of a single heartbeat.

I should let our time together end when I drop off Rachel at her dorm in Madrid. I should get the check and get out of here before she makes another Quidditch reference or charms more of my fans.

I should.

I should.

I really fucking should.

But it's too late. It was too late the moment she picked up the phone this morning and started talking hat tricks.

"Want to watch it together?" I blurt. "At my flat, I mean. *Tournament of Kings*. Maybe have a few more beers or something? Could be fun."

"There are a lot of boobs in it," she replies, teasing. "I don't know if you'll like it."

"Boobs? Pssssh. Who likes those?"

Biting her bottom lip, she studies my face. A beat passes, then another. My pulse goes wild.

This is a bad idea. Nothing good can come of extending our day together. If she comes over, all bets are off. I don't trust myself with her. Not anymore.

"All right," she says. "Let's do it."

My heart seizes. Holy shit.

Holy shit. How am I going to keep it together if she's next to me on the sofa? Do I even want to keep it together?

"All right," I manage, sucking in a breath. "You free tonight? Unless you're getting sick of me . . ."

"I am," she says at last. "I mean, I'm free tonight, not that I'm getting sick of you."

I don't think I've ever felt so high, or so terrified, after a victory before—and that's coming from a guy who won a league title last year.

When the waiter comes, I hand him a huge Euro bill and tell him to keep the change. He asks for a photo, and, hyped up on adrenaline, I wrap an arm around his shoulder and ask him to bring all the staff looking at us through that window over there so they can be in the picture too.

Cracking a dirty joke in Spanish, Rachel charms them all as she snaps the photos. Of course.

She's charmed me too. Charmed me so thoroughly I'm breaking one rule after the next with her. I can't keep throwing caution to the wind like this. I have to draw a line somewhere, or I'm going to get burned.

The thing is, though—it's too easy not to think about that burn when you're having so much damn fun playing with fire.

Chapter Six

RACHEL

It's just past four when we leave Salamanca. Tucked into the warmth of my heated seat, I watch over my shoulder as the sun ducks behind the city's pale walls, leaving behind a wide-open sky of blue and purple and amber.

My heart swells inside my chest. I feel . . . really full, I guess. Like I can't possibly process all the awesomeness that happened today. The soccer fans and Fred's giant, genuine smile and the gorgeous light that floods the city during the day, making a silvery mirror out of the river and burnishing every wall and building a uniquely Spanish shade of orangey-red.

We hit the highway, and I turn back to look at Fred. He's driving with one enormous hand on the wheel, the other on the gear shift. He took off his hat, and his hair is a wreck, sticking up every which way.

He couldn't care less.

God help me, I like this guy. A lot.

He is handsome and huge and hilarious. It's been a struggle not to touch him all day. I want to. Badly. So freaking badly.

I don't know what his invitation to go back to his place means. If it were an invitation from any other guy, I'd think for sure we were going to make out on his couch tonight.

Fred, however, told me he isn't interested in that kind of thing. Sure, we've been doing a lot of flirting. And every once in a while he'll spear me with this soft, almost tortured look that has my stomach doing this weird little somersault move. But there hasn't been any of the touchy-feely fun between us that usually happens when people are interested in each other. Fred's just been so open and honest with me about everything —his family, his past, his passions—that I have to assume he's honest about keeping things friendly between us too.

So, yeah. Maybe he really does want to watch *Tournament*. Maybe he doesn't want to be lonely, so he invited me over as a friend to keep him company—in a platonic way, of course.

I'm onboard with that. I guess.

"You all right?" Fred asks. He's turned his head to glance at me.

I blink.

Fuck, I've been staring at him. I look away, quickly, my cheeks burning.

"Yeah," I say. "Sorry. Just, um . . . thinking."

He readjusts himself in his seat, clearing his throat. I notice the knuckles on his hand—the one on the steering wheel—are white.

A shiver darts up my spine. I try not to suck in a breath. We're having such a great day together. If he finds out how badly I want to touch him, it will just scare him off. I don't want to go home to an empty dorm room tonight any more than Fred wants go to home to an empty apartment. Not when I could have some more beers with him, maybe shoot the shit about the match he has coming up next weekend.

"Thinking about what?" he asks.

"Thinking about today," I say. "How much fun I had."

He grins. "It's not over yet, yeah?"

"Yeah," I say.

"I'm glad you're coming over."

"Me too."

I mean that. I enjoy talking to Fred, picking his brain. What he said about the problems he had with his mom—that obviously cut really close to home. I wasn't lying when I said I admired his courage.

But Fred made it sound so simple, this choice between his happiness and his parents'. Between his dreams and theirs. It doesn't hurt that he absolutely knocked it out of the park with his football career. It's hard to argue that wasn't the right choice when he's taking his team to glory and making millions while doing it.

I can't help but wonder if the choice was easy—well, easier—for Fred because he's a guy. I've noticed it's easier for guys to be selfish, most haven't been raised as people-pleasers, or caregivers, like I have. Like most girls I know have. It's almost like dudes are expected to go out into the world and lose touch with their parents and do their own thing, while girls are expected to stay close to home, to take their family's needs into consideration before their own.

Not to say the choice isn't hard for everyone. But the fact that Fred's a guy, and he has siblings to help bear the brunt of the hurt his decisions cause his parents, is really a game changer.

I'm jealous. Jealous he made his choice and it worked out for him.

I'm scared, I guess, that whatever choice I make *won't* work out. There's always a chance of failure, of regret. What if I go the plastic surgery route, like Mom wants me to, and I turn into one of the appearance obsessed bullshitters who populate her office? What if I flunk the MCAT, or I just generally suck at surgery?

And what if I do sports medicine, but it doesn't pay well and I'm broke forever, or Mom and Dad disown me and I'm lonely without them, and I spend all my time wishing I'd listened to Mom and done the surgery thing?

What if, like Mom tells me, I'm not living up to my full potential by going after something as unexciting as authenticity or a healthy work-life balance?

I know I'll never get the guarantee I'm looking for—the guarantee that things will work out. But damn if I wouldn't give my left arm for it.

Damn if I wouldn't give anything for just a smidge of Fred's courage. His certainty.

No wonder I've felt so great all day. I didn't realize just how *heavy* all this stuff was until I had to pick it up again after setting it down. After getting lost in Fred and his laugh and those squinty eyes of his and his dreams of playing seeker for a Quidditch team.

Needless to say, I'm excited about tonight, even if nothing happens between Fred and me. I don't need to get naked to have fun with him. We could just talk, and I'd have a great time.

But getting naked with him—I mean, yeah, that would be awesome too.

I step inside the warm quiet of Fred's apartment behind him. I'm immediately hit by a clean smell—like freshly laundered sheets and just-washed floors. I now know I'm in a real man's apartment, a literal and figurative world away from my ex-boyfriend's dorm room, which smelled like feet and was packed with the detritus of three sophomore dudes with questionable hygiene habits.

He helps me with my coat, then I follow him into the kitchen. It's huge, with a massive, granite-topped island and a fancy French range as big as my entire dorm room.

Like the rest of his apartment, the kitchen is spotless.

"Fred, this is gorgeous," I say, allowing him to help me out of my coat. His finger brushes the nape of my neck. The muscles in the small of my back tighten as I ignore the throb of heat between my legs.

"Thanks," he replies. His voice is weirdly gruff. "Are you hungry?"

I can't meet his eyes, but I notice his cheeks are flushed. Is that from the cold? Or is it from me?

Not like it matters. I can't touch Fred tonight, and he can't touch me either.

I just . . . I didn't think the chemistry between us would be so intense. I didn't think Fred was any different from other guys I've admired but couldn't have.

Here's the thing though—Fred is different, in every way imaginable. He gets me. He likes what I like. He genuinely gives a shit about getting to know me. He genuinely doesn't give a shit about what anyone else thinks. Connecting with someone like this is uncharted territory for me. I'm not entirely sure how to navigate what's going on here.

"A little," I say, even though I'm so on edge—I'm so freaking turned on—the thought of eating makes my stomach hurt.

"Shall we order in some dinner? There's a place around the corner—"

"Why don't we just cook here?"

He looks at me like I just suggested we eat each other for dinner. "Cook? Here?"

"Yeah. Why not? You've got this gorgeous kitchen that's begging to be used. Have you never cooked before?"

"I used to, back home. I loved being in the kitchen with my mum. But cooking for one just isn't the same, I suppose. And football just keeps me—"

"So busy. You keep saying that. But you're not busy tonight. So, let's cook."

He grins, and we finally look at each other.

Jesus, those eyes. I *can't*.

"I don't have much—some pasta in the pantry and maybe some tomato sauce, I think—but all right," he says. "I'm in."

Fred

As luck would have it, I have pasta, red sauce, *and* a fresh block of parmesan cheese in the fridge. I'm so elated, I'd kiss my housekeeper if she were here. She always keeps my flat stocked with the essentials I need to get through the week.

Rachel sets her beer on the counter and dips a spoon into the pot on the stove, fishing out a squiggle of pasta.

"Don't think it's ready yet," she says, biting into a noodle. "Needs another minute or two."

I look up from the parmesan I'm grating. "So you're the master of al dente now?"

"I am. I mean, I know my way around a packet of ramen, and ramen is practically the same thing as pasta, so . . ."

She shrugs, the gesture small, unguarded. Adorably funny.

I laugh. "Definitely the same thing. I used to love that stuff."

"Me too. Lived off it my freshman year. It's a miracle all my teeth didn't fall out of my head," she says.

"Beer's got vitamin C in it."

"It does?"

"No." I'm still laughing. Have I ever laughed this hard with anyone outside of my family? "I don't know."

"Hey, I'd believe it. Something kept me from getting scurvy that year, and I don't think it was the ramen." She grabs the pot holders next to the sink and shakes some bread crumbs off them before heading back to the stove.

I try not to stare at her as she gives the pot another stir. She just looks . . . at home here, I guess. I don't mean in the kitchen. I mean *here*, in my flat. The whole place feels different when she's here. Better. It's full—full of laughter and food and good smells—the way Mum's house is always full.

Looking back at the past two years I've lived in Madrid, it strikes me how often I'm alone in this flat. I eat by myself, watch TV by myself, read by myself. It's so damn quiet here. As an introvert, I thought I needed that quiet. But now that Rachel's here, I'm starting to believe I don't need as much of it as I thought.

Maybe I need something else. I need more of this, whatever *this* is. Company, maybe. Connection.

"So, like, I hope you don't mind me asking about this," Rachel says, busying herself with the pot holders. She doesn't meet my eyes. "But why are you looking for . . . well, love, I guess? You're, what, twenty-five?"

"Twenty-two."

"So, you're in your twenties, you're a professional athlete, and you're cute. You not banging everything that moves makes absolutely no sense to me."

My lips curl into a smile. "I am quite cute, aren't I?"

She grins, turning off the stove. "Our seeker, always so full of himself."

"I've got this," I say, trying to nudge her aside. Our arms touch, my bicep grazing her shoulder. These small touches— they keep happening, and I'm not sure they're entirely accidental on my part. A charge of electricity moves between us. Her breath catches, and for a split second she goes still, her dark eyes trained on the offending bicep. The tip of her tongue, pink and wet, trails along the inside of her bottom lip as she looks, and looks, and *looks*.

Blood rushes to my groin. The head of my dick presses against my fly. I struggle not to wince. My thoughts whirl as I struggle to breathe, hot, desperate breaths that do nothing to slow my thundering heart rate.

I feel so much for this girl—all of it intense and good and deep—feeling it and thinking it isn't enough. I'd have to take her face in my hands and I'd have to kiss her mouth and her skin and her pussy to show her just how much she makes me feel. My skin feels too tight, my body too small. I'm bursting.

I'm bursting with something I should not fucking feel right now.

Rachel blinks, breaking the spell, and looks away.

My heart won't stop pounding.

"I'll get it—this is my favorite part," she says.

My mouth is dry. I lick my lips. "You sure?"

"I am."

"Okay," I say, moving out of the way to she can drain the pasta in the sink. A rush of steam billows up from the colander.

I take a long, hard pull from my beer. It doesn't help.

"As to your question . . ." I say. "I've casually fooled around with girls in the past, but I didn't like the way I felt afterward. Made me feel a bit empty, yeah? Lonely. Like there was no connection there whatsoever, and we were just using each other to get off. I was just a body to those girls. It could've been me or some other bloke, it didn't matter. I told you Mum raised me to respect women, and using them like that— it just didn't feel right."

Rachel looks at me. "I get it. There's this huge hook-up

culture back at Meryton—no one really dates—and I've felt that way too, sometimes. The loneliness of it. The superficiality. I'm all for getting your rocks off, but only if it makes you feel good about yourself, you know?"

"Exactly." I hold out my hand and Rachel gives me the pot holders. I spill the pasta back into the pot and drop in a couple pats of butter. "I've thought about this quite a bit. I'm not religious or anything, not really. But I do think sex should be special. Who you're having it with, trusting that person, caring about that person—all that stuff counts. I don't want to cheapen the experience by hooking up with some random girl who couldn't care less about me."

"You're such a romantic," she says. She's smiling, but there's something sad about her expression. Pained.

I know that pain, all too well. She's starting to hate this forced friendship—this line I've tried to draw—as much as I do. She wants more.

But where the fuck does that leave me? I'm trying to be on my best behavior here. I'm trying to respect her, to respect the boundaries I've put in place. Seeing that longing in her face though—being bowled over by that longing myself—I don't know what's right anymore. I don't know if keeping her at arm's length is the smart choice, or the choice I'm going to regret most tomorrow. Because I've never gotten on with someone so well.

I've never wanted anyone more. I get caught up in the moment with her; time always passes so quickly when we're together. I recognize that Rachel is different. Special. What if I never meet someone like her again? Will I regret not pushing my boundaries, not touching her, while I had the chance?

Will I regret not losing my virginity to the first girl who's ever made me feel so at home in my own skin?

Rachel stirs the pasta in the pot while I attempt to add a

little more butter. My hands don't seem to want to work, and I end up whacking a hunk onto the counter before I spear it with the knife and toss it into the pot.

The small space between my body and hers tightens. Narrows.

I try to focus on the food. It smells so bloody good. She nods at the pot of meat sauce beside it, and continues to stir as I slowly pour the sauce over the noodles.

I tip back the pot. There's more sauce, but I think the pasta looks good.

"Looks good," Rachel says.

I pause. Just for a second.

Just long enough for her to notice.

I look at her. Look at her pretty face and dark eyes. The pain is still there.

"What?" she asks.

I fucking like you. I really fucking like you, Rachel.

"Nothing," I say. "You just like it exactly how I do."

She smiles again, that sad thing that makes my heart clench, and meets my eyes.

"Rachel." I don't recognize my own voice. It's hard. Strained.

She hesitates. For a minute, I think she's going to turn to me. For a minute, I think we're both going to give in to the riot of things we're feeling and kiss the fuck out of each other, right here in my kitchen.

My blood burns inside my skin. I want to. Hell, I want to cross this line with her. It's a bad idea. But I want to do it anyway, taste the beer on her lips, claim that questioning little tongue as my own. Wanting to kiss this girl—it's never been more wrong.

It's never felt more right.

Chapter Seven

RACHEL

I'm shaking as Fred leans in, towering over me. The wild, almost thunderous look in his eyes scares me.

It scares me because I like it. I like that I'm making him feel these things. I like that he's clearly as unsettled by our instant, white-hot connection as I am.

And that's fucked up.

This whole thing is fucked up. But there's a perverse sort of charm in that fact too. I can't give him what he wants. He won't give me what I need. Yet here we are, dazed and horny as hell, powerless against the constant onslaught of our chemistry and our connection and our shared love of Quidditch.

I don't want to push him too far. But now he's pushing *me*. And I don't know what to do. Do I kiss him? Do I run?

I care about him. It's important to me that Fred wakes up tomorrow and feels good about whatever happens tonight. He's more than just some random guy I met. There's more between us than that.

Which means I really should keep my hands to myself. I want to respect his boundaries. I am leaving in three weeks—

I can't offer him anything more than a fling. He wants more than that. He deserves so much more than that.

I close my eyes and I square my shoulders and I turn back to the pot of pasta on the stove. It hurts—physically *hurts*—to turn my back to him. But it's the right move. If we ever did put our hands on each other, I have a feeling we wouldn't be able to stop. We'd burn each other down. Then what? We'd be left sorting through the ashes.

I can't do that to Fred.

"Should we eat at the island?" I ask. "Or the table?"

Behind me, I hear Fred release a breath. In my head, I see him tugging a hand through his hair, his eyes blue in this light, stormy. The image is so lovely it makes my heart swell.

"The island," he grinds out. "I'll get the plates."

I push back from my plate. The pasta was delicious, but I struggled to eat it. My stomach is in knots. I'm nervous, on edge, trying to keep it together. I want to be able to push Fred away if he reaches for me. But he keeps smiling. Keeps talking soccer and bringing me beer.

His hair is a mess, and his face is still flushed from standing over the heat of the stove. His eyes flit from mine to his plate to my mouth like a bee drunk on pollen. There's something almost shy about the way he's looking at me.

Shy, and honest. He's scared too, but he's not trying to cover it up. He's letting me see what he's feeling—he's sharing his vulnerability with me. There's no pretense. No agenda.

And it's killing me.

Fred is totally lethal on the football pitch. He's brutal and huge and forceful. To see this force of nature looking at me like this—with kindness and softness and sharp-edged heat— I can't freaking breathe.

I curl my hands over my knees underneath the island, my fingers digging painful little furrows in the skin there.

Dear God, why is he *looking at me like this*? Yeah, I'm a little buzzed from the beer, but I'm not drunk. I know I'm not misinterpreting or imaging the heat in his eyes. It's there. I'm sure he sees it in my eyes too. God, I want to touch him. I want him to touch me.

But we can't. We can't.

We can't.

"Did you not like it?" Fred asks, nodding at my plate. He hasn't really touched his either.

"No—no, it's delicious. Seriously. I'm just not as hungry as I thought I was."

I put down my fork. Fred puts down his and meets my eyes. A beat of heated silence passes between us.

I am not going to make it out of here alive.

Desperate for a change of subject, I say, "I needed this—a break. I've been studying like a madwoman for exams, and my mom is riding me super hard about finding an internship for next summer. I'm fucking exhausted."

"Ah. Your mum," Fred says. "She sounds . . . quite driven."

"Driven." I twirl the bottom of my beer glass to keep from looking at him. "That's a nice way of putting it. She and I . . . we have very different ideas about my future."

"Have you heard back from the athletic department back at Meryton?"

I smile. "I made it to the final round."

He holds up his hand. "Hell yeah you did! Congratulations."

"Thanks," I say, giving him a high-five. The gesture is meant to be friendly, but a shot of heat moves up my arm from the place where my palm meets his. His hand is warm, dry, enormous. "I'm excited."

He looks at me, dubious. "You don't sound like it."

I sigh. Scoff. "I *was* excited. But then I talked to my mom the other day, and now I'm confused. Stressed."

"Why?"

"Because." I take a gulp of beer. "She's got big plans for me to be this hoity-toity plastic surgeon, just like she is. But I want to do sports medicine, obviously. The internship I get this summer will kind of determine which path I'll be taking. I have to decide what my future's going to look like—I mean, I only have a year and a half left until I graduate."

"Plenty of surgeons operate on athletes—Rhys Maddox basically had his whole knee reconstructed last year. Couldn't you be one of those doctors?"

"Mom is really stuck on me going into plastics. I mean, let's acknowledge that assuming this whole scenario is actually going to happen is ridiculous. I have to get into med school, which is hard. And then I have to get into surgery, which is even harder. But Mom's convinced it will happen, and when it does, plastic surgery is what I should do. Anything else is 'a waste of my time and talent.'"

"Wow. That's some intense advice."

"No kidding. The internships my mom wants me to do, shadowing doctors and stuff . . . the med schools she keeps throwing out as possibilities . . . I don't know, none of it feels right."

Fred glides his tongue along his bottom lip. He puts his forearm on the island and leans into it. Leans toward me. "None of it feels like you."

"Yes." I try to swallow the sudden rise of feeling at the base of my throat. "Yes, exactly. But I'm terrified of disappointing her. I'm terrified the balance I'm looking for in life will disappoint *me*. That what Mom says is true—it won't be enough. That it will be boring."

He cocks a brow. "Balance?"

"You know, work-life balance. I want to have a life outside

of work. A *real* life, one that's not wrapped around making tons of money or impressing other people. I want to have time for hobbies, friends. Eventually a family."

"I've never thought about life like that," he says, blinking. "The balance part. It's been all football, all the time for me—"

"I know." I grin. "You're such an American when it comes to work."

One side of his mouth quirks up. It's an adorably boyish expression, and it's so very *Fred*. Honest, unguarded, genuine.

My pulse hiccups.

"What does that mean?" he asks.

"You have to admit you wrap your life around your job."

"Well, yeah." Fred shifts on his stool. "I didn't plan for it to happen that way. Football's just the only thing I've ever been good at."

I'm leaning forward now too. It's like there's a string that connects Fred's chest to mine, and he's slowly reeling it in, pulling me toward him centimeter by centimeter.

I need to pull back. I know that.

Maybe it's his grin, or his insightful questions, or his genuine interest in what's going on inside my head—whatever it is, it has me falling into him instead. I can't resist the pull of his gravity.

I don't want to.

"I disagree," I say. "You're good at other things. Really good. Like taking selfies, obviously."

"Too bad it took me twenty-two years to meet you so I could figure that out," he says, grinning for the hundredth time tonight. I love it when he grins and his eyes get all squinty. I don't know how he can be so freaking adorable while also being so smoking hot, but he does it, and he does it well.

"Better late than never," I say. "I mean, you've got this super successful career, obviously, so making football your life has served you well. But in a way, you live to work. I think I want something different. I want to work to live. Not to get, like, all Oprah on you or anything . . ."

He looks at me. "Why would you want that? To work to live? I'm not asking to be a dick. I'm asking because I'm genuinely curious."

I pause. I've thought about this so often, and for so long, I'm not really sure where to begin. I'm also a college student, so I know how ridiculous it sounds for me to talk about work-life balance when I've yet to hold down a real job.

But I've seen how my mom lives her life. Or doesn't, really. For all the money she makes—she makes a *lot* of money —Mom doesn't seem to enjoy the things she works so hard for. We have a big, beautiful house, but Mom is never home. She's too busy being important—too busy impressing her colleagues and her patients and her fake friends with clothes and cars. On the outside, she has a beautiful, successful life. But on the inside, it's empty. She's always stressed. Always unhappy. Her relationships—the few real relationships she has, with me, Dad, my aunts and uncles—have suffered on account of her work.

"Because," I say. "Because I think we miss out on the things we're looking for in life by thinking we're going to find them in our work. Don't get me wrong, I think work is an important piece of the self-fulfillment puzzle, and a girl's gotta pay the bills. But in terms of finding meaning there, and a sense of real and lasting purpose—I don't know. I haven't found any of that in the jobs or internships I've had so far. I haven't found it in my studies either. I know I won't find it in plastic surgery. But I have found it in my friends. My hobbies. Travel. That's the stuff that lights up my life, you know?"

Fred's got this funny look on his face as he meets my gaze. I can't tell what he's thinking, he just looks at me, and looks, his green-blue eyes going soft again. Soft, and hot.

The kind of hot that makes my stomach flip.

"Christ, you're a knockout," he says at last.

I shut my eyes. I have to change the subject again. I have to change the fucking subject now, or I am going to tackle this guy and not get off him until we're both naked and panting and spent.

"You're just saying that because you're bored with talking and you want to get to the vampire boobs, don't you?"

"No." He shakes his head. "Quite the opposite. I love hearing you talk. You're so passionate. Well spoken. I admire that. I admire you."

"Admire me?" I scoff, even as a rush of pleasure moves through me. "Why?"

"Because you have a life," he says simply. "A full, real life. And it's making me realize that I want one too, because you make it look so fucking good."

I cock a teasing brow. "I'm making you want a life? That sounds dangerous. I hardly think your coach—and, um, all of Spain—would approve."

Fred shrugs, like it's no big deal that he is, in fact, a really big deal. "Who's to say I can't strike that balance you were talking about? Perhaps I can have my fun on the pitch and off it too."

There's a joke here—one about me being included in off-the-pitch fun—but I don't make it. We're skating on thin enough ice as it is. I have to respect Fred's boundaries.

I have to, or we'll both end up doing something we'll regret.

"I obviously can't tell you what to do," he says. "I've been in a similar situation with my mum, and I had to make a difficult decision. I want you to have all the information you possibly can before that happens, so you can make the best possible choice, yeah?"

"Yeah," I say. "But how do I do that?"

"I know you probably have Valentina's email—"

"I do."

"—but I'll try to get the emails for the other physios and doctors next time I'm at the training facility. You could chat with them about that internship Valentina was talking about —could be a solid backup plan for next summer?"

I pull back, stunned. "That'd be awesome. But you've already done so much for me. You don't have—"

"I want to." Fred meets my eyes. "You're obviously torn up about what to do. I've been there, Rachel. The thing that helped most was knowing deep down in my gut that I was doing something I truly loved. That I was capable of being great at it. Because doing something you love, and knowing that passion will help you work hard enough to get really, really good at it, is a solid recipe for happiness. No matter what path you choose, it's going to be fucking hard. But if you have that feeling in your gut, you have what you need to push through the doubt and the regret. Let me do this for you."

Stop it, I want to say to him.

Stop making me want you. Because you said you can't want me.

I meet his eyes. "Thank you. Seriously. For making this happen. And for talking me out of going on a murderous-mom rampage, like Empress Marina does on *Tournament of Kings*."

"Speaking of," he says, "shall we start our marathon?"

I mean. Come on. Could this guy be any more perfect for me?

Three episodes later, we're huddled on Fred's cushy couch in his living room, glued to the TV. I vaguely register the room's clean, tidy gorgeousness—he's definitely had the flat professionally decorated. It seems almost *too* tidy though, the pillows too fluffed, the furniture too pristine. Like Fred's never really used any of this stuff.

The episode we're watching ends on a shot of Queen Lorena's dead body in a coffin. Suddenly her eyes pop open. Fangs sprout from her mouth. And then the credits roll.

"No fucking way," Fred says, throwing up his arms in genuine, enthusiastic distress. "No fucking way! Are you joking? It can't end like that. This show is bloody killing me."

You're bloody killing me.

I've been a huge *Tournament* fan ever since the show saved me from a major *Lord of the Rings* hangover a few years back. Just when my Aragorn obsession was starting to get weird, Queen Lorena and her dysfunctional family showed up. I've been a fan ever since.

Usually, I'll watch the show on my own. Mom, of course, won't bother with "campy vampire smut" and my roommates aren't all that into fantasy. I've never experienced *Tournament* with someone else, which I was cool with because I didn't know any better.

But watching it with Fred takes the experience to a whole new level. He loves picking apart the finer points of the show —the powerful female leads, the themes of loyalty and fate— even more than I do. I pick up on stuff I didn't see before, like seeing the story through a new pair of eyes . We laugh about the ridiculous preponderance of not only boobs, but butts too. We discuss how awkward it must've been to film all those sex scenes in the castle moat.

Basically, we indulge our inner nerds to our hearts' content. And it. Is. Awesome.

So awesome it almost makes me sad, because I know Fred and I won't be watching *Tournament*'s new season together in February. I wish, I really, really wish, that things were different—that Fred and I didn't have lives on opposite sides of an ocean. I've met enough guys to know hitting it off like this is rare. It never happens. Not this quickly.

I want to touch him and kiss him and come with him. But I can't. Even if I could, it wouldn't last. It wouldn't change the fact that we were never meant to be.

I clutch the pillow I'm holding a bit tighter against my torso, but it does nothing to alleviate the painful twist inside my chest. This is agony.

"It's addictive, right?" I keep my eyes focused on the screen, even though the credits are still rolling. "Just wait until they introduce the gargoyles. Oh! The Princes of the Desert too. They have this, like, crazy power of being able to see the future through the eyes of these killer bees. It makes absolutely no sense, and it's amazing."

"I can't believe I've been missing out on this brilliance. Now I know why the lads are constantly talking about it."

I grab my phone off the coffee table while Fred fiddles with the remote, scrolling to the next episode.

My pulse hiccups when I see the time.

"Shit," I say. "Fred, it's one thirty! How am I going to get home? The Metro just closed. I have an eight o'clock class too."

Fred turns from the TV to look at me. "Stay here. I'm not drunk or anything, but I did have a couple beers, so driving is probably not a great idea . . ."

"I can take a taxi," I say, untangling myself from the pillow.

He puts his hand on the pillow, holding it against my chest. My blood throbs. "I don't like the thought of you taking a taxi alone at night. Please stay, Rachel."

I pause. Look at him. What does he mean, asking me to stay? Stay in his guest room as a friend? Or stay in his room—in his bed—as something more?

He's looking at me with heat in his eyes again. Heat and want and pain.

I know that pain. Oh, do I know it.

I'm not sure what I should do here. Neither of us meant for our little day trip to last this long. But it's going so well, and I'm having so much fun.

I am so turned on.

This is a bad idea.

"Okay," I find myself saying anyway.

"C'mon," he says. He stands up and offers me his hand. "I have some sweats for you to sleep in."

I take his hand. It swallows mine, his palm warm and dry. Little sparks of heat ignite and move up my arm. I let him pull me to my feet. He holds my hand for a beat too long before he drops it and tugs his fingers through his hair.

He's going to have none of it left if he keeps tugging at this rate.

I emerge from Fred's bathroom in a sweatshirt and a pair of shorts five sizes too big for me. His number—seven—is emblazoned in purple all over my new outfit.

The clothes are clean, but they still smell like him. Soap, sandalwood. Heat flares between my legs. I am wide awake. My heart feels swollen, tender almost.

Fred is standing beside his bed, plugging his phone into a charger. He looks up.

Looks at me.

I attempt a smile, because I'm nervous as hell and still shaking a little and don't know what else to do.

His bedroom is cozy. I try not to look at the enormous bed in the center of the room. Being in here feels unbearably intimate. I want to be the girl who sleeps in that bed with him.

I'm not though. I will never be that girl.

"Your clothes are just a *little* big," I say, holding up my arms. The sleeves of his sweatshirt hang several inches off my hands.

Fred's expression hardens as his eyes move over my body. "Just a little."

"Look." I do a sort of half-dab, holding the crook of my elbow to my nose. "I could use your sweatshirt as an invisibility cloak."

The *Harry Potter* reference is a shameless attempt to get Fred to laugh. But he doesn't. The look in eyes just gets harder. Darker.

My heart thuds inside my chest. What is he thinking? Is he mad? Does he want me to leave? I can't read this guy tonight, and it's driving me crazy.

"I'd also fit right in at Queen Lorena's castle," I say. I'm starting to babble, but *I don't know what the hell else to do*. I tug one arm out of the sleeve and wrap the soft material around my neck. "The collars on her ladies' dresses—they're huge. I don't know how they fit through all those tiny medieval doors. Maybe they have their servants follow them around or something, so they can crowbar them out if they get stuck."

Fred sets his phone on the nightstand. Spears a hand through his hair, giving it a solid pull before he lets go. The muscle in his jaw jumps.

I swallow, hard, and clench my teeth. I'm shaking so hard I'm worried they'll start to chatter.

His gaze slides to meet mine. There's a crease in his brow now, like he's worried. Like he's scared.

My heart dips.

Oh, Fred.

I want to take your face in my hands. Smooth that crease with my thumb.

I want to fucking kiss you until neither of us can see straight. But I won't. Not unless you want to.

My pulse is thumping.

My breath catches when he crosses the room and reaches for me, towering over me. He's so damn huge. He's close enough I can see the stubble dotting his chin, the hair growing there is so blond it's almost translucent.

The look in his eyes—it's violent. Dark. So open and honest it's hard to look back.

I didn't know feelings could be so excruciatingly *real* until this moment.

I didn't know people could be so real with each other.

I struggle to breathe. The relief that floods my chest is crushing. The relief, and the anguish too.

I just found what I've been looking for. I found real. I found something true in a world full of bullshit.

Of course I found that truth in someone I can't have.

Fred slowly—carefully—unwinds the sleeve from around my neck. His small touches raise goosebumps on my arms and legs. What I would give for him to touch me like this all over.

My eyes flutter shut. My body screams.

We can't be together.

But that doesn't stop me from wanting Fred to burn me down.

That doesn't mean I wouldn't let him turn me inside out if he wanted to.

Chapter Eight

FRED

Rachel trembles with the effort to keep tabs on the desire pooling between us. She wants to touch me as much as I want to touch her.

But she doesn't. She keeps her arms glued to her sides, eyes screwed shut as she stands in front of me, hardly daring to breathe.

The effort is killing her. Just like it's killing me to stand here, the floral scent of her shampoo filling my head.

Still, she doesn't touch me.

She's respecting my boundaries. She's respecting *me*. And she's doing it while cracking nerdy jokes about *Harry Potter* and my new obsession, *Tournament of Kings*.

In other words, she's bloody perfect.

Perfect for me.

I've tried—hell, have I tried—to be smart with her. To not let her in. But how can I not let this girl in when we're clearly made out of the same stuff?

I should've known my fucking rules would go out the window the minute this girl started talking patellar dislocations and beer at Olivier's party.

I should've known I'd break every rule and cross every line with Rachel.

I should've known she'd be different, right from the start.

All my life, I've worn layers of armor to protect me—protect my heart—from girls who wouldn't stick around for the long haul. I promised myself I wouldn't take it off until I met my forever girl.

But here I am, taking it off for the girl who's leaving in three weeks' time.

Here I am, tucking her hair behind her ear, watching the sinews of her throat move as she swallows.

I'm still scared shitless about what's going to happen at the end of December. Now, though, the thought of not experiencing everything I possibly can with Rachel in the small amount of time we have—*that* scares me more.

I've been hanging on to this V-card for a while. Who better to swipe it than the girl who makes me feel more at home—who likes me for me, no matter how dorky I am—than I have since I left Germany?

I take her face in my hand, cupping her cheek. Her skin is warm. Smooth. She draws a sharp breath.

"Hey," I say, softly. "Hey, love. Open your eyes."

Rachel swallows again. Then she does as I tell her, revealing black, wet eyes.

"You're shaking," I say.

"So are you," she says.

I bite the inside of my cheek. "I know."

"This is so not okay, Fred."

"I know," I repeat. I pull my thumb across her bottom lip. Her eyes go soft. "For the record, I would gladly crowbar you out of a doorway in High Castle."

She grins, slowly, like she's savoring it. "Always such a gentleman."

"My mum raised me right."

"She certainly did."

I search her eyes. Her grin fades. My heart pounds.

"Yes," she says to my silent question. Her eyes move to my mouth. "Yes, Fred. Please."

I adjust my hand on her face, rocking her in time to my movements. I bend my neck and she goes up on her toes, closing her eyes. I close mine too.

And then I press my lips to hers. Her mouth is soft, hot, so bloody perfect I groan. For several heartbeats I keep the kiss small and clean. I want to savor the feel of her. The taste.

But my blood is rioting inside my skin, and soon enough impatience takes over. I've wanted to do this all day. I can't help myself.

I tilt my head and move my lips, opening hers to me. Electricity bolts through me as my mouth slants over her mouth, every corner of my being blinking awake, throbbing with need. Rachel tilts her head too, deepening the kiss. I drink her in, the taste of her lips—chapstick, *her*—the smell of her skin. I drink and I give slowly, thoroughly, and she takes.

I bury my fingers in her hair. I haven't kissed a girl in ages, but even I know it's never this good on the first go round. It's never this deep, this sweet.

I want to kiss her like this for hours.

I fall into her, giving, giving, exploring her mouth and her tongue and her lips slowly, like we have all the time in the world. I nudge her with my nose, wanting more, wanting to deepen the kiss further. Now that this is happening—now that I've let myself cross a line—there is so much I want to do and know and learn that I don't know where to start.

Her body rises to meet my kiss. Her hands uncurl at my sides and she holds me just above my hips. She turns her head in my hands, changing the angle of our mouths. She's sexy and soft. In this moment, she is mine and I am hers. I've never . . . never felt so possessive of someone, or so possessed myself.

I can't believe I've been missing out on this for so long.

I drink her in like a man dying of thirst.

Because that's what I've been all this time. A man dying of thirst. And now I finally get to drink my fill of Rachel's sweetness.

To hell with my rules. This girl, this bloody moment, makes breaking them worth it.

I step forward, tucking her body against mine as I guide both her legs between mine. Our hips meet.

I tug at her bottom lip.

She moans. The feminine, almost desperate sound sends a rush of sensation straight to the head of my dick.

I back her toward my bed.

Rachel

Fred's kiss is hard and soft all at once, slow and fast, patient and piqued. It's making me dizzy in the best, best, *best* way.

He holds nothing back. He doesn't try too hard, or put any cheesy moves on me. He's just kissing me, touching me, adoring my body, his only agenda our enjoyment.

He savors my bottom lip between my teeth. Heaviness gathers between my legs. My knees buckle.

Like he can read my body like a book, he steps into me, nudging his hips against my hips, using his own legs to hold me up. It's sexy and it's cocky and I like it too much.

I like this guy—this guy I can't fucking have—way too much.

I could kiss him for ages, and it still wouldn't be enough.

I reach behind me for the bed, but before I find it, Fred curls an arm around my waist and lifts me, tossing me gently onto it. I gasp, he smiles, and my heart and need feel several sizes too big for my body as I watch him climb on top of me, over me, blocking out the rest of the world.

I sink into the fluffy duvet. My back almost aches, it's so comfortable.

He supports his weight on his hands, which are on either side of my head. I run my hands up the length of his forearms. They're huge, rigid with muscle, a roadmap of thick, ropey veins taut against his skin.

Fred brushes a wisp of hair from my forehead. He smiles, and the way his eyes get all squinty makes my pulse dance.

"You taste so fucking good, love," he says, and then his mouth is on my mouth and his lips are moving in that deep, passionate way of his. Behind my closed eyes I feel like I'm falling, falling into his caresses, dizzy and terrified and turned on. His weight comes down on me, bit by bit, making me breathless, holding me down.

I'm greedy for the feel of him. I grab fistfuls of his shirt and try to pull him even farther on top of me.

"I don't want to crush you," he says, resisting. "You're so little, and I'm . . . uh, not."

"I'll be okay," I say. "I like feeling you."

I nuzzle his neck as he lowers himself on top of me. My body lights up at the deliciousness of his weight pinning me down. He's heavy, but he's also really, really careful not to put *too* much weight on me. He's on his elbows now, his lips trailing along my neck as I try to get my bearings. This feels . . . this feels *real*. Right.

This feels like heaven. Which means it's going to hurt like hell tomorrow when we wake up and remember it can't last.

I want it to last, more than I've wanted anything in a long time.

I want my time with Fred to last.

"This feel good?" His voice is husky, his German accent really coming out.

"Fred," I plead.

He looks up from neck. His eyes, wild, wet, green now, meet mine.

"It's all right," he says. "We're going to be all right."

"Liar," I say, the last half the word stalling in my throat when Fred's hand moves up my torso and cups my breast. A bolt of heat spears me right through the center of my sex. I already know I'm wet. Dripping wet.

I take his face in my hands and pull him toward me, lifting my head to press my mouth to his mouth. In the space of two heartbeats, the kiss goes wild, a little messy, and the heat between my legs tightens. I run my fingers through the hair at the nape of Fred's neck, and he groans, nipping at my lips with his teeth.

I break the kiss, move my mouth down his jaw. His whole body tenses when I start kissing his neck.

"Oh, love—" he stutters.

"This okay?" I ask, licking the place just beneath his ear.

He closes his eyes. "Fuck. *Yes.*"

So I keep kissing him like this, and he wedges a knee between my legs, spreading them apart. My hips roll toward him, begging for friction, begging for more.

He settles his hips between my legs. Presses his groin right where I want him to press it.

My eyes roll to the back of my head. This feels amazing. Better than that.

I was *so* not prepared for the onslaught of goodness tonight—today—would bring. I knew Fred was different and we'd have fun together. But I didn't know how terrifyingly *good* things between us would be. I didn't know he'd love sports and Queen Lorena and beer as much as I did.

I was attracted to him before, but I didn't know our connection would lead to such smoldering chemistry.

Fred grinds his pelvis against me. I cry out, my hips rising to meet his. I want him to touch me. To taste me. To fuck me.

I want to experience everything with him.

He ducks his head and starts kissing my neck. Pulses of electricity move through me from the places where his lips meet my skin. It's my turn to start making noises. Emboldened, Fred scrapes his teeth against the side of my throat, and I arch against him, gasping.

Using my hips, I roll us onto our sides, and then I kiss him, and he kisses me back, and somehow—

Somehow I know that this is the beginning of the end. My control is slipping. He's too good at this. He makes me feel too good. Too turned on.

Too sexy.

Fred's kissing me slowly, deeply, driving me wild. Waking up corners of my body and of my being that I didn't know existed.

That I worried I didn't have at all.

His enormous hands are on my waist, they're on my ass, they're gently exploring my breasts. I grab onto him, holding on for dear life as he touches me with awed confidence. I'm writhing beneath him, baring myself to him, and he is so gentle with me and so thorough I'm overwhelmed.

Fred bites my bottom lip. He runs his palm up the length of my back and then curls his hand around the nape of my neck, his grip firm, possessive, confident as he pulls my mouth toward his. The way he touches me—I've never been touched like this. I've never been so worshipped.

I've always loved making out. But this—this is on a whole other plane compared to the make-out sessions I've had with guys back at Meryton. I'm not worried what Fred thinks of me or what he'll say to his friends. I'm not sweating whether or not he'll acknowledge me if I see him on campus tomorrow—whether or not I'm in a popular enough sorority to merit his attention outside of his dorm room.

Fred is real, he's honest.

I can trust him in a way I've never trusted a guy before. Which means I'm more myself with him than with anyone else. The sense of liberation this gives me is exhilarating.

I could become addicted to it.

I slip a hand underneath his sweater, allow my fingers to explore the expanse of muscle and skin and wiry hair there. I pull back, take a breath, swallow.

"You okay?" His pale eyes search mine for several long, excruciating heartbeats. In the half-light of the lamp on the bedside table, Fred is handsomer than ever. An eviscerating handsomeness.

"Not okay," I say. "We should stop now."

"We should."

I wait for him to take his hands off me, but he doesn't.

I wait for the fierceness of my feelings for him to fade. But they don't. They burn hotter the longer we make out.

We roll around in his bed for what seems like hours, kissing until our lips are swollen and the skin on my cheeks and chin is raw from rubbing against Fred's stubble. I'm horny as hell, and judging from the distinct bump I feel every time he grinds against me, he is too. But neither of us makes a move to go any further. I don't want to push him, for one thing, and for another, I'm enjoying taking it slow. I get to savor Fred, savor the experience of our bodies touching and tasting and teasing.

I get to savor him like we have more than just three weeks together. I decide to let myself live in that fiction, just for tonight. Just for right now.

Eventually our kiss becomes less fevered. Our bodies

begin to slow. Fred turns me around and hooks an arm across my middle, pulling my back to his front.

"Fred?" I ask sleepily.

"Yeah?"

"Why Harry Potter?" I don't know where the thought comes from, but I'm curious all of the sudden. "Why are you such a giant fan of a teenage wizard?"

He pauses. His breath his warm on the nape of my neck.

"I suppose I can relate to the lonely boy underneath the stairs," he finally replies. "You know, the boy living with people who don't understand him."

My heart clenches.

"What about you?" Fred asks. "Why do you like the books so much?"

I take a breath. Let it out.

"Because the boy with the good heart becomes a badass wizard who saves the day, all because he's true to who he really is, no matter how much it costs him. He had to give so much up to become who he was. But it was worth it."

Now Fred's pressing kisses onto my neck. A delicious shiver moves through me.

"I like that thought," he murmurs.

I fall asleep curled into the solid bulk of his body.

Fred

It's dark in my room, but I can still see the outline of Rachel's body as she rides me, legs spread around my hips. Her pelvis grinds against mine, her pussy clenched tight around my cock. I reach up and take one of her breasts in my hand, thumbing the nipple. Her head falls back, her long hair tickling the tops of my thighs.

"Fred," she breathes. "Oh my God, Fred—"

I sit up, somehow managing to keep myself inside her as I curl her into my arms. Her nipples brush against my chest, and we both suck in a breath. My balls tighten. I don't want to come, not yet. This has to be good for her. This has to be the best sex she's ever had, because I want her to come back. I want her in my bed like this every night, moaning my name.

I duck my head and take her nipple in my mouth.

"I'm—Fred, I'm coming."

Her hips move frantically against me now, sucking me to completion, urging both of us to heights I didn't know existed. She moves exactly how I need her to, and I do the same for her, like we're reading each other's minds. The intensity of our connection—it's almost too fucking much to bear.

This is what I want, I think to myself. *This is what I've always wanted.*

I use my body to press her down onto the bed. We're in missionary now, and I hike her leg up over my hip as she comes and comes and comes, crying out, clutching the sheets. I see stars as I feel the first stirrings of my own orgasm. It's too much—can I come inside her—I don't know how we got here, this can't happen, I don't want her life and she doesn't want mine—

My eyes fly open. I'm breathing, hard, burning up.

My skin is covered in a sheen of sweat. I've got a hard-on the size of a bloody tree. When I kick off the blankets, I suck in a breath as the soft glide of the cotton against the head of my dick has me wincing in pain.

I cover my eyes with my thumb and forefinger. *Fuck*. Another dream about Rachel. This was the most real one— the most explicit dream—yet.

I glance at the shapely form in the bed beside me.

Rachel's breathing is even and deep. I didn't wake her, thank heaven.

My heart thumps at the knowledge she's so close. An arm's length away, maybe less. I could easily reach out, touch her, wake her, reenact everything I just dreamed about.

Christ, I want to fuck her. Brand her. Give her the virginity I've been holding on to for far too long now.

Maybe then she'd stay in Madrid with me. Maybe then I could convince her—the way I'm convinced—that we really are forever material, even though I've known her all of a week.

I need this girl with me. I know this sounds crazy, but I'm ready to take the next step. Maybe Rachel would consider applying to that internship at the training facility—the one Valentina mentioned. Then she could stay in Spain *and* chase her sports medicine dream. It'd be win-win.

But I'd still be asking her to give up the internship back in the States—the one she really wants. I'd be asking her to take a massive leap of faith that, from the outside, looks quite foolish.

I sit up and drag a hand through my hair, cursing. My eyes burn because I forgot to take out my contacts last night. I check my phone. It's half past six.

I send up a silent prayer of gratitude. It's early enough that I can grab a shower and take care of this raging woody, hopefully before Rachel wakes up.

Rachel. The girl who is breathing and sleeping and dreaming in my bloody *bed* right now. What is she dreaming about, I wonder? Probably about that wanker Prince Jacoby in *Tournament of Kings*—the guy with the puppy dog eyes who just happens to be shirtless in every scene. Tosser, that one.

I blink at the jealousy that spikes through me. It's not a familiar feeling. I'm not a jealous bloke. Never have been. I've no right to be jealous when it comes to Rachel.

But this girl has me feeling all sorts of fucked up this morning.

I head for the bathroom, pausing at the door. I glance back at the bed. Rachel turns over, her hair forming a dark halo on the pillow around her face.

Get in the shower, I tell myself. *Get. In. The. Bloody. Shower.*

My dick throbs.

I flick the lights on in my bathroom and turn on the shower, jamming the dial to the hottest possible setting. Almost immediately steam starts to curl inside the glass enclosure.

I step inside. The water, so hot I can hardly stand it, stings my skin.

Good.

Gritting my teeth, I lather my hands with soap. I reach for my dick and groan at first contact. I don't know if I've ever been this hard. If I've ever been in this much pain.

I close my eyes and there she is. Rachel. Naked and hot to the touch, her intelligent eyes glassy with desire. She gets on her knees. Takes me in her mouth, slowly at first, then faster, until the head of my cock presses against the back of her throat.

It only takes three, four strokes, and I'm coming so hard my legs almost buckle. The orgasm pounds through me, obliterating every thought except the one that screams *I want her*. I want her, every part of her, her mind and her laugh and that mouth of hers. Her eyes. Her pussy.

I want to claim her.

She's making me an animal.

The shockwaves finally subside, leaving my body limp and boneless. I lean hands on the wall and hang my head, the steam that swirls around me making it difficult to breathe. My heart is beating hard and fast. I can't get a grip on it.

Fuck. I'm in trouble.

We're both quiet on the drive over to Rachel's dorm building. There's no traffic for once—seven fifteen is early for Madrid —and I can't tell if I'm relieved or annoyed the ride doesn't last longer.

I pull up to the building and park illegally up front. I'm blocking a lane, but it's still early, and this street seems pretty quiet anyway.

Rachel yawns.

"Tired?" I ask.

"I am," she says, bending down to grab her purse. "I don't know if it was those boobs in *Tournament* getting me all hot and bothered or what, but I haven't made out like that . . . well. I guess I've never made out like that. Ever."

I glance at her as she sits up in her seat. She looks more beautiful than ever. Her hair is a mess of waves that fall over her shoulders and her lips are still the tiniest bit swollen.

Her face is flushed.

"So many boobs," I say, flicking my gaze teasingly to her chest. "And yet I can't seem to get enough of them."

"Is it my boobs you can't get enough of," she teases back, "or is it the vampire boobs?"

I laugh. "Your boobs, clearly. I imagine vampire boobs are quite cold to the touch, no?"

Rachel pulls a funny face. "Totally."

"I'd like to do it again," I say. "The making out, *and* the vampire boobs marathon."

She looks at me, her eyes dark and vulnerable. Her lips quirk upward, just enough to let me know she's flattered.

Fuck me, I want this girl.

"Me too," she says. "As long as beer's still involved. That stuff you have is awesome."

Of course she wants beer.

Of course what she wants to do tonight is exactly what I want to do. The thought of curling up with Rachel, cozy on my sofa or in my bed, fills me with a lightness so exquisite I can barely breathe.

I want to get cozy with her every night. I want to take her home and talk football over beers and watch *Tournament* together and read Potter in bed afterward, the two of us comparing notes as we work our way through the series again and again and again.

"The internship Valentina was talking about," I blurt. "The one at the training facility next semester—would you consider applying for it?"

Rachel rolls her lips between her teeth. Shifts in her seat.

"I would, yeah. It's a great opportunity. It's also extremely competitive. But sure—I'd check it out." She focuses her gaze on her lap. "Why do you ask?"

I take a deep breath. "Look, Rachel, I know we've only known each other for a week—"

"Fred, we've spent all of—what, twelve hours together?"

"—but I bloody like you. A lot. Don't tell me you don't feel it—the connection we have. The chemistry."

Her fingers worry the handle on her bag. "I do. I definitely feel it."

"This—what we have—it's different. Special. I think we should give it a shot."

"A shot in the long-term?"

"Yes. I'm not asking you to make any decisions yet. I just want you to think about it."

"Fred." She meets my eyes. "What the hell does this mean? One minute you're telling me you only want to be friends, the next you're asking me to stay in Spain for another semester. You have to admit this whole thing is crazy."

I reach across the seat and take her hand in mine, tangling our fingers. She lets out a short, hot breath.

"It *is* crazy, absolutely," I say. "But my gut's telling me it's right. I've never met anyone like you. I don't usually like having people around this much, but I'm already counting down the hours until I can see you again."

"Oh?" she arches a brow. "And when is that going to be?"

"Tonight. If, of course, you're free."

She's trying not to smile. "I am."

"Then it's a date." I give her hand a squeeze. "Just promise me you'll think about the internship, yeah?"

Rachel looks at me for a long moment before she starts to nod.

"Yeah," she says. "I will."

My heart contracts. I haven't had my coffee yet, but already my blood buzzes with anticipation, excitement too.

She keeps looking at me. I look back. After a beat, we both start to laugh.

"I can't believe this is happening," she says.

"Me neither. I never thought—"

"What? That you'd fall for some American chick who wishes Quidditch were a real sport?"

I grin. "Yeah. Something like that. So, when can I pick you up tonight?"

"Well," she says, sighing. "I have my last round interview for that internship—the one back at Meryton—this morning"—my heart falls, just a bit, at the mention of Rachel's plans to head home—"and after that I need to go do some research at the Reina Sofía Museum. Want to just meet me there and we can figure something out after?"

"Yes," I say, a little too quickly. "What time works for you?"

I've never been to the Reina Sofía—it's one of Madrid's

most famous art museums—but I don't tell Rachel that. It's pretty much a given at this point that I don't know about or do much outside of football.

I'm excited to go to the museum. But not nearly as excited as I am to see Rachel again.

"Around seven sound okay?"

"Seven is perfect."

"Great."

"Great."

Rachel's smile breaks through.

I can't stop looking at her. Even as my heart pounds, everything inside me feels soft. Hungry.

The girly scent of her perfume fills my head.

But really. What the hell is happening? A week ago, I would've been completely content holing up in my flat with Voldemort for company on a Monday off. But now the thought of eating pre-made meals by myself, and watching match footage by myself, suddenly seems . . . I don't know.

Sort of lonely, I suppose.

When I'm with Rachel, I don't feel lonely at all. I feel . . . found, as cheesy as that sounds.

"I should go," she says. "I'm going to be late for class."

"All right," I say, reluctantly releasing her hand.

She looks at me. I look back.

She's still smiling. Her eyes flick to my mouth.

Quickly she leans in and kisses me. Her lips are soft as they move over mine. She tastes like toothpaste. Toothpaste and Rachel. She must've used one of the spare toothbrushes I keep in the guest bathroom

My whole body jumps. I groan. "You sure you can't meet me any earlier?"

"Trust me, I'd stay all day with you if I could," she says, looping the strap of her bag over her shoulder.

"Good luck with your interview. Not that you need it, but . . ."

She grins. "Thanks, Fred."

Rachel hops out of the car. I wait until she's safe inside the building before I drive away.

Chapter Nine

RACHEL

I'm unlocking my dorm room door, my hands shaking like the rest of me, my lips still burning from kissing Fred—still sore from our marathon make-out last night—when I hear a familiar voice.

"Um. Did I just see what I thought I saw?"

I turn and see Laura peeking out of her room two doors down from mine, a look of happy disbelief on her face.

Damn it. I forgot she's been staying at the dorm these days, and her window looks out onto the street. Usually she's shacked up at Rhys's apartment. I should've known I'd run into her—we have the same class schedule on Monday mornings.

"See . . . uh . . . what?" My voice is uneven. It's a dead giveaway.

"See you tongue kissing Fred Ohr in his car."

I swallow, turning the key in the lock. "Maybe?"

"Holy shit, Rachel." She steps out of her room and stands in front of me, peering at my face. "Are you guys, like, a thing?"

"Um," I say, fighting a smile. "We're . . . well. I honestly don't know what we are."

"Holy shit," she says again. "Did you guys do it?"

I open the door, shaking my head. "No. We just made out for, like, ever. It wasn't supposed to happen, but . . ."

I step inside my room, and Laura follows me in.

"But if you guys just made out, then why do you look so . . . blissed out, I guess? It's like he fucked you until you found nirvana. It's scary. And kind of hot, actually."

"The way he kissed me last night—it was good. Really, really good." So good my pulse throbs from the memory of it. That look in his eyes as he came in for the kill—he was scared and hungry and so intent. So focused on me.

I put my bag on my desk and start stuffing random notebooks into it.

I glance at Laura. She's looking at me, tilting her head. "You like him, don't you?"

"I do. He's charming, and smart, and hot as hell." I look away. "He asked me to think about staying in Madrid for another semester."

Laura pulls back, eyes wide, jerking her head side to side. "*What*? Didn't you guys, like, meet two days ago?"

"We met a week ago, but yeah, it's pretty crazy, right?"

"Crazy? Rach, it's *insane*."

My pulse hiccups. Hearing my friend say it out loud makes me realize just how nuts this whole thing is.

"Fred wants a girlfriend," I say with a shrug. "Like, wants to settle down with someone for real. And I like him. A lot. I'm just worried—"

"Your internship," Laura says. "The one you want back at Meryton. If you stayed here for another semester, you'd miss out on it."

"Exactly. That internship starts at the end of April, and the semester here doesn't end until June."

Laura purses her mouth and sighs through her nose, deep in thought. "That's tough. I know how important this internship is to you. You've been working your ass off to get it. I mean, you only talk sports, like, *all* the time."

"Sorry," I say, grinning.

"Don't be. I bet Fred loves it."

I bite my lip. "He does."

"Maybe you guys really are meant to be together," she says.

"I mean, there is another sports medicine internship I could apply for, one that's here in Spain. I have to do more research, but it's a possibility. I'm just not sure it'd be as great of a fit for me as the internship back home would be."

"Worth considering," Laura says. "So, don't get me wrong, I like Fred. But you're talking about taking a pretty giant leap of faith with him here."

"I know." I shrug. "We just . . . we have a lot in common, weirdly enough. We both love sports, and books . . . beer . . . we like the same TV shows. We even like our spaghetti the same way. I've been into a guy before, but this . . . this just feels different. He's so real, Laura. Authentic. Like he doesn't give a shit what people think. There's not a superficial bone in his body. He's confident in who he is. There's something incredibly sexy about a guy who's confident like that."

Laura smiles. "I have to agree. Rach, I think you like Fred. A lot. Even though you *are* playing with fire, making out with him like this," Laura says. "What if you end up falling for him, but the internship here doesn't work out—for whatever reason—and you have to leave at the end of the month? Obviously, you can't pass up the internship at Meryton. Aren't you worried you'll be a little crushed?"

I blink. Look away. "Well—yeah, of course I'm worried about that. Really worried, actually. But I've never hit it off with someone like this before. Part of me thinks getting involved, seeing where things go, is worth the risk. The other part of me—that part of me doesn't know what to do."

"I'm sorry, friend," Laura says, wrapping me in a hug. "To be fair, a lot would need to happen between now and the end of December for you guys to go from first-kiss-butterflies to oh-my-God-our-forbidden-love-is-doomed. And who knows? Maybe he turns out to be a total weirdo. A serial killer."

I laugh. "Fred is many things, but a serial killer isn't one of them."

"You never know." She pulls back and holds me by the arms. "Then again, this *is* your semester of hashtag-YOLO."

I nod. "It is. Well. It's supposed to be."

"So maybe you should live a little. Realistically speaking, the chances of you two falling in love and having a Romeo and Juliet moment are slim to none. But the chances of you having super-hot hook-ups with a super-hot footballer are way better. So why not have some fun with him, I guess, and see where it goes?"

I take a deep breath, let it out. My body aches with exhaustion, but I'm somehow wild with excitement at the same time. Excitement and anticipation.

I have gotten pretty good at living in the moment in Madrid. And the semester isn't over yet. Why not end it with a figurative (and hopefully literal) bang?

Besides. Laura is right—the chances of Fred and me falling for each other, really *falling*, are tiny at best. I mean, we've only known each other for a freaking week. Yeah, it's starting to feel serious now. But maybe it won't be serious after this honeymoon glow wears off.

Maybe I really should just enjoy the moment and see where this thing goes.

Because really, even if Fred is different—even if he's genuine and fun and hot as fuck—could I truly want someone more than I want to chase down my dreams and make this sports medicine thing happen?

I don't think I could, honestly.

So I guess the decision would be easy enough, if I had to make it.

I guess I'm safe, then.

Later That Night

It's so quiet in the gallery that the scratch of my pencil across my notebook makes me squirm. For the hundredth time I set the notebook down on my lap and glance around, but the gallery is empty. Just like it was fifty seconds ago, when I last checked. It's only half past six, which means Fred won't be here for half an hour at least.

Since when am I so impatient?

I curl my legs underneath the bench and attempt to get back to work. The painting I'm writing this paper on hangs on the nearest wall, it's Herman Anglada Camarasa's *Sonia de Klamery (lying)*. It's a dark and moody portrait of a black-haired woman, her shoulders and chest bare, lying down beside a peacock in an exotic garden landscape.

I don't know why I was drawn to this painting when we had to select our topics. I've always been a fan of portraiture, I guess, and I liked that this one was bright and weird and different.

I didn't think the painting was especially sexy at first. But suddenly, I do. I see sensuality in Sonia's naked arms, in the shape of her waist as it curves into her hip. I see sex in the bright, flaring red of the peacock's tail feathers. I feel the living throb of the darkness that surrounds her.

Something else throbs between my legs. My lips tingle

with the memory of Fred's mouth on my mouth, his mouth on my body.

His *mouth*. It's like Fred and his tongue and his hands are breathing new life into this painting for me. I had to experience the sort of deep, unsettling, wild sensuality I did with Fred to be able to see it in Sonia.

The world is literally more colorful, and more interesting, now that I've made out with Fred. I can't imagine what the world would feel like if we went further. If we did more than feel each other up. The intensity—it'd be unbearable.

I swallow. Look at my notebook. It is not okay to be this turned on in an art museum.

It is not okay to be this turned on by a guy who says things like *sex should be special*.

I look up at the distant rumble of voices. My heart rate, already elevated, takes off at a sprint. I start scribbling in my notebook again, some bullshit about the birth of sensuality in art in the pre-war period, in a lame attempt to look like I haven't been waiting for this moment all day. My palms are sweaty so the pencil slips in my grip.

This is it, a man says in Spanish. His voice echoes off the tall ceiling. *Room 201.*

Thank you, another man says.

I know that voice. I know that man and his German accent.

Good luck this weekend, the first man says. *Granada is garbage this year, you shouldn't have trouble defeating them.*

Fred laughs, a giant, genuine sound. It makes me smile.

Granada is actually quite good, he replies. *A fair opponent. We'll do our best.*

I look up and there he is.

Fred's shaking the other man's hand—the guy is in a museum uniform—offering him a smile before he turns his head. His eyes meet mine. They're more green than blue in this light. His smile broadens, the skin around his eyes crinkling in unselfconscious pleasure.

Oh, dear.

"Hello, love," he says.

My heart contracts.

He looks good, like he always does. Jeans, sneakers, jacket —same Tomás Rincón hat—he wears it all well. I'll never get over just how big he is. How handsome. I've never been with a guy this good-looking. I doubt I ever will be again.

"You're early," I say, happy with disbelief. "Like, half an hour early."

He digs a hand into the hair at the nape of his neck and looks at me, sheepish. "Sorry—I was a bit impatient to see you. Do you need more time to work? I'm happy to wander about on my own . . ."

I dig my nails into the palm of my hand. I can't maul him. Not here. Not in public.

"No. No, I'm good," I manage to say. I close my notebook and stand. He walks over to me and puts a hand on the small of my back as he leans in and kisses my cheeks. He smells delicious, like sandalwood and soap. My knees are doing that funny thing again where they feel like jello. "Hi. Hello."

He only pulls back part of the way. His face is close to mine as is his body. His hand is still on my back. We've crossed into touching territory—where it's okay to touch, I guess, now that Fred's hands have been on my boobs—and I don't mind it. Not one bit.

"How's the paper coming?" he asks. His eyes move over my face. It's a careful gesture, a caring one too. Like he's making sure I really am good.

I swallow. "Eh. Shitty."

"You'll get it done. And the interview? How'd that go?"

"That went well, thank God."

"Brilliant. We'll have to celebrate."

"No celebrating yet—I don't want to jinx it," I say. I bend down to grab my notebook, grateful for the space this creates between my body and Fred's. It's overwhelming, being so close to him. I put the notebook in my messenger bag and hike it over my shoulder. "How about we just take a stroll around here instead? It's my favorite museum in Madrid—I know it decently well. I take it you've never been to the Reina Sofía?"

Fred grins. "How'd you know?"

"Lucky guess," I say, and now I'm grinning too. "Hang with me, Fred, and you'll see more of Spain in the next three weeks than you have in the years you've been here."

"I know. Why do you think I like you so much? Besides the fact that you're beautiful. Here, let me take this." Fred gently takes my bag and ducks underneath the strap, crossing it over his body. "Ready?"

I bite my lip. "Yeah. I'm Ready."

Fred

Rachel leads me through the museum's highlights: Picasso's *Guernica*, several Dalí masterpieces, an exhibition on Egyptian surrealism. Before I met Rachel, I never would've jumped at the idea of going to an art museum. But now that I'm here, listening to her talk about how this sculpture makes her feel, or how that painting is an interpretation of the Spanish Civil War, I'm smitten—smitten with the art and with the girl who knows so much about it.

Now that I'm experiencing more of Spain—more of life— I want to experience *everything*. And I want to experience it with Rachel. She makes the world come alive. She gives meaning to everything I see. Everything I do.

Today was boring without her. Lonely. I went through the motions, watching film, eating lunch. But the silence of my flat pressed in on me in a way it never has before. It drove me mad. I missed the sound of Rachel's voice, chatting about football, or vampire boobs, or Quidditch. I missed the smell of her perfume. The knowledge that she was *there*, with me, just an arm's length away. I was dying to watch more of *Tournament of Kings*—really, I need to know what happens next now that Queen Lorena is a vampire hell-bent on revenge—but I didn't want to watch it alone. It wouldn't be fun without her.

I'd hoped, foolishly, that I'd enjoy the time by myself after the . . . er . . . intensity of the past twenty-four hours. I am, after all, an introvert, and I usually do need to be alone after spending so much time with someone. I hoped that my burning desire for her might cool a bit. Out of sight, out of mind—that sort of thing.

But I didn't stop thinking about her, not for one bloody second.

Now that I'm with her again, drinking in her knowledge, the two of us laughing about all the boobs in Pablo Picasso's work (Is it just me, or are there suddenly boobs everywhere since I met Rachel?), I realize how electrified I feel when I'm with her. How respected.

How at home.

This—whatever *this* is—it's not going away. I don't want it to.

I want to take her home tonight. I want to take her home every night, even though—as of now—she's heading back to the States in less than three weeks' time.

I am so beyond fucked it's not even funny. It's a risk, letting Rachel in. Letting our relationship go any further.

But maybe—just maybe—it's a risk worth taking. Who

knows what will happen in the next month? Maybe Rachel gets her internship at Meryton. Maybe she doesn't.

Maybe she applies the internship at the squad's training facility and gets that one instead. Which means we'll have far more than three weeks together. Rachel did say she'd think about it.

I can't stop thinking about *her*.

"You okay?" Rachel asks as we make our way through one last gallery. "You look a little . . ."

She doesn't finish her sentence. She doesn't need to.

"Distressed?" I try to keep my voice light. "I'm all right. Well. Maybe not. I'm not all right. Christ." Instinctively my hand goes to the crown of my head, but my hat prevents me from tearing my fingers through my hair. I slide my hand to the bill and give that a solid tug instead.

Rachel slows down, falling in line beside me. She tucks her hair behind her ear. "I didn't think—I don't think either of us thought—"

"I missed you today." Bloody hell, when am I going to stop blurting shit out when I'm with her?

"I missed you too," she says, quietly. "But if you're not one hundred percent sure about taking this further . . . I mean, we can just be friends, Fred. It's not too late. Chalk up the make out to the beer and just . . . I don't know, pretend like it never happened?"

I meet her black eyes. They're clouded. Uncertain. She hates that idea as much as I do.

The soft parts in my chest swell. They fucking burst.

"I don't want to pretend with you, Rachel."

"And I don't want you to do anything you'll regret."

I chew on the inside of my cheek. Study her face. She's so damn smart. Respectful. Almost too respectful, if such a thing exists.

Like I could ever regret anything I do with this girl. Anything that happens between us.

I reach for her, twirling a lock of her long, silky hair around my fingers. Her eyes darken. "Let me worry about that, yeah?"

"No," she says. "I'm worried about it too. How you feel— Fred, it matters to me."

I give her hair a small tug. "I feel fine, love. You make me feel very fine indeed."

Her features relax with relief. "You sure?"

"I'm sure."

"I promised you I'd think about the internship with your team," she says. "In return, I want you to promise to talk to me. Tell me if things are happening too fast for you, or if we're going too far. Okay?"

I smile. I smile so hard it hurts.

"You have my word," I say.

Rachel grins. She angles her head back ever so slightly. Just enough to invite me to kiss her.

I lean in, tilting my head so I don't catch her with the bill of my hat. I press my lips to hers. They're soft, warm, wet on the inside. Familiar heat spreads up my thighs and in my stomach, settling between my legs. I'm dying for this girl.

I'm dying to put my hands on her again.

I recognize that now would be a good time to address my virginity situation. But I also recognize it could stunt the magic of this moment. Rachel's already concerned we're breaking too many of my rules too fast. If I tell her I'm a virgin, she'll insist on slowing things down. She respects me too much to swipe my V-card on the third night we're together.

But I don't want to slow things down. Especially if we have only a couple weeks left before she's due to leave.

I'll tell her later, when things between us aren't quite so new.

In the meantime, I want to get her naked. Make her come.

"Come home with me," I murmur against her mouth. "We can figure out dinner—"

"Screw dinner," Rachel says. She looks a little dazed when she pulls back. "Let's make out again instead."

"I was hoping you'd say that," I say.

I grab her hand and make a beeline for the exit.

Chapter Ten

RACHEL

We don't say a word on the way to Fred's apartment.

The air between us crackles with anticipation as we hurtle through traffic. Fred shifts gears with impatient, authoritative thrusts. A muscle in his jaw twitches.

By the time we get there, I'm so wet I could wring out my underwear.

I'm nervous. Excited.

The elevator ride up to the fifth floor of his building feels like it takes a year. When we get there, we practically run down the hall to his door.

He opens it and lets me go in first. He follows me inside.

Fred reaches behind me to close the door, trapping me against it. Slides the deadbolt home with an audible *whack*.

I fall back against the door. My bag falls to the floor. Fred faces me, taller and broader than ever. In the shadowy hall, his eyes go dark, gleaming with heat and intent.

I'm breathing hard, all the sudden, my skin prickling with the need to be touched.

"Fred, we should take it slow," I say.

"Take it slow." He puts his hand on the door beside my

head and leans into it. Leans into me. "Tell me, love, how the fuck am I supposed to do that when I've wanted to touch you all day?"

Love. I freaking adore it when he calls me that.

"I told you," I say, swallowing, "I don't want you to have any regrets."

He looks at me. My heart is pounding.

"I could never fucking regret anything I do with you," he says. And then he ducks his head and covers his mouth with mine. I rise to meet his caress, sighing.

Well all right then. Starting off with a bang. I like it.

Like he did last night, Fred steps into me, nudging his leg between mine. A flare of heat shoots through me, landing between my legs. His lips move over mine, kissing me, kissing me hard and deep. I feel trapped. Surrounded.

Adored.

Keep kissing me, I silently beg. *Please don't stop kissing me like this*.

The door is hard against my back, but I don't care. His tongue is in my mouth now, his breath in my lungs. He smells *so* good. The spicy sandalwood scent wafts off his skin and fills my head, making my sex pulse in agony.

His hard-on presses against my hip. It appears I'm not the only one who's already hot and bothered.

I can't help it. I am greedy with need. I want to touch him everywhere, to feel him all over me. I roll my pelvis, rubbing against him. He makes this noise in the back of his throat, something between a growl and a groan. He takes my hip in his free hand and guides me against him again, and again, and again, thrusting just the tiniest bit against me when we meet.

The heat pulls and prickles and intensifies between my legs. I want him there, now. I want him inside me, moving, hurting, soothing.

I bite the edge of his mouth. He moves his lips to my jaw,

my throat, and my head falls back against the door, sensation spiking through me. I put my hands on his chest, my fingers fisting the fabric of his jacket, pulling him to me.

His hand drops from my face and reappears on my leg, just behind my knee. Before I know what he's doing, he's hiking one leg around his hip, then the other, settling himself between my legs as he spears me against the door.

I cry out.

He goes still. "Rachel." He pulls back to look me in the eye. "Are you okay?"

I am not okay.

I am *so* not okay.

And I have never been better. Fred holds me, his hands on the back of my thighs, his weight pressed against me. I've never felt more precious or more turned on in my life.

"So much for slow," I breathe.

He scoffs. "No kidding. I can't—I don't want to hold back, Rachel. I'm not hurting you, am I?"

I shake my head. "No. Keep going."

And he does. I drape my arms around his neck and then we're kissing again. Or really, he's kissing me, slaughtering me with every stroke of his tongue, every tease of his lips. His hands creep up my legs to cup my ass. The last two fingers on either of his hands settles in the aching crevice between my legs.

Yes. A million times yes.

He hardens his grip on me and lifts me off the door. Usually I'd never trust a guy to carry me like this—I mean, how embarrassing would it be for us both if he dropped me— but I trust Fred. He's huge and strong and his grip on me is confident. Possessive.

I never want him to take his hands off me. Ever.

I sink my teeth into his neck as he moves down the hall, his stride long and just the littlest bit hurried. My entire body throbs with need. I'm all sensation, all feeling and need. I'm out of my head and in my body.

I inhale the clean scent of his skin. My body goes wild with need.

I somehow manage to wrangle free of my jacket, dropping it on the floor.

Fred moves down one step, then another. Carpet swishes underneath his boots.

His hands move back to my legs, and then he tosses me gently onto a sofa. I land with a gasp on the cushy upholstery, my eyes flying open.

"Too much?" he asks, green eyes flashing with concern.

"I'll tell you if it's too much."

I glance around. We're in his living room, where we had our *Tournament of Kings* marathon last night. The pillows are squished and misshapen; a blanket's thrown on the floor. The room actually looks like it's been lived in. Because we *did* live here last night, laughing and teasing and flirting. My heart folds in half at the happiness of that memory. I love it here. I love being so unabashedly myself with him.

"Hey," he says. "Eyes on me."

I look up at him. God, that smirk of his. I knew he'd be good in bed.

He's a natural.

I watch Fred as he tugs off his jacket, rolling his shoulders back, stretching his sweater against his enormous chest. He takes off his hat and runs a hand through his hair, mussing his usual tidy swoop. He looks unkempt. Flushed.

Fucking hot. As. Hell.

I'm not grinning anymore. The beat between my legs is starting to get painful. Needy.

He removes his sweater, the hem of his button-down popping out of his jeans as he pulls the sweater of his head.

"Fuck, Fred, stop teasing me."

"You're incredibly sexy, love. I won't last a bloody minute if I don't slow this down."

"Oh," I say. "Of course."

Truth be told, I'm flattered. That Fred wants to take his time with me makes me feel . . . adored, I guess.

I've never been adored before.

Popping open the first few buttons at the throat of his shirt, he moves toward me. My body leaps in anticipation.

I take the loose hem of his shirt between my first two fingers and give it a small tug. My pinkie brushes his erection, straining against his jeans. He winces. His nostrils flare.

I swallow.

And then he's lowering himself onto the couch, my legs falling apart to accept the breadth of his body between them. He supports his weight on his elbows, but I still feel him on top of me, still feel a bit breathless. I sink further into the sofa. He's so huge but so gentle. Gentle and rough, all at once.

Oh, God, I am done for.

I put my hands on his waist. I love the feel of him here, all muscle, solid and taut. It's a little intimidating, having him so *close*. Having him all to myself. I want to remember every-thing about him, every muscle and movement, but I also want to close my eyes and lose myself in the frenzy of what's to come.

There isn't enough time in this life to do everything I want to do with Fred.

He ducks his head, tugging at my earlobe with his teeth. My eyes flutter shut as his mouth moves down my neck to my collarbone. He rolls his hips, pressing against my center, hard, and I moan. My hips surge upward, seeking more of that deli-cious pressure, that painful friction, but he's pinning me down. Making me wait.

"Fred," I beg. "Fred, please."

He looks up at me from between my breasts. He's starting to unbutton my top; my nipples are so hard you can see them through the silky fabric.

"What do you want?" he asks.

I blink. *What do I want?* I don't know why, but that question—it hits me squarely in the chest. It feels so much bigger than the simple words that make it up.

"You," I say.

"You want more than that," he says. "I see it in your eyes."

I look at him for a beat, then another, his eyes never leaving mine as he nudges open one button after the next, and the next. What are you looking for, I wonder?

What am *I* looking for?

Fred opens my shirt and kisses the swell of my breast. I arch against him, sensation spiking through me, and close my eyes.

I bury my fingers in his hair. It takes him a couple seconds longer than it should, but he pops open the front clasp of my bra and the cups fall apart.

Cold air rushes against my nipples, pulling them to painful points. Fred nicks one with his teeth, then the other, and for a hot minute I think I'm going to lose my fucking mind. Desire bolts from each caress to my core, making it throb against the seam of my jeans. He licks and he sucks and he bites down, hard, just hard enough to be both painful and sweet.

I whimper. He growls. I buck against him, hard, wild and needy. I'm suddenly tearing at his shirt, trying to pull it over his head, and he's reaching for the fly of my pants.

"Here," I say. "Sit up for a minute."

Fred pulls back and somehow manages to kneel at my knees. He rips his shirt over his head—I hear a tear, probably a button or two—and after I toe off my booties, I try to shimmy out of my jeans. He reaches down and helps me, dipping his fingers inside my underwear to bring those down too, while I raise my hips.

He drops my jeans and undies on the floor.

Immediately the scent of my arousal blooms between us.

I'd be embarrassed if it wasn't for the dark, almost sinister desire that clouds Fred's eyes as he looks down at me, his eyes roving over my body.

I figure it's only polite if I return the favor. He's shirtless now, and oh God, *oh God* is he gorgeous. I shamelessly drink in the glorious wonder that is his body. The sculpted ridges of his shoulders move into biceps that literally bulge with muscle. And then there are those forearms I love so much. A single vein snakes down the length of his right arm. I notice the skin on that wrist is paler than the rest of him; he must tape it. I'll have to remember to ask him about it.

Fred's chest is broad, his pale skin smattered with hair a shade darker than the stuff on his head, and works its way into a subtle *V* that dips into the front of his pants. And his abs—let's just say you could do laundry on those babies.

Everything about him is ragingly, aggressively masculine. I don't know what to touch or explore first.

He's still kneeling. He reaches between my legs.

I moan when his first two fingers glide between my lips. I'm wet. Really, really wet.

"Fuck, Rachel," he breathes. "You're so bloody soft."

I'm rolling my hips against his fingers. I reach down and cover his hand with mine.

"Put one inside," I say, and guide his middle finger into my vagina. He goes slowly. Carefully. But with confidence. "Perfect. That is . . . wow, that is perfect."

I use my first two fingers to work my clitoris.

"You like it inside and outside?" he breathes.

I nod, the heat between my legs twisting tighter. Higher.

My back arches off the couch.

"Hold on," he says, and reaches for my leg with his free hand.

He guides that leg up over his shoulder and does the same with the other, pulling me up against him so I'm balanced on my shoulder blades, my knees bent over his shoulders.

Immediately the angle of his finger inside me changes. Deepens. We both watch our hands between my legs, which are falling farther and farther apart with each passing heartbeat.

After intently studying my fingers, Fred bends his neck and covers them with his tongue. The feel of his tongue against my clit—it's warm and it's soft and it's so incredibly arousing my legs start to shake.

Oh fuck. Oh, holy *fuck*.

My fingers fall away. He slips another finger inside me, increasing the pressure, while he sucks on my clitoris, pulls at it with his lips. I've never been fingered and eaten out at the same time, and it's just as incredible as it sounds.

I'm seeing stars. I grab at him, locking his forearm in a death grip.

"Fred," I pant. "I don't know—I can't hold myself up—"

He curls an arm around my back. "Relax. I've got you."

I let him hold me like his, not because I want to, but because I have to. I settle my weight into his arm, the skin of his bicep warm against the skin of my back. My shirt is scrunched up around my shoulders; I have no idea where my bra went. I think it's somewhere behind me maybe?

I don't care. I have to come. Soon. Now. Or I am going to die.

I'm rolling my hips against his mouth, he's moving his fingers in and out of me. The muscles in my low back tighten as the throb in my clit and deep inside my vagina reach a crescendo, halting on the edge of the spasm.

The release.

"Oh," I breathe. I take my nipple between my fingers and squeeze it. "Oh . . ."

I plunge over the edge. I cry out, the orgasm making my entire being throb in time to the pulse of my sex. The roar of my heart fills my ears. I spasm around Fred's fingers, against his mouth, and he growls, an anguished, satisfied sound.

Behind my closed eyelids, a universe of color explodes, a welcome distraction from the pain that wracks my body. I've never had an orgasm feel so good it actually *hurts*. It's sharp and white-hot.

It's intense, intense enough to make me forget myself.

It's unfair and savage and *so fucking good* I would sell my soul to the devil in this moment if it meant I could have orgasms like this every day for the rest of my life.

My sex pulses, the waves hitting me again and again until at last they recede, leaving me a panting, sweaty mess.

This is dangerous. Already I want more. I want to come again, be with Fred again, do this again tomorrow and the next day and the day after that.

Lord, am I tempted to make this a *thing*. An every-night thing where I come ten times and so does he.

"Fred," I say, keeping my eyes closed.

He runs his tongue up my slit one last time, like he's finishing the last lick of an ice cream cone. "Good?"

I scoff. "Stop being modest. You know that was better than that. To be so considerate—you put my orgasm first—and to be so freaking *good* at it—"

"Blokes don't make you come first?"

"Not usually, no."

"Wankers, that lot." He scoffs, ducking down to kiss me. I taste the tang of my arousal on his lips. It turns me on all over again.

I reach between us and thumb the tip of his erection through his jeans. "You want me to return the favor?"

Chapter Eleven

FRED

Sensation, hot and tight, shoots from the head of my dick to my balls as Rachel's thumb moves over me.

I was supposed to take it slow. But then I kissed her, and in a single instant, I got caught up in the moment. Caught up in her.

It was over for me the second we stepped into my flat.

Looking down at her now, naked and panting on my couch, my fingers still wet from being inside her, a possessiveness takes over me. A softness. I want to protect her. Take her. Give to her.

I like this girl so bloody much, I want to give her everything. Including my virginity.

I've always believed sex should be with someone special.

Rachel is special.

We're not in love. Not yet. But deep down, I know having sex with her would be special. I know this is not just some random hook-up with a random girl. It's more than that.

I care more than that. And I want to show her. I want to do this.

Maybe I'll regret this tomorrow. Maybe I won't.

It just feels right. That's all I've got to go on. That seems to be enough for now.

"I've got condoms in the loo," I say. "I'll be right back."

"Condoms?" She grins. "I like the sound of that."

In the bathroom, I grip the edges of the sink and lean into my hands and try to catch my breath.

I'm shaking. Almost as much as Rachel shook when she came.

This is happening. I'm finally losing my virginity. I always imagined the girl I'd lose it to. But Rachel blows all those imaginary girlfriends out of the water. She's smarter and hotter and more interesting. She is everything I didn't know I wanted.

I'm so bloody pleased I could make her come.

I am actually good at something other than football.

I am also officially obsessed with Rachel's pussy. I loved how she smelled and felt and tightened around my fingers when she came. She was so swollen. Swollen and so fucking wet and soft. My cock throbs at the memory of it. At the sweet, salty smell of her.

Now I just need to keep from blowing my load in the first five seconds I'm inside her. I've overheard the lads say that condoms help with this . . . er, issue.

I glance in the mirror above the sink. I don't recognize the man looking back at me. I imagine this is what I'd look like if I ever ran into J.K. Rowling on the street—pleasantly shell-shocked. Bewildered in the best way.

I put a couple condoms in the front pocket of my jeans and head back out to the living room.

Rachel sits up on the sofa when she sees me, leaning against a pillow. Her hair, long and loose around her shoulders, is wild, and so are her eyes. Her lips are swollen, red.

She is swollen and soft *everywhere*.

I want to bury myself inside the softness between her legs. The thought of how good that's going to feel—

I stop a few paces from the sofa, gritting my teeth.

"You're gorgeous," I manage. I don't recognize my voice.

She laughs, and the sound hits me squarely in the chest, like I'm hearing it for the first time all over again. "You sound like you're in pain."

"I am," I say. Rachel moves to cover herself back up with her shirt. "Don't. Don't you fucking dare."

Her dark eyes go wide. Not with fear—with arousal. "Oh —okay."

"I want to see all of you. As a matter of fact, take it off. Take everything off. Now."

She looks at me for a long moment. When this whole encounter started, I took control because I didn't want to ejaculate in the first three minutes of kissing her. I thought if I was in charge, I'd have a better chance of making it last.

But now I'm discovering I like being in control. It turns me on.

From the look of it, it turns Rachel on too.

Her gaze latches onto mine. She takes off her shirt, one arm at a time, and grabs her bra from behind her back, tossing it to the side. Her eyes are burning now.

"Open your legs," I say.

Slowly, she draws her knees up to her chest. Then lets them fall apart.

Her pussy is just as gorgeous as the rest of her. Red, pink, swollen. It glistens in the low light of the room.

"Here," she says. She reaches down and sinks her first finger inside herself. "I need you right here, Fred."

My pulse roars at the lewdness of the gesture.

At its perfection.

I cannot get enough of this girl. I'm scared I'll never get enough of her. But I'm not going to think about that now.

I toss the condoms onto the coffee table, and then I take off my belt, unbutton my jeans. She reaches out and helps me tug my pants and boxers off my hips.

"Oh my God," she says when my dick springs free.

It's my turn to grin. That's a good *Oh my God* if I ever heard one.

"I'm negative on all fronts," I say, kicking my clothes off my ankles. "But I want to be safe with you, Rachel, and the condoms might help me slow things down a bit, yeah?"

She nods, eyes still glued to my dick. "I'm negative too. I actually have an IUD, so the birth control part is taken care of. But I'm definitely cool with condoms."

"I can send you a copy of my medical records—"

"I trust you," she says. Her eyes are dark and serious.

My heart thumps. "I'll send them to you tomorrow anyway."

I lower myself onto the sofa on top of Rachel. The hardened points of her nipples brush against my chest. I groan, reaching down to take one of her breasts in my hands. She sighs when I pinch her nipple.

Being able to touch her like this—knowing I turn her on as much as she turns me on—it's fucking overwhelming. It's so much better than I thought it would be. I guess a small part of me didn't let my imagination go this far. I guess deep down I thought I'd be better off putting all my focus on footy, because I was never going anywhere with girls.

Because I'd never find a girl as genuine and as sexy as Rachel.

The tip of my cock throbs against the soft skin of her belly. She reaches between us and takes me in her hand, and my entire body goes rigid.

"You okay?"

In response, I slip my hand between her parted thighs and

touch a finger to her slit. She's still wet, still very, very wet, and hot.

She's ready.

I swallow. *Please let me last long enough to get her where she needs to be.*

I lift my head and press my lips to hers. She pushes mine open with her tongue, and then we're kissing, really *kissing*, demanding something of each other we haven't yet given.

The kiss gets messy. She bites my lip and I buck my hips, forcing my dick farther into her hand. She's rolling her hips against me, and I'm playing with her clit, and suddenly I can't take it anymore. My arms are shaking—I can't get a grip, my hands are sinking into the sofa cushions—and I feel like I'm going to come or die or both.

I fasten her against me with my arms. She draws a breath.

I roll onto the floor, a swift, sure movement that has Rachel crying out in surprise. I land on my back, careful to hold her tightly so I absorb most of the impact.

"Okay?" I ask.

"Okay," she says.

I roll over again, pinning her beneath me on the carpet while I kneel between her legs. Her hair is spread out around her head, a dark halo that complements even darker eyes.

"Please," she pants, reaching for my cock. "I can't wait. I don't want to wait, Fred."

I slam a hand onto the coffee table, searching for a condom while I part her legs farther with my other hand, guiding one of her knees up onto her chest. I can see her pussy better this way, and she liked it when I did something different before. Maybe she'll like it again. I hope so.

I rip open the foil packet with my teeth. I've practiced this too, and I have the condom rolled onto my dick in a heartbeat and a half. I put my hands on either side of her head, careful not to pull her hair, and lean forward.

Rachel reaches down and guides me to her center. I close my eyes, and suck in a breath through my teeth. She already feels delicious. I can already imagine the fucking insane pressure of being surrounded by her. Being *inside* her.

"Go. Please," she whispers. Begs.

It makes me wild. I feel like a fucking animal.

I buck my hips, hard, and she gasps when I surge inside her. She's hot and tight and soft and bloody *hell* I want to live here, I want to live inside her throbbing heat. For a second my mind goes blank. All my focus is on this place where our bodies are joined, on the sweetest, most intense sensation I have ever felt.

When I come to, I notice that Rachel winces, closing her eyes.

Fuck.

"Rachel. Christ, Rachel, are you okay? Did I hurt you?"

She shakes her head. She doesn't open her eyes. "It's just been a while for me. I needed a second to, um, adjust. But I'm okay now."

"You sure?"

Finally her eyes meet mine. "Fred, I'm so much better than okay. This—this feels—"

I start to move inside her, a little baby thrust. The rug burns against my knees, the heels of my hands, but I don't care. With her knee so high up—with her so spread open—the angle is deep.

"—so fucking good. So *fuck*ing good," she says.

Her pussy flutters around me. A rush of blood gathers in the tip of my dick and my balls tighten.

Oh, no. Not yet. I've got to last more than fifteen seconds.

I pull back and close my eyes and take a deep breath through my nose. I corral my focus, will my body to do what I need it to do. It works on the pitch. I hope it works in the bedroom—or on the floor, I guess.

Rachel rocks her hips. It's a small movement, a gentle one, and when I open my eyes and see her looking at me, her eyes glassy and soft and satisfied, my confidence comes back in a rush.

I've got this. I can trust my body.

I can trust Rachel.

My knees are on fire, but I don't care. I keep moving. We've both started to sweat. I roll my hips against hers. She grasps my forearm, like she's holding on for dear life. I tighten my abdominal muscles, use them to thrust a little harder, harder, harder, the slap of our bodies coming together only egging us on.

She's rolling her hips too, moaning, coming apart.

I pull her leg out from between us and settle even farther in the cradle of her pelvis. Her tits bound in time to my thrusts. I'm really moving now. Holy *fuck* we're really animals.

This is really fucking good.

My low back stiffens as my orgasm gets closer. This time, I know I can't hold it back. I've used up all my control, all my strength.

I bend my neck and kiss her. She takes my face in her hands and makes the kiss hers, like she knows I'm about to fucking lose it.

I pound inside her one last time. Her pussy swells around me, clamping down on my dick. And then I really do lose it.

Something goes soft inside my chest at the same moment my orgasm explodes through me. I bite back a yell and squeeze my eyes shut. It's too much. The release is too bloody much, too much relief, too much sensation. My body throbs and my vision goes blank. Rachel is milking me to completion, her tight heat pulling on me and pulling on me, pulses of hot cum filling the condom.

I come for what feels like days. I don't want it to stop, but then again I do. I do because it's so intense it scares me a little. I don't know what I might do or say.

I'd give this girl bloody anything right now.

Her hands are still on my face when I open my eyes. The hair at her temples flutters as I breathe, hard, into her face. Her hairline is damp with perspiration.

Rachel leans forward and kisses my mouth, softly.

And then she smiles. I notice then what it is about her smiles I love so much. They take over her whole face— cheeks, eyebrows. *Eyes*. She smiles with her eyes, the dark brown lit up with all sorts of good things.

My heart skips a beat.

"Holy *hell* that was excellent," she says, and holds up her hand for a high five.

I scoff. I give her the high five, but then I lace my fingers through hers, pressing our palms together.

"So. Bloody. Good," I say, and we both laugh. I look at her. "How was it for you?"

"I'd fucking hate you if you weren't such a great guy. You have, like, ridiculous physical talent in *all* areas of life—it's not fair! You may be a gifted footballer, but you're, um, gifted in other ways too. You're the best lay I've had. Ever. I'm not exaggerating."

I grin, reaching down to play with her pussy. I know she's on the brink of another orgasm. I felt the first spasms when I was inside her just a minute ago. "Yes you are. But thank you nonetheless."

"No I'm not, Fred." She gasps when I thumb her clit. "You're—you're amazing at this. Seriously. And I am seriously about to come again. Oh, *oh* my God."

That softness in my chest—it's back, and it makes me want to be close to her in every way possible.

"Look at me," I say when she tries to close her eyes. "I want to see your face when you come. Your eyes."

She gives me a little nod, swallowing.

"It's just my back—I'm going to have a wicked rug burn," she says.

I go still. "Come on, Rachel. Why didn't you say something sooner?"

"I'm okay," she says. Her lips part when I press my thumb against her clit a little harder. I'm still inside her and the spasms are happening again, small at first. "Please don't stop."

I duck my head and put my mouth on the skin just beneath her ear. She tastes like skin, sweat. I suck her there, her pulse beating against my tongue. All the while I keep my eyes on her face.

Trailing a long, ardent kiss down her throat, her shoulder, her collarbone, I finally reach her breasts. I know she likes this.

So I go for the kill. I take her nipple in my mouth and bite down, hard.

She comes. Her eyes go wide and her body arches up and she clenches around me. She whimpers; I growl, my dick getting hard all over again.

This hurts.

This is the best fucking thing that ever happened to me. It's like I've stumbled on a whole new world—one I didn't know existed outside of the football pitch.

This world of Rachel and orgasms and dinners in and TV marathons and museums.

I want to keep living in this world.

I want to be with Rachel. For good. This is happening fast, I get it. But a girl like Rachel doesn't come around that often. A connection like ours is rare. I would know, I've been looking for it for years.

I want Rachel to be my girlfriend. My real, long-term, maybe-forever girlfriend.

For that to happen, though, one or both of us will have to give something up. Something big. I can't do long distance with Rachel. I like having her here, by my side, too bloody much. And I travel so often during the season—almost every week—I'd rarely have the time or the energy to jet across an ocean to see her.

But how can I ask her to give up her dream internship back at Meryton if she gets it? Granted, there's a chance she can also get the internship here in Madrid at the club's training facility. But I respect her ambition—I admire it— and if that ambition takes her back to the States, then what?

I'd have to leave Madrid, just when my contract is being renegotiated for a number that made my eyes water the first time I saw it. It's a big number. A wildest-dreams number.

I mean, I love my job here. I work well with my managers and the lads on my squad. I've worked hard to earn my place on what is probably the best football team in the world right now. How could I give all that up?

How could I give it up for a girl I've known all of a week?

It's crazy. And I don't know how Rachel and I will make it work. But I think it's worth trying.

I want to try.

I wait until the spasms subside to pull out of her.

"No!" she says, her arms going to the small of my back in an attempt to keep me there.

I brush my lips against her forehead. "Your back, love. And I'm worried if we go again that—"

That what? We'll cross a line that cannot be uncrossed?

Because that's already happened. Somewhere between the kissing and the coming and the fucking, we crossed a line.

And now I want Rachel to *stay.*

So I hold her. I curl her into my arms and I hold her

against me. I hold her so close I can feel the hammering beat of her heart against my chest.

I want to go again. But I am concerned about Rachel's back, for one thing. And for another, we have some TV to catch up on.

Tomorrow. Maybe tomorrow I'll feel her out. Tomorrow we can talk about making a relationship work.

Tonight, though, I just want to enjoy her company.

"Let's take a little break," I murmur into her ear. "I'm bloody dying to know whose throat Lorena rips out first with those new teeth of hers, yeah?"

I feel Rachel's lips move into a smile against my shoulder. "Yeah."

Chapter Twelve

RACHEL

The Next Morning

I wake up slowly. I'm on my belly. Somewhere in the back of my mind it registers that I'm super warm and super comfy. This bed is *heavenly*. It's soft and it smells clean and somehow so very cozy—flannel sheets, maybe? I burrow farther underneath the duvet, luxuriating in the happy sensation of it all. What a delicious change from the cruddy mattress and scratchy sheets back at my dorm room.

Somewhere in the background, a door closes, quietly and I hear a voice murmuring.

A *male* voice.

Fred's voice.

My stomach flips, jolting me fully awake. My eyes fly open.

Pale streamers of morning light unfurl across a tidy bedroom. I'm in a massive bed dressed in impossibly gorgeous, impossibly spotless white linens.

I turn over and sit up against the fluffy pillow. I suck a breath through my teeth at the unpleasant tightness of the skin on my back.

Rug burn. From the crazy animal sex we had on the floor last night.

Dear God.

I hold up the blankets and glance down at myself. I'm in a man's shirt—it's huge, more like a dress on me—that has a giant purple number seven across the front. Fred's number.

I'm not wearing anything underneath the shirt. My vagina clenches, tingling with arousal. I reach down and touch myself.

I'm dripping wet. And *sore*.

I've been awake for, oh, twelve seconds, and already I'm so turned on I can barely stand it.

What the hell did we do to ourselves last night?

We were supposed to take it slow. And we ended up fucking on the floor of Fred's living room.

I hold my forehead in my hand, even as I fight back a smile.

We *fucked* on the living room *floor*.

Hell. Yes.

Fred's voice gets a little louder. It's still a murmur, like he's trying to be quiet, but I can hear him nonetheless.

He's speaking German, that much I can tell. He uses the word *Mama*.

How cute. He's talking to his mom.

I hear him laugh. I can't understand what he's saying, obviously, but from his tone I can tell he's enjoying the conversation.

My heart twists. That must be nice, having a fun conversation with your mom. I wouldn't know. All my mom talks about during our weekly calls is *how's your GPA looking?* and *when are you going to sign up to take the MCAT study course? Time is running out . . .*

Needless to say, I get the worst stomachaches ever when I

talk to her. A tiny part of me doesn't want to get the internship back at Meryton because I know I'll have to call Mom and tell her. That call, if it happens at all, is going to be bad. Really, really bad.

I check the time on the alarm clock next to Fred's side of the bed. A little past eight. Whew. Luckily, I don't have class until eleven on Tuesdays.

I climb out of bed and head for the master bathroom, a giant expanse of white marble with a huge tub and even bigger shower. I pee, wash my hands, and brush my teeth with my toothbrush I "borrowed" from the vanity. When I'm done, I sneak out of the bedroom into the hall.

I follow Fred's voice through the living room. Pillows and cushions are everywhere; foil packets litter the coffee table.

I wasn't lying or blowing smoke up Fred's ass when I told him he was the best lay of my life. I've never had sex like that —urgent, messy, intense sex that leaves its mark.

The Madrileñas always talk about the crazy sex they have with studly Spaniards. I wanted to have that kind of sex, but I never have. Until last night, I thought maybe I just wasn't the type of person who has crazy, delicious sex. Maybe I wasn't sensual enough, or good enough at this stuff.

But now I see my somewhat lackluster sex life wasn't so much about me as it was about the guys I've been with. Being so turned on and so in synch with Fred last night showed me that. It's like we were speaking the same language without having to say a word.

I just wish I had a shot at being that forever person he's looking for. I like Fred. Really, really like him.

Maybe I'm starting to want him to be *my* forever person. Which scares the hell out of me, because we have lives on opposite sides of the Atlantic.

Then again, I haven't officially gotten the internship at

Meryton yet. Fred *did* ask me to think about applying to the internship with his team here in Madrid.

I've thought about it. Well—I'm thinking about it now, anyway.

And I think I'm going to apply. Why the hell not?

Am I an idiot to hope that Fred and I actually have a future together? I mean, I've only known the guy for a week. But he's so deliciously different from everything and everyone I know. He stands out in all the best ways.

He makes me feel like it's safe to be myself. Makes me feel like it's *okay* to be myself. All my life, I've pretended to be someone else. Someone who would make my mother happy. Proud. But when I'm with Fred—I can be who I really am.

I love him for that. I don't *love* him love him, obviously. I mean, hello, the sex may be great, but I have only known this guy for eight days. That kind of love—I can't go there. Not yet.

I pass a doorway and catch a glimpse of Fred. I immediately back up and turn into the kitchen.

He looks as rumpled and bed-mussed as I do. His hair sticks up every which way. He's wearing a pair of clear-framed glasses that make him look like the most adorable, sexy smarty-pants ever.

God, I love guys who wear glasses.

He is wearing a pair of white athletic shorts—emblazoned with his team's logo, naturally—and nothing else.

Let me repeat that: Fred Ohr is standing in his kitchen in his glasses and shorts and *nothing else*.

The heaviness between my legs throbs.

I try—and fail—not to stare at his naked torso. He's ripped. So very ripped. Those muscles that dive between his hips and arrow down to his groin—Jesus mother, they do something to me.

He looks up when I enter the room and grins. His eyes get all squinty with pleasure. They look more green than blue today. I like how they're always changing. Always different, depending on the light.

Relief floods my chest. He doesn't look angry, or regretful, or guilty.

He looks blissed out.

Something inside me tightens. Hurts. This *guy*—I always thought he was hot.

But I was not prepared for how everything about him—his eyes and his grin and the sound of his voice—would full me with such sharp-edged longing.

He's still on the phone and mouths "sorry." I wave him away.

Don't rush, I want to tell him. *I love hearing you talk to your mom.*

It's adorable, for one thing. For another, its ordinariness is sort of soothing. Intimate. I love that I'm here, now, warm and cozy in Fred's kitchen, instead of sweating over an essay in the library or pacing my dorm room, worried sick about my future.

It doesn't hurt that hearing a guy speak a different language is really, really sexy. I wonder what other languages Fred knows. Like a lot of Europeans, I bet he knows three, four, half a dozen. Makes me feel lame for being so proud of the fact that I'm fluent in Spanish.

I settle onto a stool and hold my chin in my hand. My stomach growls. I'm not usually much of a breakfast person, but I guess I worked up an appetite having crazy floor sex last night.

"All right, Mama," Fred is saying, switching to English. "Okay. Yes. No, I've got plenty of undershirts . . . no, really, you don't have to . . . yes, I did get the socks. Yes, they are very warm. Thank you for sending them. I love you too . . . yes, we all need to practice our English. Okay. Yes. Really, you don't need to worry—I know I work too much . . . I'm fine, I promise. All right. Goodbye."

He hangs up and sets the phone on the counter. He looks up at me, fisting his hair in his hand. His bicep bulges, the muscles along the sides of his torso bunch and ripple. He's huge in every way imaginable.

I mean. *My God.*

"Good morning," he says, grinning.

"Morning," I say, suddenly shy. "Hi."

"How are you feeling?"

"Good." *Turned on. Sore. Awed.* "You?"

"Bloody perfect."

"Really?"

"Yes."

"You're not just saying that to make me feel like less of a dick?"

"No. Why would you feel like a dick?"

"Because things . . . uh, kind of got away from me last night. I was supposed to take it slow with you—I asked you to make out—and then we end up having crazy animal sex."

Fred moves around the island toward me. "Rachel," he says.

"I'm sorry," I say. "I know how much sex means to you—"

"Rachel."

"—and I swear, I didn't come here with the sinister intention of, like, taking advantage of you or whatever. I want you to feel good about what we do together. I hate that I got so caught up in . . . in everything. In you. I know better—"

"*Rachel.*"

"—and I should've stopped us before things went too fa—"

He takes the last half of that word into his mouth, pressing his lips to mine as he cups my face in his hands. For a second I remain rigid, too stunned to move. He tastes like toothpaste. Clean. Fresh.

His tongue slips inside my mouth. I melt. How could I not?

I moan when he pulls away. His face is an inch from mine. He's so close I can see the individual hairs that make up his pale eyebrows. I can see each freckle dotting his nose and cheeks.

"I feel good about what we did last night," he says. My face is still in his hands. "In fact, I'd very much like to do it again."

"Oh," I say, crumpling with relief against him. "Oh, thank God. I was so worried—"

"I'm worried too," he says, softly. "But I'm not going to let that keep me from you. Last night—it was unbelievable."

A beat of silence passes between us. We're playing with fire, like Laura said, and we both know it. But what can we do?

"How's your back?" he asks at last.

"Hurts a little. I'll live."

"I'll be more gentle next time."

"Please don't. I kinda liked how intense you were. It was *really* hot. How are your knees? I imagine they're in rough shape too."

"Rug burn hurts less than a patellar dislocation, I'll tell you that much." He grins, running his fingers through my tangled hair. "Your hair looks an absolute state."

"So does yours. I like it." I'm grinning now too. "We forgot to eat dinner last night. Which means I'm kinda starving right now."

"Then we've got to feed you. I'm hungry too."

"No rush—I don't have class until eleven," I say. "Was that your mom on the phone?"

"It was. She's hell-bent on sending me socks and under-shirts this winter. I told her I'm perfectly capable of buying my own, but she's worried I 'won't be warm enough.'" He shrugs. "Piece of work, that one."

"I think it's adorable." I say. "So she really did forgive you for leaving, huh?"

Fred nods, slipping his arms around my waist. Our groins meet, and for a minute I think I might faint. "Back when I was deciding whether or not to go to Munich, I was so worried my decision would make her unhappy. But now I understand her happiness is not in my hands. Mama will choose whether or not she is happy. Yeah, my decision upset her. She was disappointed. But she's always been happy, and she stayed happy after I left. So now she is happy, and so am I."

A hand grips my heart and squeezes. "She sounds like a lovely person."

"This is what you're struggling with, yeah? Worrying about making your mom unhappy if you choose sports medicine over plastic surgery?"

"Good guess. Jeez, Fred, I thought those glasses only made you look smart, but now I see they've turned you into a real genius."

He uses his first finger to slide the glasses in question up the bridge of his nose. "A charming genius, surely?"

I bite my lip. "You did charm my pants right off last night . . ."

"I did. It was delightful."

"*Very* delightful. Want to do it again?"

"Hm." He looks down at my naked legs. "It appears my charm is still working. You aren't wearing any pants."

I wiggle my eyebrows. "Nope. And right now I wish you weren't either."

"You're starving." He bends his neck and plants a quick kiss on my throat. "Let's make breakfast, and then we can—you know. Take care of my pants situation. But how about some stuffed French toast first?"

Chapter Thirteen

FRED

I slice the stuffed French toast in half, and a thick slab of Nutella oozes out of the center. It looks heavenly and smells even better, if I don't say so myself. I've never really loved breakfast, but now that Rachel is here and we're both half-naked, cooking in my kitchen, I fucking adore it. I feel like I'm back at home on a Saturday morning, roused from bed by the delicious smells coming from downstairs.

I feel . . . complete. So bloody happy it scares me.

It should scare me. Because last night I decided to give in to my feelings for Rachel. I literally gave myself to her. I let myself fall for this excellent human being.

And being with her this morning, touching her, laughing, cooking breakfast together—it's only making me fall harder.

I want to be with her. I want to eat breakfast with her for more than just a couple weeks. I can't stand the thought of letting her go. Of not having her here for dinner tonight, and breakfast again tomorrow, and a *Tournament* marathon every day after that.

I can't fucking let this girl go.

"Holy moly, Fred," Rachel says, eyes glued to the plate I set in front of her. "That looks amazing."

"It should. Only took us, what?" I toss a towel over my shoulder, glancing at the clock on the stove. "One and a half hours to make?"

She smiles. "You were the one who suggested we 'whip up' stuffed French toast."

"Perhaps a tad ambitious of me, but I wanted to impress you with my culinary skills, so . . ."

"So now your kitchen is covered in powdered sugar, your neighbors are pissed because we burned a batch and set off the fire alarm, and we're both going to be late."

"But you *are* impressed, aren't you?"

Her dark eyes dance. "Hell yeah, I am."

Those same eyes roll back in her head as she chews on her first bite. Yeah, it's probably going to take me a day and a half to clean up from this French toast fiasco, but seeing that expression on her face—that fucking smile of hers—makes it all worth it.

"This is good, Fred," Rachel says. "Really, really good."

"As good as the orgasms I gave you last night?"

She looks at me, mischievously, from the corner of her eye. I've been sporting a half woody all morning, but that look has me fully hard in the space of half a heartbeat. "Almost. Those orgasms are pretty tough to beat, not gonna lie."

I swallow. The urge to pick her up and throw her on the counter and fuck her hard and fast and mercilessly is overwhelming. I know she's wet too. I can smell the faintest trace of her arousal.

I know she's not wearing underwear. Which means I could be inside her in two seconds.

But she's hungry, and I'm not about to send her home with an empty stomach. Plus my dick is a little sore from last

153

night—she's *really* tight—and my knees and hands really do sting from rug burn. Rachel and I could probably both use a little break.

Then again, I'm not sure I can keep my hands off her much longer. Her lips are still swollen, and her hair is all over the place. She looks so bloody fuckable right now I can hardly stand it.

I want to be with her.

I turn off the hood and sit down at the island beside Rachel to eat.

As we eat our French toast in companionable silence, I compose a grand speech in my head. I'll start off by telling her how much I enjoy doing new things with her, and how she's pushed me to expand my world, and what an absolute joy she is to be around. I'll tell her how sexy she is. How I'll support her dreams in any way I can. I'll tell her how much I admire her for chasing down what *she* wants, even though her mom wants her to do something completely different. I'll say I can't keep my hands off her and that only having three weeks together is a fucking terrible joke and we both know it.

Then I'll ask her to be my girlfriend. I'll ask her to take a stab at forever with me. I'll ask her if she's thought any more about applying to the internship with the squad.

Rachel looks up from her plate at me. Grins. She's got some Nutella on the edge of her mouth. I don't tell her, because she looks adorable.

In that tiny bit of time, between on heartbeat and the next, my speech goes out the window. I don't want to waste another second.

So instead I blurt, "Be with me."

"Be with you?" She's still grinning. "I am. I'm with you right now."

"You know what I mean. Be with me, Rachel, for real. I don't want to be with anyone else, and I hope you don't either. So let's make this exclusive. Let's make it real. Be my girlfriend."

Her brows come together when she realizes that I'm being serious. She draws a sharp breath but doesn't let it out. "You're talking about making this—us—a long-term thing, even though there's absolutely no guarantee we'll have any time together past the end of December."

"Not if you apply to the internship here in Madrid."

Rachel takes another breath. This time she lets it out. Swivels her head to look at me. Her hair falls over her shoulder onto her chest.

"Have you thought any more about that?" I ask.

"I have," she says.

My heart skips a beat. "And?"

She grins. "And I'm going to apply."

Before I know what I'm doing, I'm pulling her to me, wrapping her in my arms as I give her a tight squeeze.

Holy shit.

Holy *shit* this might actually happen.

Rachel might actually stay in Spain with me.

My chest is going to explode.

"Don't get ahead of yourself," she says, laughing as she pulls away. "I still have to do some research—I know the deadline is coming up. And the program is really tough to get into. But I'm willing to give it a shot."

"You're willing to give us a shot," I say. I reach over and swipe away the Nutella from her lips with my thumb. Then I bring my thumb to my mouth. "Be with me."

A beat passes between us. Her grin broadens. Reaches her eyes.

"Okay," she says. "It's crazy, but yes. Yes, I'll be with you."

I'm leaning in to kiss her when I hear it—the unmistakable chime of a mobile.

Rachel pulls back. "That's my phone. I think I left it in my bag last night? I'm actually waiting to hear . . ."

She gets up and runs to the hall outside the kitchen.

I look down at my French toast. I know I'm smiling, probably a big, goofy smile, but I don't care.

Rachel is my girlfriend. We are going to try to make this work.

We are going to be together.

I look up when Rachel comes back into the kitchen. She's holding her phone in her hand. She looks up at me.

She's got this stunned expression on her face.

My stomach twists.

"Everything all right?" I ask.

"Yeah. Yes," she says, setting her phone down next to her plate. She looks away. "I just . . . um. I got the sports medicine internship at Meryton. They called me earlier and left a voicemail—guess I didn't hear it ring."

My stomach twists again, harder this time. She meets my eyes. This means—

We both know what this means. The chances of Rachel leaving Spain for good at the end of the semester just got bigger. Much bigger.

Which means the chances of us having a real shot at something long-term got much smaller.

I can't ask her to pass on such a brilliant opportunity. I never would. But Christ, do I wish that opportunity was a bit closer to Madrid.

"How do you feel about long-distance relationships?" she jokes, but neither of us laughs.

I don't want to piss on her parade. This is a huge accomplishment. I want to celebrate with her. We can think about what to do next later, I suppose.

So I smile, holding my arms open. "Congratulations, love.

I'm happy for you," I say, and I mean it. "I know this is your dream internship, and you got it. You bloody got it!"

"Thank you." She climbs into my arms. She fits perfectly against me, her soft curves the answer to my hard edges. "I, like, can't believe it. This is insane. I've worked for three years—"

"Not so insane. You're incredibly bright. I'm sure you interview well. And you're truly passionate about the field. Of course you got it."

She tilts her head to look at me. "Don't forget I'm also applying to the internship with Valentina. We could still . . . you know. Be together in the long run."

"I know," I say. "I just don't want you to give up something you've been dreaming about for so long. I know how badly you want this."

"Dude. Having the world's most valuable sports franchise on my résumé—that'd also be a dream come true."

"Well," I say, sighing, "we'll cross that bridge when we get there. Right now, we have to celebrate. You free tonight?"

"I am."

"Perfect. I'll be at training until late—but I can pick you up after?"

"Sure." She spears me with a look. "But in the meantime . . . how's that pants situation looking?"

I grin. "I've had the most fucking painful hard-on all morning. What time is it—?" I glance over my shoulder at the clock. "Shit, Rachel, you're going to be late to class if we don't leave now."

"Really?" I try not to smile at the disappointment in her voice. She enjoyed last night as much as I did, which is a huge turn-on.

"Really. By the time I drive you home—"

"I can just wear what I did last night to class. That way you can drop me off right at school—might give us a few extra minutes?" She reaches down and hooks a finger into the waist of my shorts. My dick pulses in agony.

I grab her by the wrist. "I'd love nothing more than to spend a few extra minutes with you—naked—this morning. But you'll not be late to class on my account. And I do have training."

"Fuck," she breathes. Her shoulders fall. "You're right. But I really wanted—"

"Me too. You have no idea how much I want that." I meet her eyes.

We stand. I take Rachel's face in my hands and press a long, lingering kiss on her mouth, taking her bottom lip between my teeth as I pull back. She moans. She tastes sticky, sweet. Perfect.

My whole body lights up with need.

"And Rachel?"

"Yeah?" her voice wavers. Her eyes are still closed.

"Wear a dress tonight."

She pulls back. "A dress?"

"Yeah. A dress. I've got an idea."

Chapter Fourteen

RACHEL

I spend a good chunk of the afternoon sending a frenzy of emails and texts to Fred and chatting on the phone with Valentina. The application deadline for the football club's spring internship is tomorrow (go figure), so I have less than twenty-four hours to write essays, gather recommendations, and coordinate with the Meryton University's bursar's office to get a sealed copy of my transcript delivered in time.

I have no idea how I'm going to pull it off. But I have to try. Valentina promised to help.

Getting this internship just got really important all of the sudden. Because if I get it, that means I get to stay in Spain for another semester—at least. Which means I'll get to be with Fred. I'll get to be with Fred, *and* I'll have an internship opportunity that's so incredible I didn't even know to dream about it.

I'll have my cake and eat it too.

It's almost too good to be true. Which makes me think it won't work out. It can't, because no one deserves that much awesomeness. But maybe—just maybe—I'll get lucky this time.

Maybe the happy, well-balanced life I've dreamed about might actually happen.

Every so often, when I get up to use the restroom, or I shift in my seat, the skin on my back smarts. It feels tight, and even my softest sweater feels uncomfortably rough against it. Still, I have to smile. That rug burn is a reminder of Fred. Fred and his smile and his glasses and the confident way he touched me and teased me and made me come. My heart flutters, literally *flutters*, when I think about him.

I'm definitely playing with fire here. But it's too late to tuck tail and run. I like this guy. A lot. Not only because he is excellent. And genuine. And open-minded. Kind too. And Lord does he look good in a hat.

Fred's also making me feel more confident about following my own career path. About doing what I want to do, what is right for me, instead of doing what I've always thought I should do—what my mom wants me to do.

What he said this morning about not being responsible for his mom's happiness really opened my eyes. I mean, maybe I really don't have an obligation to make her happy. Maybe I can't. I've tried very, very hard for a long time, and it hasn't made her any happier. But it's certainly made me less happy. It's stressed me out, big time.

Maybe, no matter what I do or say or accomplish, Mom is always going to be . . . well, Mom. Maybe she's always going to be unhappy until *she* decides otherwise. That choice, like Fred said, is in her hands.

Just like the choice to be happy and follow my dreams is in mine. I can't make Mom happy. But that doesn't mean I can't be happy myself. That doesn't mean being happy and doing what I want is some kind of crime. I'm not doomed to live a stressful, shallow life like her. I don't have to be unhappy or superficial in sympathy.

I know my happiness will come at a price. That sucks, and

it's unfair. But who knows? Hearing Fred talk to his mom this morning made me think that maybe one day I'll be able to talk to my mom like that too, despite the fact that I disappointed her.

I'm still scared shitless to tell her I not only got an internship in sports medicine, but I've also been pursuing this career path for years behind her back. I know the call is not going to go well. But now, thanks to Fred, I know that it (hopefully) won't be the end of the world. It's not the end of our story. There's still a chance for a happy ending. Look at Fred and his family.

I just have to be brave and hope she'll understand one day why I did what I'm about to do.

Between the emails and frantic phone calls, I somehow manage to throw myself together in anticipation of my date with Fred tonight. The Madrileñas notice that I put a little, er, extra time into getting ready. Vivian all but whistles when I walk into the library.

"Are you wearing *eyeliner*?" she asks, peering at my face like I've suddenly sprouted a fascinatingly horrible skin disease. "And a dress! Wow, Rach, are you, like, planning to seduce our professor or something? Because I'm totally on board with that."

I try to laugh it off—"I just took a shower, guys, no big deal"—but no one buys it.

"So tell me, Rach—who's this new guy you're fucking?" Maddie asks.

I almost choke on my soda. "I'm not—what—"

"You're glowing," she says. "Which means you're fucking someone hot. Good for you. Now tell us everything."

I try to bite back my smile, but it doesn't work.

So I do. I tell them everything. Well, not everything—I want to keep the most delicious details for myself—but it fills me with the loveliest, giddiest joy to share Fred with my girl-friends.

"He is so swoon-worthy," Laura says. "I had no idea!"

"I'm very curious about the dress," Viv adds. "Does he, like, want to finger you in public or something? You're not wearing underwear, are you?"

"I mean, I am," I reply. "But it's the tiniest thong I own—very easy to, um, get around, if you know what I mean."

Maddie grins. "That's my girl. I hope everything works out for you guys. But what if you don't get the internship here in Madrid? Are you going to stay anyway?"

My joy clouds over, just for a minute. "I don't know. I'm trying to think positive thoughts. I get it, everything is so new between Fred and me. It's crazy to make plans like this. But the way I feel about Fred . . . I just . . . I'm falling for him. Hard."

Viv drops her pencil. "Holy shit, Rachel, are you falling in love with this guy?"

Love. Honestly? I could see it happening. Which is terri-fying and thrilling, all at once.

"Wow," Viv says, interpreting my silence as an affirmative answer. "Well in that case, let's form a prayer circle and make sure God lines up this internship for you. Because . . . *wow*."

I put my head in my hands. "I'm really setting myself up to crash and burn, aren't I?"

"We have a week or two left before the end of the semester." Maddie squeezes my shoulder. "A lot can happen between now and then. Things will work out. They always do, right?"

"Right," I say, even though I'm not sure I buy into that belief.

I honestly don't know what we'll do if I don't get this

internship. I want to work in sports medicine one day, which means I shouldn't pass up the spot at the Meryton athletic department. I've dreamed about that internship for years now, and I've worked toward it ever since I was a freshman. It's a slam dunk. An amazing, life-changing opportunity.

But now I also want Fred. Which means I'll have to pass up the Meryton internship and stay in Madrid. Or—total long shot—I guess he could come to the States. Fred is a legit soccer star, though. He can't just uproot his life and his career —his insanely lucrative career—to come live with me in Durham, North Carolina. I mean, we do have professional soccer in the States, but the small American league is a bit of a backwater compared to the famous, lucrative leagues here in Europe. Who the hell am I to ask him to give up money and fans and opportunity like that?

I guess we could try long distance. But four-thousand-some-odd miles is a *lot* of distance. And we're both so busy, Fred with soccer, me with school and, later this year, an internship. To make it work long distance would be nothing short of a miracle. Could we do it, though, if push came to shove? Do I want this enough?

I don't know.

I don't know what's going to happen.

No matter how hard I try to think about what Fred might be plotting for this dress I'm wearing, my mind spins. A lot has happened in the past week—the past twenty-four hours—and I'm struggling to process it all. Fred, my future, my mom—it's all coming at me so suddenly and so quickly it's almost paralyzing.

I'm sure everything will work out one minute, and then

I'm crushed by the certainty that it won't the next. Should I hope for the best? Should I cut and run?

Am I being a complete and total idiot by allowing myself to fall for a guy I'm probably going to have to leave behind? Am I an idiot to think we're forever material even though we've known each other for all of two weeks?

I glance at the clock at the far end of the library. Half past five. Fred isn't supposed to pick me up for another hour or so, but I can't keep sitting here. I need to get up. Walk. Think.

I bundle up and head outside. I walk for a long time, block after block, until I hit Salamanca, passing by the Prado Museum. The enormous building is all lit up at night. It's pretty, worth taking a stroll around the block to see.

I check my phone. I have another twenty minutes or so until Fred comes. I shoot him a quick text, telling him to meet me around here instead of at the university. He says he'll be heading my way shortly.

My dress flutters in the breeze as I make my way around the museum. I'm glad I wore over-the-knee boots underneath my dress because it's cold tonight.

Good-looking couples huddle together as they pass. One couple kisses, a loud, wet kiss that would've had me rolling my eyes in disgust a week ago. Now, though—I find myself smiling. I wonder what Fred and I look like when we kiss.

A shiver of anticipation darts up my spine. I can't wait to see him.

I turn the corner onto Gran Vía, the street that runs lengthwise alongside the museum. The building is illuminated in a rainbow of colors, a bright behemoth against the black night sky. I've been in Madrid for almost five months now, but stuff like this never gets old. I love this city. Love the way it smells and how it looks and how much it appreciates day drinking and dancing until six A.M.

I'm going to miss it if—when—I leave.

I raise my head at the sound of approaching footsteps. A big guy in biker boots walks past me, his footfalls echoing off the museum walls. I blink, my eyes moving to the street.

They land on a tall, broad figure, really just a shadow from here, leaning against a car at the curb.

The man's hands are in the pockets of his jeans and his ankles are crossed. He's looking the other direction, away from me. Something about the set of his enormous shoulders says he's waiting for someone. They're just the tiniest bit tense.

He turns his head, revealing the outline of a familiar nose. Full lips. Tidy swoop of hair.

Glasses.

A rush of awareness douses my skull and moves through my body, leaving behind a tingling sensation in my knees, the tips of my fingers.

Fred.

I am suddenly so, so glad. Glad for what, I don't have a fucking clue.

I'm close enough now to see him smile as I approach. He stands, keeping his hands in his pockets, and pivots a little to face me. He looks good. Really fucking good. The kind of good that makes my entire being throb with longing.

I don't want to leave this guy. Ever.

"Hello, beautiful. I hope you're not too cold in that dress," he says, eyes narrowing.

If anyone else said that right now, it'd sound cheesy. Trite. But in Fred's earnest, slightly gravelly voice, it sounds just right.

"I'm fine," I say, drawing to a stop a few paces away from him. The space between our bodies—I don't know any other way to describe it except that it's *hungry*. My heart swells.

I guess I'm just glad to see Fred.

I'm glad that he's here.

Chapter Fifteen

FRED

The light from a nearby street lamp catches on Rachel's long, silky hair, gilding it in shades of gold and copper. My heart skips a beat. I feel the blood moving inside my skin, filling every square millimeter of my body with excitement. Want.

I want to reach out and pull her to me, but she's standing just out of arm's reach. It's bloody killing me. All day long I've thought about this moment. About when I'd see her again.

I was in a happy daze during training this morning. My surly manager, William Wallace (not his real name, we just call him that because he is scary and Scottish) told me more than once to "wipe that silly fecking smile off yer silly fecking face." Olivier, our captain, asked, "Are you on some-zing, like ze drugs?" Alexsandr, in true form, teased me about the rug burns on my knees.

I shrugged them all off with excuses of feeling well rested. I didn't quite know what to say about the rug burns. I just pulled up my socks and got on with it. I don't want to tell them about Rachel. Not because I'm ashamed—quite the opposite—but because I don't want to jinx it. Us. Me and Rachel.

I thought losing my virginity would be the best fucking thing ever. And it was great. It was so much better than I could have ever imagined.

"Ready to celebrate?" I ask.

The sinews in her throat move as she swallows. "I am. I guess."

Her voice stretches over those last two words. I blink. Shit, something is wrong.

I take a step toward her. I can see her eyes now. They're glassy. Wet. Tired, like she's been struggling.

"Rachel." The dip in my voice betrays my concern. "Are you all right?"

She turns her head and looks away for a moment. She swallows again. Christ, did I hurt her last night? Is she in pain? The thought that she's tired or hurting on my account makes me fucking angry as hell at myself.

"I've been thinking a lot. Too much," she says, meeting my eyes again. She puts her hands in her coat pockets. "I had amazing sex with a famous footballer and got my dream internship and applied to *another* dream internship, all in one day."

"No big deal," I say, grinning.

She scoffs. "Small beans for sure."

"I know I'm putting a lot on your plate right now," I say. "Is there anything I can do to help?"

"You've already done way too much," she says. "And it's all good stuff you've put on my plate. Really, really good stuff. I'm just worried that . . . you know."

I look at her. "That things won't work out."

"Yes. Exactly. There's a lot on the line for me."

"I know," I say. Bloody hell, do I know. Because there's a lot on the line for me too. I've been so careful with my heart. So protective.

And now I'm giving it away to a girl who might run halfway across the world with it.

We'll figure something out. I'll pull every string and call in every favor to make sure Rachel stays by my side. The club loves me right now. There's no way they'd stand in my way. Not on this.

"You're going to get the internship. I'll make sure of it, all right?"

"C'mon, Fred, you don't have to do that. I'd actually prefer that you didn't. If I'm lucky enough to be chosen, I want it to be on the awesomeness of my application, not on the fact that I'm some player's girlfriend. I want to feel like I earned it. That I deserve it."

"I understand that," I say. "And I know the awesomeness, as you say, of your application is going to put you at the top of the pile. But what if Valentina is deciding between you and another candidate, and it's my call that tips the balance in your favor?"

"Fred," she says. "Don't, please. I want to do this on my own. I'm super proud of the fact that I got the internship at Meryton—mostly because I did it all on my own. If I get the internship here, I want to feel just as proud. I want to know there was no favoritism involved."

"No favoritism?" I ask. "Then what do you call the tour I organized for you? You would've never met Valentina if it weren't for me. You didn't do that on your own."

Rachel lets out a sigh. "Fair point. But when I accepted the tour, I had no idea that any of this"—she motions between us—"would happen. I had no idea the internship program at your club even existed. So would you pretty please butt out and let my stellar transcript speak for itself?"

"Stellar transcript?" I tease. I don't want this to turn into a fight. "Someone's a little full of themselves."

"Hey, I worked hard for those grades," she replies, grinning. "Just . . . promise me you won't say anything to Valentina, okay? This is important to me."

I put my hands on my hips. Look down at Rachel for a long beat. Then it's my turn to sigh.

"I promise," I say. "Although I don't agree, not for a moment. I want your dreams to come true, but it'd be even better if they came true here. With me. And for that to happen, you need to get this internship."

She looks away. "I know. It's a risk we'll have to take."

"We've been taking a lot of risks lately."

Rachel doesn't reply. A beat of silence passes between us, full of all the things we haven't said. All the things we're afraid of.

"You wore your glasses," she says at last, looking back at me.

"You liked them." I shrug. "They also make me smarter, and you seemed to like that too."

"Smart *is* sexy."

"Want to get going?" I motion to the car. "I imagine it's quite chilly in a dress."

"The dress," she says, wiggling her brows. "I've been wondering all day what that's about."

It's about me being able to fuck you the literal second we walk through my front door. I've got it all planned: I'll unzip my fly and wrap her legs around me and push aside her panties and then I'd be in.

I'd be so fucking deep inside her she'd cry out, and I'd struggle not to come, and we'd fuck hard and loud against the wall like the animals we are.

"That reminds me," I say, hustling to open the passenger side door for her. "I have something to send you."

I close the door behind her and get in the car. I start the

engine, and right away the heat comes on. I made sure it would for Rachel. Then I unlock my phone and hit a few keys. It makes a *whoosh* sound through the speakers of my car —I've got it connected via Bluetooth—when I send her the text.

"That was for me?" she asks, holding her phone while she locks in her seatbelt.

"It was." I glance over my shoulder before merging into traffic.

"Ah," she says, scrolling down. "Your health exam. Says you're 1.83 meters tall—that's what, six one ish?"

"Don't be stingy, love—that's six one and a half."

"Right. Can't forget the half. So you're six one and a *half*, one hundred seventy one pounds . . . Greek god levels of body fat . . . blood work looks good, except for . . . oh! Says you have an incurable and particularly virulent case of syphilis."

I nearly swerve into the next lane. "It does not!" I say, leaning over to look at her screen.

She keeps it just out of my reach, laughing. "No it doesn't, but I couldn't resist busting your balls."

"My syphilis-ridden balls. Nice, Rachel. Really nice."

We both laugh at that. I'm always laughing with her. Makes me realize how little I've laughed in general up until I met her.

"But really, thank you for this. I appreciate you being so up front about things," she says. "Here, I'll send you mine— should have it in my email somewhere . . ."

I glance at her, shifting gears. "I trust you."

She looks at me. "You do?"

"I know you better than I've known any girl. Ever."

"Well, yeah, you know me like *that*—"

"I do," I say. "I can't wait to keep knowing you *like that*. But I'd like to think I'm a good enough judge of character at this point in my life to know you wouldn't lie to me."

"I wouldn't lie to you," Rachel replies.

I look away, focusing on the road. "I've met a lot of girls, Rachel, but you—you're different. I knew that right away when we met."

A smile flutters at the edges of her mouth. "I'm different?"

"Yeah," I say. "Obviously. You're my girlfriend, remember? And I don't have many girlfriends."

"I know," she says. "By the way, I just sent you my physical exam results. If you want to read them."

"Thanks," I say. "I know you've been struggling with which direction to take in your life, but the fact that you're struggling at all shows you've got something inside you that's genuine. Something that tells you to stop trying to be someone you're not."

"Wow. That's really lovely of you to say—thank you." She curls into her seat. Sighs. "You know, it took meeting you for me to finally grow the balls to choose sports medicine over plastic surgery. It took having someone who's unconditionally on my side—someone who's been through the same thing— for me to get here. So thank you, Fred, for being such a wonderful friend."

I smile. I smile so bloody hard it hurts.

Out of all the things I've ever wanted in a girl, I never considered wanting a *friend*. But now I see how important friendship is. How it should come first and foremost, because that is where the magic is. Not to say there isn't magic in the bedroom, because holy hell, there certainly can be. But it's the magic that comes from being friends—listening to one another, being there for one another, having fun with one another—that really glues us together. That makes what we have special.

"You're an even better friend to me," I say, softly. "What can I do to return the favor?"

When she turns to look at me, her eyes are dark. Saucy.

"You can fuck me," she says.

My pulse hiccups. "I was going to do that anyway. But if you've got a lot on your mind—if you need some time—"

"I don't need time." Her hand falls out of her hair. "I need you to have sex with me. Now. Fred, please. Last night, I felt so—I don't know. Amazing. I want to feel like that again. Get out of my head for a little, you know?"

I look at her. She looks back at me.

I nail the first turn I can. We're somewhere in the old town, Madrid's medieval quarter where the streets are narrow, quiet, a labyrinth of cobblestones and shadows.

Perfect.

It's loud driving over the cobbles, but I don't slow down. I take a left, then a right, working my way farther into the labyrinth. It gets quieter. Darker.

I pull into an alley and, seeing that no one's around, throw the car into park and turn it off.

"Get in the back," I murmur, unbuckling my seatbelt.

"Wait," Rachel says. "Are we—the sex—are we going to do it here?"

"You said you wanted me to fuck you. Now." I look up at her. "So that's what I'm going to do."

"But we're in public!" She gestures out the windshield, a smile of disbelief breaking out on her face. "Someone will see us—"

"No they won't," I say. "But it could make things a bit more exciting, yeah?"

"I didn't know you were an exhibitionist."

"I'm not. I just want to repay the favor, remember?"

She looks at me for a beat. Then another. "You're fucking excellent, Fred. You know that?"

"I do. Get in the back."

"Okay." She takes a deep breath. "Okay."

Rachel unbuckles her belt and, putting a hand on my shoulder, climbs into the backseat. I'm too big to manage the same maneuver, so I turn off the car and get out. Glancing around one last time, I open the car door and slide onto the back bench beside Rachel.

It's dark back here, the only light coming from a nearby window. I can just make out Rachel's face. She's breathing hard. Looking at me with parted lips. Her dark eyes aren't wet anymore, but I hope—I think—she's wet somewhere else.

Her eyes flick to my mouth. She runs her tongue along her bottom lip.

This girl. *This fucking girl.*

I reach for her, putting my hands on her neck. Her head falls back when I bring my mouth down on hers. I lean into her and her hands go to my chest. I drink her in, opening her to me with my tongue. She kisses me back, hard, her breath coming hot and fast against my face. She tastes clean, like water, a hint of gum.

I'm hard in the space of a single heartbeat. My dick throbs against the crotch of my jeans, seeking her tight heat. Seeking release. Christ, I've been dying for this all day. Dying for her.

Her hands are on my face now, and she's climbing on top of me, straddling my lap. The front slit in her dress falls to the side, revealing the top of her thigh.

I groan when she settles her weight on me. I curl my fingers around her waist, slide them to her hips, and I guide them in a slow, grinding circle against my dick. She gasps. Bites my lip.

She's got her arms around my neck now, moving against me in a steady grind. My dick is throbbing. I lift my hips, just a little, roll against her.

I reach around her neck and gather her hair in my fingers, pulling it across her back to drape it over one shoulder. This leaves one side of her throat completely revealed—completely vulnerable. I sink my teeth into the soft skin there, gently sucking it until she cries out.

"Fred," she moans. "Oh, please. *Please*."

With my other hand I tug her dress up her thighs. Reach between her legs.

I pull back when I encounter the thin lacy strap of a thong.

It's soaking wet.

I meet her gaze. "Oh my God, Rachel."

"All day," she pants, closing her eyes. "I've been wet like this all day, thinking about you."

I swallow, hard. I knew Rachel and I had chemistry. I didn't know our attraction would go this deep. Would haunt both of us like this.

I'm so fucking turned on it hurts.

"My jeans," I grunt. "Unbutton them."

Rachel goes right to work, reaching between us. She pops the button and tugs down the fly, reaching inside my jeans. She cups my dick through my boxers, giving it a squeeze.

For a second my vision goes blank. I can't resist the idea of fucking her raw, without a condom, but I'm also worried I'll last all of three seconds. Everything about her just feels so bloody good.

I hook my first two fingers in the center strap of her thong and yank it aside. The tip of my middle finger meets with her center. She's hot, pulsing, practically dripping with arousal.

"Jesus Christ, love, I thought you were wet last night, but this—"

Her face hovers above mine. She smirks. "This is insane. I know."

I guide my finger up to her clit and she gasps, her eyes going dark. "I want to make you come first."

"I'm—" Another gasp when I work her clit between my knuckles and give it a tug. "I'm already so close, Fred. Let's just go."

"You sure?"

In reply, she reaches inside my boxers and grabs my cock. I suck a breath through my teeth at the strength of all this sudden contact—skin on skin, her palm on my length. She rears up on her knees, her hair falling in my face as she positions her pussy over the head of my dick.

I reach between us and put my hand on hers. I want to be here for this—for the moment when I slide inside her.

"Wait," she says, pulling back just enough to meet my eyes. "You didn't look at my exam results."

"I already told you," I reply, "if you say you're negative—if you say you've got birth control covered—you're fucking negative. We're all right."

Her eyes contract, but in a pleasant way. A surprised way.

"All right," she says.

Together we position my dick at her entrance. My head grazes her heat. Then she cants her hips, rolling them back just the tiniest bit.

Her eyes never leave mine as she sinks down on me, slowly. They're glazed over with pleasure. Satisfaction.

Her mouth falls open.

I want to fucking howl as her grip on me, hot and wet and so bloody soft, intensifies. She takes me in, one inch at a time. She's wetter and tighter than before—I don't know how, but she is, maybe because we're bare this time, maybe because we know each other. Whatever the reason, it's so good it's almost painful.

Her hands are on my shoulders. She goes still, an inch or two from swallowing me whole.

"I can't," she whimpers. "Fred, I can't. It's too much—you're too big—"

I brush the hair out of her face, reaching up for a kiss. "Do you want to stop?"

She closes her eyes. Shakes her head. "I don't ever want to stop with you."

I help her the rest of the way, lifting my hips as she sinks down the last little bit. She winces.

"Does it hurt?" I ask.

"A little," she says, going still. "It's really—intense this way. And I'm still a little sore."

"I am too."

"You're sore?"

"You're tight as fuck, Rachel. So yeah, I'm sore. Don't think the half woody I've had all day helped much either."

She scoffs at that.

I take her chin in my hand. Swipe my thumb across her lips. She's soft and wet here too. She is soft everywhere.

She's making me feel soft, right in the center of my chest.

"What can I do to make it feel better for you?"

She opens her eyes and searches mine. Our noses are touching, and our shared breath stirs the strands of her hair trapped between us.

"This," she says, and grabs my hand. We reach between her legs, and she guides my fingers to her clit. I let my fingers wander for a moment, she's swollen, engorged with me. I fucking love it.

Her forehead falls against mine when I touch her where she wants. She moans, whispers my name.

Her pussy spasms around me, just once. It's enough to have both of us cursing. My *God* I'm going to fucking die here. I'm going to die, and I don't give a shit. This is so bloody good.

She starts to move, rocking against me. I work tight, hard circles around her clit. I kiss her. She bites me.

My heartbeat is racing.

Headlights slice through the darkness, making me blink. Rachel goes still. Taking her by the nape of her neck, I curl her into my body, shielding her from any prying eyes that might be about.

"Can they—did they—"

I glance over her shoulder at the street in front of us. Nothing.

I glance over my shoulder at the street behind us. Again, nothing.

"We're fine," I say, releasing her.

But the prospect of getting caught must motivate Rachel, because suddenly she's moving against me, really *moving*, grinding her hips against mine. We're gasping for air and we're kissing, violent, messy kisses, and I'm playing with her pussy, my fingers slick with her arousal as I touch her everywhere she'll let me. I wrap an arm around her waist, crushing her against me. We're as close as we could possibly be right now, but it's not close enough.

Her legs start to shake. Her pussy contracts again, gripping me in hard, sudden spasms.

"Fred," she gasps. "I'm coming—"

I grit my teeth at the spiral of sensation in my balls, the head of my dick. "I know. I think I'm going to too. I'm gonna pull out—"

"No!" Rachel grabs the front of my shirt. "You can come inside."

"Rachel—"

"You said you trusted me," she says. "The IUD—we're good. I promise."

I look at her.

She comes as our eyes meet, falling apart around me,

milking me, making *me* come, a rush of blood and heat and so much searing sensation I feel like I really am dying, being burned up from the inside out.

Rachel gasps, cries out, and I take the back of her head in my hand and press her face into the hollow where my neck slopes into my shoulder.

She fits perfectly there.

I hold her and I hold her, I hold her until the spasms subside and she releases her death grip on my shirt. She collapses against me, curling into my chest, breathing hard.

I'm breathing hard too. I can't get a fucking hold on my heart rate. I run ten kilometers in any given match—I run like mad for ninety minutes—and I'm always able to recover quickly. I can always get back to where I need to be.

But right now I'm struggling. With the warm weight of Rachel resting on my chest—with the smell of her hair in my head—my heart is beating so hard I worry it's going to burst.

I take a deep breath through my nose, let it out through my mouth. An old trick one of my coaches from way back when taught me.

It works. A little.

I still don't want to let her go. I never want to. How do things keep getting better between us? More intense?

"That clear you mind?" I manage.

"Just a bit," she says, laughing.

We clean ourselves up with some tissues Rachel has in her bag. Bare sex is amazing, but Jesus is it messy. We leave more than a little DNA behind on the back seat, but I couldn't care less. Who knew christening your car was so damn fun?

Only when I duck outside and come back in at the front do I realize how different it smells inside now.

My car has never smelled like anything except—well—a new car, I guess.

Now it smells like sex. Like pussy and sweat and perfume.

It smells like Rachel.

Fuck. *Yes*.

Chapter Sixteen

RACHEL

Saturday Morning

"So," I say, flopping down on the couch next to Fred. "Are you getting nervous?"

"About playing Málaga tonight?" He pulls a face. God, he's cute. "Not particularly. I appreciate what they're doing to try and turn the club around there. But their management leaves quite a lot to be desired."

I grin. It never gets old, shooting the shit about sports with Fred. "They should've never hired Hanover. The fans hate him. He totally blew up Bordeaux—that club won't recover for years. Wouldn't be surprised if Málaga is his next failed experiment."

"You know you're giving me a hard-on, right?" Fred asks.

"I do." My gaze flicks to the tent he's pitching inside his athletic shorts. "Usually happens less than a minute into our conversations about Spanish football."

"Less," Fred says, eyes latched on my mouth. "Way less than a minute."

I'm leaning toward his lap when my phone starts to vibrate on the coffee table.

I glance at the clock on the cable box. 9:59.

My stomach flips. *Shit*. I forgot that Mom was supposed to call me this morning—she texted earlier this week, something about a form "we" needed to fill out so I can shadow one of her douchebag doctor friends in Dallas this summer.

Needless to say, I ignored the text. But if I ignore this call too, Mom will know something's up.

"Sorry," I groan, sitting up and reaching for my phone. "I'll be quick, I promise."

I glide my thumb across the screen.

"I was worried I wouldn't get you," Mom says after I tell her hello. "You never responded to my text. You know that's one of my rules, right? I pay your phone bill, which means you answer me. Always."

I roll my eyes. I'm a lot calmer than I usually am when I talk to Mom, but my pulse still skips at the condescending tone she's taking with me.

"I know," I say. "I'm sorry. I've just had a busy week—I finished up a big paper."

Mom makes this small, impatient noise, something between a scoff and strangled choke. "Rachel, *I'm* busy at work. I don't have time to chase you down."

Fred grins at my second eye roll.

"Really, I'm sorry. I'll try to respond sooner next time."

"So I spoke with Dr. Roby on Wednesday," she says, talking about one of the anesthesiologists she works with at the hospital. "He said he'd love to have you shadow him this summer. It's an amazing opportunity, Rach—his practice is one of the most prestigious in Texas. The guy drives a frickin' Bugatti and owns a yacht down in Nassau, for God's sake. He's a total success story."

It's all I can do not to gag. This is the closest I've ever come to actually puking in my mouth.

"Good for him," I say evenly.

A beat of silence passes between us.

"So?" she demands.

"So what?"

"So I need you to finish filling out this paperwork so we can get you all set up at the hospital. Nothing you haven't seen before. But I want to make sure you hit the ground running—maybe you can even have lunch with Dr. Roby over Christmas break, while you're home? Get to know him a bit, kiss the ring, that sort of thing."

I let my head fall back onto the sofa. Mom doesn't even ask if I want to shadow Dr. Roby, or if I'm interested in anesthesiology. She just assumes, because he's successful, because he drives a stupid expensive sports car, I'm going to fall all over myself to shadow him.

I glance at Fred. He looks at me, the hazy desire in his eyes replaced by sharp concern.

"You okay?" he murmurs.

I nod, even though I'm starting to feel a little shaky. I have a feeling that this is going to be the call—the call I've been dreading for years now.

The call where I fess up, and tell Mom about my sports medicine plans.

"You can thank me anytime now, you know," Mom is saying. "I had to pull a lot of strings to get you this opportunity. Med students would kill to get their foot in the door with a doctor like Roby."

Fred takes my hand and gives it a soft squeeze. I love how big his hands are, how warm and dry.

"I don't want to do it," I say.

Mom goes silent. My heart begins to pound.

"What?" she says after a beat. "What do you mean, you don't want to do it?"

"I mean I don't want to shadow Dr. Roby this summer. I don't want to shadow any of your doctor friends."

Again, silence.

Again, that awful noise Mom makes. "Just what do you think you'll be doing this summer, then?"

I swallow. Fred offers me that smile of his, his eyes getting squinty and cute.

You got this, he mouths. *Sex in the shower when you're done?*

Despite being so nervous I really do want to puke—despite the hammer that's about to come down on my head—I giggle.

"Rachel," Mom says. "What the hell is going on over there? Are you with someone?"

"No-o?"

"That's it," she says. "I'm going to FaceTime you. You're clearly not paying attention to what I have to say."

My stomach tightens, a cold wash of panic seizing my insides. If Mom sees me in this apartment with Fred—

"No," I say. "No, Mom, wait, I'm listening—"

But I can already hear her fiddling with her phone, cursing as she hits the wrong button. For a second I think I'll get lucky—maybe she accidentally hung up—but then I hear her saying my name, her voice different, smaller, now that we're on FaceTime.

Shit.

I glance at Fred. He's looking nervous now too.

"I'm sorry for whatever she says," I whisper.

And then I pull the phone away from my ear and hold it out in front of me.

"There," Mom says. There's a second or two delay in the video feed, so she doesn't say anything about the apartment yet. "That's better. As I was saying, I just need you to finish filling out these forms, and then you can scan them and—"

Oh, God. Here it comes.

"Whoa, whoa. Rachel—that doesn't look like your dorm

room. And why is your shirt so big?" Her eyes bulge as the realization hits her. "Just where the hell are you?"

I roll my lips between my teeth. Best to just get it out and tell her the truth.

"I'm at my boyfriend's apartment."

If Mom's eyes were bulging before, they're literally about to pop out of her head now. "Boyfriend? I didn't know you had a boyfriend. We've talked about this before. I don't like the idea—"

"Mom, meet Fred Ohr."

I tilt my phone, leaning into Fred so both our faces fit into the tiny square in the corner of my screen. Of course he's still scruffy from sleep. I think he always looks handsome, but I know Mom is going to be put off by his five o'clock shadow, his glasses, and the ratty sweatshirt with the stretched collar he wears in the mornings.

He couldn't look more different from the slick, polished, impeccably groomed surgeons who inhabit Mom's world.

My phone slips out of my hand; my palms have gotten really sweaty all of the sudden. I catch it and hold it back up.

"Hello, Mrs. Collins," he says, and gives her an awkward little wave.

Another painful pause. She's clearly not impressed. "So. When did Fred come into the picture?"

My face burns.

"A couple weeks ago. Maybe a little less than that."

"How long ago, exactly, did you meet him?"

I look at Fred. "Ten days? Twelve?"

Mom does something I've never heard her do. She laughs. A giant, disbelieving cackle that would make Cruella DeVille proud.

Beside me on the sofa, Fred goes still. My heart clenches.

"Ten days? And here I was starting to worry. Just blink twice if you need to be rescued, okay?" She laughs again. The sound grates on my nerves, already stretched taut. "Listen, you're clearly distracted this morning. Why don't we talk about your summer plans when you get home in a couple of weeks?"

Fred gives my leg a squeeze. I feel slightly less like dying.

I feel like now is not the time to chicken out. In for penny, in for pound, or whatever that expression is.

"About that," I say. "I'm actually trying to get a summer internship here in Madrid."

Her smile disappears. "In Madrid? Doing what?"

"Sports medicine," I say. My voice is high and thin. "I'd be interning at the facility where Fred's football team trains. It's also a prestigious program. I'm just not that interested in surgery—I'm sorry."

Mom stares at the screen. Her mouth pinches.

I wait for her response.

I wait.

And wait.

Somewhere in the background, our cat meows.

"Mom? Say something. Please."

When she speaks, her voice is cold. Hard.

"We've talked about this, Rachel—sports medicine is a dead end. So is this guy. Are you really going to plan your entire future around a man you've just met? Get real, Rachel. You're coming home, and we're getting you in with Dr. Roby's anesthesiology team. End of story."

My nervousness expands, burns to anger at the edges. "I told you. I'm not interested in surgery. I'm not taking the MCAT."

"You're not interested in surgery," she scoffs. "So what are you interested in, then? And don't say sports medicine, because that's just ridiculous. What are you going to do for the rest of your life? Stretch out some guys on a soccer field?

You can't make a real living that way. You'll get bored. You'll never be able to buy a house, take nice trips . . ."

"That's not true."

"You know what happens to people who don't have a plan, Rachel? People who don't care about their future? Nothing happens, that's what. You want to be nothing? A nobody?"

I grit my teeth. Beside me, Fred squeezes my leg again.

"Be calm," he says, quietly. "You don't want to say something you'll regret." Right. Be calm. I take another deep breath.

"Listen, Mom. Just because I don't want to be you, doesn't mean I'm going to be a nobody. I know you're not happy with my decision. But I hope one day you'll be able to accept it. Accept me for who I am. I love you, Mom, and I always will. I have to do this. I have to go with my gut. I'm not a surgeon. I never will be. I think we both know that."

"You have the potential to be anything you want, Rachel. As long as you don't get caught up with the wrong guy," she says.

"I want to be in sports medicine. You know I love sports. I am so freaking excited about this internship—not only about how prestigious it is, but also about actually doing the work there. It's going to be the best summer ever. I'm excited, and I'd love it if you were excited for me too."

She releases a long, low breath. "I don't think I can be, Rachel. I'm disappointed in you. Very, very disappointed."

Tears burn the backs of my eyes. Fred wraps his arms around me, and I fall into his chest. His heartbeat is steady. Strong.

"I have to go," she says. "But this conversation is not over, you hear me? We have a lot more to talk about when you come home. *When* you come home. Not if."

"I don't think we do," I say. "Mom, I've made my decision."

She huffs. And then she hangs up.

My hand drops from my ear. I look down at my screen as it goes blank.

For a minute I just sit there, letting the last charges of nervous energy work their way through me. I'm lightheaded. Relieved. Destroyed.

Sad.

"Breathe," Fred murmurs. "Don't forget to breathe, love."

When I do, I'm attacked by a fresh wave of tears. The burn behind my eyelids is unbearable. I hold my thumb and forefinger against them. It helps, a little.

"Fuck, this is hard," I say. I look at my phone. All I'd have to do is pick it back up. Call Mom again. Tell her I'm sorry, I was wrong, I'll shadow those anesthesiologists for the next ten years if that's what she wants me to do.

If that's what would make her happy.

"I know," Fred says.

I straighten. Scoff. "How long are things between Mom and me going to suck for?"

"Probably a while." He tucks my hair behind my ear, meeting my eyes. "But you've got me in the meantime. Small consolation, I know—"

I laugh, and he smiles.

"—I'll do my best, though. I know how much it hurts. And how the temptation to turn back is always there. But you've taken the first step in making your life your own. That's a good thing. That's huge."

"I thought it'd feel better." I unravel the tissue in my hand, then crumple it into my fist again. "I mean, I feel good that the call is over. But the doubts I've always had about making this choice—it's like they're howling inside my head."

"Yeah, but isn't the voice that told you to take this path also howling?"

I manage a smile. "It's screaming. I guess it always has

been. I've just been scary good at ignoring it. And then I met you . . ."

"And everything fell apart," he says, smiling back.

"No." I shake my head. The heaviness inside my chest releases, just a bit. "Everything came together."

He strokes the top of my hand with his thumb. "Your happiness is important to me. It matters, Rachel. You matter."

Oh, God, I'm going to start crying all over again. I know, somewhere deep down inside, Mom wants me to be happy too. She's not a total monster. But she's buried so deep in her own shit that sometimes the message—the intent—gets distorted. Our relationship is complicated. I think most mother-daughter relationships are. There's love, but there's also jealousy. Miscommunication, misunderstanding.

I've never had someone in my life so unconditionally on my side the way Fred is. My girlfriends are great, of course, and I love them to the moon and back. But Fred is different. We're closer. And I'm not just saying that because we have the best sex on the planet. He just understands the battle I'm trying to fight in a way no one else can.

He's holding my hand through it in a way no one else would.

I look at him through a film of tears, some of them sad, others happy. Because as much as disappointing Mom sucks, knowing that I have this new, amazing friend-slash-boyfriend-slash-studly-soccer-player by my side makes it bearable.

It makes it all worth it, even though I really did only meet him twelve days ago.

It lets me know I'm going to be okay. Eventually. And until I get there, I'll have stuffed French toast and shower sex to get me through.

I only hope it can last. *Please*, I pray. *Please, God, let me get the internship with Fred's club*. I don't know if I can fight this battle on my own back home.

I don't know how I'll choose between Fred and the Meryton internship I've been dreaming about for years.

I don't want to have to make that choice.

Then again, I might have to. I bought my plane ticket home way back in August and it's a one-way ticket for a flight to Dallas on December 23. I keep waiting for the chance to change or even cancel it—hell, if I get the internship at the club, maybe I'll just go to Germany with Fred for Christmas —but I don't want to jinx myself.

Maybe I should've let Fred make that call to Valentina. I'm getting nervous now. Really nervous.

Whatever—what's done is done, and worrying like this is just a waste of time and energy. It's all pretty much out of my hands at this point.

"So," I sniff. "Still up for that shower?"

Fred's pale eyebrows jump. "Fuck yeah I am. Maybe catch the bowl game after?"

I smile. Few things make me prouder than knowing I turned Fred into a college football fan.

It's in that second, suspended between heartbreak and happiness, that I think I've fallen in love with Fred.

Then again, is it even possible to fall in love with someone you've only known for all of two weeks? Are we really forever material even though we've just met?

I've heard stories of it happening with my parents' friends. You know, boy meets girl, boy marries girl a month later, and now they've been happily married for thirty years. I guess I didn't believe it could happen for me. I believed that kind of love died out with soda shops and saddle shoes.

Modern love is complicated—or it's supposed to be, isn't it? It's supposed to be angsty, impossible, distorted by our internet-driven indifference. It isn't supposed to happen so quickly.

So happily.

But it's happening. And the way I feel about Fred doesn't seem complicated at all. Yeah, our situation is difficult, to say the least. We're hinging all our hopes on this random internship application working out. I'm very much aware that we're skating on thin ice.

But it's *happening*. And I kinda sorta love it.

Chapter Seventeen

FRED

Rachel and I steal away every chance we get during the next week and a half. Sometimes we'll travel to a new city— Segovia, Toledo. Other times we'll hole up in my flat, where we'll catch episodes of *Tournament of Kings* or watch American football between marathon naked sessions on the floor, in my bed, on the counter. We fuck until we're both so sore we have to resort to oral.

Having Rachel suck my dick is even better than I fantasized it would be. I always make sure to repay the favor once, twice, three times over. I feel like my mouth is between her legs morning, noon, and night.

I wouldn't have it any other way.

We take cooking lessons. We go to museums. We watch the *Fifty Shades of Grey* movie (boring) and read the book (amazing, mostly because Rachel insists on reenacting the sex scenes after we read them). Rachel crashes my training session when she can—it seems the training facility is the happy place for both our inner sports nuts. We go to Madrid's famous flea market, *El Rastro*, one Sunday morning, and see a flamenco show in the afternoon. We shop and we eat, and then we burn off what we ate in the shower.

I am ravenous all the time.

"It's strange—I feel like Rachel and I have been together forever, even though it's only been a few weeks," I tell my sister, Sophie, on the phone. I just dropped Rachel off at class, and now I'm tidying up my flat, folding my shirt she sleeps in. "I have no idea what the hell I did before I met her."

"You didn't do any of the things, Fred. Except play the football," Sophie replies. She's been working on her English in anticipation of meeting Rachel, and she's still a bit rusty. "Rachel has opened your eyes to the world. I am so very glad of this. We worry about you, Uncle Fredrik, being so far from your family."

I put the folded shirt on Rachel's nightstand—yes, the nightstand is hers now, crowded with her perfume, hair ties, a stack of books—and I smile. I fucking adore how lived in my flat feels. Maybe because I'm actually living in it now that Rachel's around. I cook here, I have sex here, I spend time here.

I feel like my life—this life I started when I left Germany to come to Spain—is finally starting.

"I can't wait for you to meet her."

"Oh? And when will that be? Baby Lilli is getting very so impatient. We hear these many wonderful things about Rachel, but we do not get to meet her!"

"Soon, I hope," I say. I glance at Rachel's laptop, charging on my dresser. She's supposed to hear about the internship at the training facility any day now. Of course she crushed her interview with Valentina last week. It's still taken every ounce of self control not to pick up the phone and call Valentina myself.

I've started to get nervous when I think about what

happens next. Because then I have to think about what we'll do if things don't work out—if Rachel doesn't get the internship here in Madrid. Now that she's committed to sports medicine, she's more excited than ever about spending her summer working in the field.

Things are great between us. Really, really great. But when push comes to shove, I'm worried Rachel is going to choose her career over me.

I'm worried that it might be the right choice for us both. The sane choice. I can't forget that it's only been three bloody weeks since we met. If you look at it on paper, we'd be crazy to give up anything to be together—much less our careers.

"How soon? Will she visit us for the holidays?"

The hope in Sophie's voice makes my heart twist. "We'll see, Soph, all right? I told you we are waiting to hear about this internship Rachel wants to get. After that, I guess we'll figure out the holidays."

"Well." Sophie grunts, and a second later, I hear Lilli coo into the phone. I grin. "It sounds like you are very smitten with the lovely Rachel woman. We are eager to meet this one girl who has given claim to you heart. Mama—"

"You didn't tell Mama about her, did you?"

"Tsk. Of course I told her. She was so happy."

My stomach flips. Now I'm really in trouble. If I don't bring Rachel home over the holidays, shit's going to hit the fan. Mum will be crushed. I've already broken her heart once. I don't want to do it again.

"C'mon, Sophie, I told you—"

"You told me about a girl you very much liked—and you have never, ever told me about any girl. I could not keep so juicy a secret forever! Mama would discover your truth anyway."

"True," I say. "She's better than Sherlock when it comes to her children's love lives."

"Yes. She sniffed up Peter just after our first date. She knew I was pregnant too, before I did."

"That's . . . bizarre."

"Very much bizarre. But that is who she is. And she knows you are in love with Rachel. We all do."

I blink. "I never told you I was in love with Rachel. I don't even know—"

"You are," Sophie says. "You would never let someone so close if you weren't in love with her. You have always protected your heart. You have not met anyone worth risking it for. But you risk it with Rachel, because you believe she is like nobody else you meet. She is lovely, and wise, and very sexy, yes?"

"Oh, God, please just—let's not—just don't—I can't talk about that with my sister," I say, holding the bridge of my nose between my thumb and forefinger. My heart's popping around inside my chest. "The sex, I mean. Rachel being sexy. It's not a brother-sister approved topic of conversation, all right?"

"All right. But you love her in the sexy way too, right? I hear it in your voice."

"Oookay, this is getting weird. I've got to be off—"

"Soon," Sophie says. "You promised we would meet Rachel soon. Do not forget that!"

"But I didn't promise anything! Just like I didn't tell you—"

"I am your sister," she replies. "I've known you since the day you were born. What a fat baby you were! I still know you now too, when you are not so fat. I know you are in love with Rachel. And I know we will meet her soon."

I sigh. "All right, Nostradamus, I really do have to get to

training. We'll talk soon. And please, for the love of God, stop telling Mama about Rachel."

I hang up, and then I hang my head.

I am in love with Rachel. I've known it for a while now.

And I am scared out of my fucking mind I'm going to lose her.

I launch one ball after the next at the goal, savage, hard kicks that make the inside of my right foot and ankle burn. They all soar past Alexsandr, except for the last shot—that one hits him right in the bollocks.

He goes down like a sack of potatoes, hands clutched to his groan.

"What the fuck, mate?" he cries out before he begins to roll back and forth in apparent agony.

"Jesus Christ," I murmur, running up to help him. "I'm so sorry. I didn't mean to hit you . . . uh, there."

He squints up at me. "But you did. Total asshole move."

"I know. Can I get you anything? Do you need the physio—"

"No. I'll be all right. I may never be able to have children, but I'll be all right."

I offer him my hand. "I'm really sorry. I don't have an excuse—I wasn't paying attention. I'm sorry."

Alexsandr grabs my hand and lets me pull him to his feet.

"What's up with you today?" he asks.

"What do you mean?"

"You're murdering the ball. Did it, like, sleep with your girlfriend or something? Because that's how bloody hard you're kicking it."

I dig my hands into the hair on the back of my head. It's slick with sweat.

I hold a breath in my cheeks. Let it out.

"Rachel," I say. "The girl you met—"

"A couple weeks ago. Yeah, I remember her. She's the pretty brunette."

"Yeah. Wow, you've got a good memory."

"You never bring girls round. Rachel stuck out."

"Yeah, well . . . I'm in love with her."

Alexsandr's grimace softens into a grin. He pounds me on the shoulder. "So I wasn't very far off, asking for an invitation to the wedding. Good for you, mate."

"Thanks. She's . . . she is everything to me. She means everything."

"But?"

"How'd you know there was a but?"

He motions to his groin. "Because you just knocked my dick inside out. That's how."

"Oh. Right. Yeah, there *is* a but. I'm in love with her, but there's a very good chance she's heading back to the States—for good—next week."

"That is a pretty big but."

I roll my eyes at the joke.

"Then you've got to make her stay," he says. "Use your . . . er, German wiles or what have you and convince her she can't live without you. Have you talked to her about it?"

I shrug. "Not recently. I think it'll just hurt too much for the both of us. Our strategy, I suppose, has been pretending that December is going to last forever. It's the only way I've been able to cope."

"No offense, mate, but that's just stupid."

"I know," I say. "I know I'm being stupid. Which is part of the reason why I'm so out of sorts. I'm angry with myself."

"It's fucking with your head, and that needs to stop." Alexsandr looks me in the eye. "You've got to talk to her. Come up with a plan to keep her here. Everyone thinks footballers have girls coming out of their ears, but the ones you want to keep around—the good ones—they are few and far between."

"I know. Rachel is a good one. The best."

"Then make your move. Make her yours. If only so my dick can survive the season intact."

I laugh. "All right. I'll talk to her. I'm just worried—"

"No more worrying. It's time to *do*, Fred. Do what needs to be done."

"All right." I look at him. "Thanks. For talking me out of being an idiot."

He grins. "No problem. Now go and talk to your girl before I steal her. All's fair in love and war, and considering the sorry state of my balls right now . . . well. You owe me, mate."

I'm making my way through the training facility, determined to call Rachel as soon as I'm showered up, when I pass the hall that leads down to Valentina's office. I shouldn't—Rachel told me not to meddle—but I find myself backtracking and weaving through the maze of physio offices anyway. It's on the way to the locker room.

Sort of.

My heart skips a beat when I see Valentina at her desk. She looks up as I approach.

"Fred!" she says, smiling. "Might I help you?"

Hello, I reply, switching to Spanish. It's easier for her. *No, I'm just . . . uh. Coming in from training. About to hit the showers. How are you?*

I am well, she says. Her smile fades. *I'm sorry about your friend Rachel. She was a fantastic candidate, really top notch, but we only have one spot for an intern this spring, and Antonio's nephew—*

"Wait," I blurt, my stomach turning to ice. "Wait. *Waaaait*. Rachel didn't get the internship?"

Valentina's eyes widen. "I am sorry, I thought you knew? This morning, I send the email—"

"I didn't know," I say, more harshly than I mean to. *What the fuck?*

What the fuck, what the fuck, what the *fuck*.

Valentina is looking at me funny. "Is everything all right?"

"No." I start to panic, wave after wave of thumping heartbeats. "I mean. We—Rachel—she was really hoping to get it. The internship. There must be some mistake. She got everything in on time. She has fantastic grades, and a stellar résumé . . ."

"All this is true," Valentina says. "But Antonio, his nephew—"

"Who the hell is Antonio?"

She looks at me like I have two heads. "Antonio Gonzalez. The club—he is the owner of it? Surely you know Antonio."

Of course I know Antonio. He's a Spanish billionaire—tires, I think, or maybe telecommunications—and the majority stakeholder in this football club. He's one of the most powerful, and most well connected, people in Madrid.

And I know—I just bloody know—he used those connections to get his wanker nephew this internship. He made the calls Rachel wouldn't let me make.

God*damn* it. The irony of it—the unfairness of not being able to be unfair—does not escape me.

Still. I wish I'd made those fucking calls.

The fluorescent lights seem to press in on me, making me dizzy.

"Antonio Gonzalez's nephew is nowhere near as qualified for this internship as Rachel."

"Pardon me," Valentina replies, suddenly stern. "We

vetted each candidate very . . . how do you say . . . with much care. We chose Antonio's nephew. I am sorry."

I look at her, my mind racing. I'm still sweating, but somehow I'm cold too. It's a cold sweat, and it's awful.

"Then create another position," I blurt. "Surely you can have two interns at a time? This place is massive, and you've got loads of staff to help."

She shakes her head. "I am afraid that is not very possible. We desire to give the intern the best training possible. Also, it is very much work for me, yes? I am busy already without an intern to look over."

"Who do I have to call to open up another position?" I grind out. "Who? Antonio? Because I will go that high to get Rachel a spot here."

"Rachel, she is your . . ." Valentina furrows her brow. "Friend?"

"She's my girlfriend."

"Ah. I see."

"No, you don't see. I need her—I need—" I spear a hand through my hair. Where to even begin?

"I am sorry," Valentina repeats. "But there is nothing I can do for you, Fred. Rachel might apply for next year, if she likes."

"She'll be gone next year!" I shout.

Immediately I regret raising my voice. Valentina's hands clutch the edge of her desk, her knuckles are white. I've scared her.

Jesus Christ.

"Look, Valentina," I begin, softer this time. "I didn't mean to shout like that. I'm sorry. There's just a lot on the line for me here, all right? I need this to work out."

She just looks at me. "I'm afraid it is out of my hands."

I tap the side of my fist against the doorjamb. There's got to be someone I can call. Some way to make this right.

I can make this right.

But deep down, I'm not so sure. How can I compete with the bloke who owns this bloody place? I'm important to the squad, yeah, but it's not my billions keeping us afloat. My agent is working to renegotiate my contract, but it does expire next year. If I cause a fuss, they can cut me loose without much trouble.

Fuck me.

Seriously, seriously fuck me for life.

"I'm sorry, really, I am," I say, turning to go. "Thank you very much for considering Rachel for the internship. We—I —appreciate it."

I move back into the hall.

I can't breathe around the sharp, black pain inside my chest, my belly.

This is bad news. Really, really bad news.

Chapter Eighteen

FRED

My fingers shake as I tear my bag out of my locker. A couple of the lads are hanging about talking, laughing. They go quiet and stare as I rip open the zipper. I dig for my phone, sweat dripping in my eyes, making them burn. Where the hell is this bloody thing—

I pull it out from the bottom of the bag. I've got a missed call and three texts from Rachel. I don't bother reading them. I stalk to the nearest empty room—massage therapy—and slam the door shut behind me. I dial her number.

It rings. And rings. All the while my mind is racing. It's difficult to breathe. I pound the flat of my hand against a nearby wall. Shit.

Shit. This was not supposed to happen. Things were not supposed to go this way. What are we going to do?

I am so fucking in love with this girl.

But I also love my job. That job is here, in Madrid. That job is with this club.

I gave a lot up to get this job. I left my family behind. I've worked my ass off to get where I am. Years—almost a decade

—of sacrifice have led me to the stadium where I play football every weekend with the best players in the world.

I can't give that up.

I also can't ask Rachel to give *her* career up.

Shit.

"Fred." My heart trips to a stop at the thin, high sound of her voice.

It hits me then just how fragile this whole thing's been since the beginning.

How did I not know we'd inevitably cut ourselves on broken pieces of promises we didn't have time to make?

"I got an email this morning—" she says.

"I know. I just spoke with Valentina."

"Oh."

"Where are you?"

She starts to cry. "Fred, I didn't get the internship. You know what that means."

"It doesn't mean anything. Not yet."

"What are we going to do?"

"Where the hell are you, Rachel?"

"I'm in my dorm room." She sniffles. The sound sucks my heart right out of my chest. "I skipped my last class. Couldn't stop crying, so . . . yeah. I went home."

"I'm coming to get you. I'll be there in half an hour."

"Fred," she says. "What are we going to do?"

"I'm going to call everyone in this bloody organization for starters. See if we can't work something out."

"I don't want you calling in any favors, remember?"

"Jesus Christ, Rachel! The kid who got the internship— you know he's the owner's nephew, right? You think Antonio Gonzalez didn't hound Valentina day and night, throwing his billions in her face? You think he didn't call in every favor he had? Please." I let a beat pass. "Please let me fucking do this for you."

For us.

I'm begging now, but I don't care. This girl has got to bloody stay in Madrid. I am going to get my girl, and get my contract, and we'll live happily ever after. I refuse to believe we can't have our cake and eat it too.

"Okay," she says.

But we both know this is not okay.

I have a feeling we're not going to be okay.

Rachel

This morning started off so freaking great. Fred went down on me for about an hour (no joke), and then we got out of bed and made some eggs. We've burned through all six seasons of *Tournament of Kings*, and we talked about what we wanted to watch next. Fred mentioned another vampire show we'd read about on a *Tournament* fan blog we visit religiously every day after coffee.

"Apparently there are even more boobs in this show than in *Tournament*," Fred said.

"Then we definitely have to watch it. Because . . . art."

"Art." He smiled his handsome, squinty smile. "I like art. Your art, in particular."

I made it to school a little earlier than usual, so I had some time to check my email before class. Truth be told, my stomach has flipped every time I've opened my inbox this week. I knew I'd be hearing from Valentina about the internship. It's the only time of the day I let myself feel nervous.

It's the only time I can bear to get real about my future with Fred.

We've gotten absurdly great at pretending like we have all the time in the world together. Pretending we have nothing to worry about and that everything is going to work out in our favor. I feel so high when I'm with him. It makes it too easy to ignore reality.

Now we can't ignore it anymore.

So I open my email this morning and there it is—a short but kind rejection from the physiology team at Fred's football club. I knew the second I saw the line item, in bold, at the top of my screen that I didn't get the internship. If I had, they would've called with the news.

A hot rush of sensation moved from my chest into my head, settling behind my eyes. My throat closed up. I tried to breathe, tried to get a hold on the panic and disappointment and fierce sadness, but I couldn't.

I started crying. Big, fat, warm tears that were impossible to hide. I ducked out of class and tried to call Fred, but by that time he was in training. I didn't know what to do.

I came here, to my dorm room, where I've been crying on and off all afternoon. For the first few hours, I couldn't move. I just curled up in the fetal position on my bed and lay very still. *Maybe getting that email was just a dream*, I thought, half delirious. *Maybe this is all a bad dream and I'm going to wake up and laugh very hard about it.*

But after that I couldn't sit still. Now I'm pacing, my chest hollow, eyes swollen, my thoughts coming and going so quickly I can hardly keep track of them.

I did not get the internship at the club. Maybe Fred can pull some strings and change that. But my gut is telling me the door's shut on this opportunity. I did a quick Google search on that guy Antonio Gonzalez. Not only does he own the club, he practically owns all of Madrid. Fred's an important guy in this city, but he's small beans compared to Antonio.

And if that's the case, then what? Do I give up my other

dream internship—the one at Meryton—to stay in Spain with him? To be Fred's forever girlfriend?

I guess I could try to find another job here in sports medicine. But what if I don't find another one? Or what if I do but it's not nearly as great as the one back home? I'd be passing up what could be the professional opportunity of a lifetime to be some dude's girlfriend. I'd essentially be putting my life on hold. Maybe even doing irreparable damage to the résumé I've worked so hard to build for the past couple years.

I mean, Fred and I have known each other for *three weeks*. Twenty-two days. That's it. Am I crazy for even thinking about staying in Spain?

I think I'm in love with him. We have the best, best, *best* time together.

Then again, this could just be a honeymoon phase. We haven't exactly been living in reality. What happens when the sex stops being exciting or he gets bored or I get resentful—what then?

I'll have given up everything for nothing. I pretty much put a stake through my relationship with my mother to pursue my dreams—pursue sports medicine. What little goodwill is left between us will be destroyed if I decide to stay in Madrid with no real plans for my future.

I've been braver than I ever have before with Fred. But I don't know if I'm brave enough to do this. To take this leap of faith. We have to be reasonable. We have to think like adults.

I know it's not reasonable to ask him to move with *me* back to the States. He'd be giving up—well, I don't know how much money he'd be giving up, but it'd be a lot. He's also sacrificed his relationship with his family to get where he is now. He'd be an idiot to move with me. There will be other girls for him. Nice, pretty girls who can *stay*.

I suck in a breath. The thought of Fred with someone else

—fuck, that hurts. It physically hurts, in a spot somewhere between my heart and stomach. The spot in the very center of my being. Fred touching someone else like he's touched me —Fred *finding* someone the way he found me—I can't.

I can't go there.

Does this mean I'm really, truly in love with him? I don't know.

I don't know what to do.

I look up when my phone chimes. It's a text from Fred— he's outside. I take a quick glance out the window. My stomach dips. He's standing at the front door. He's still in his practice clothes, just like he was that first afternoon I took the tour at the training facility. His face is a little red when he turns it up to look at my window.

He's taller and handsomer than ever. Right now I wish he wasn't so handsome. Maybe this would hurt less. Maybe I'd want him less.

He looks worried. Fred's always been a steadfast guy. Confident in the way he moves. But now he's jerking back and forth, checking his phone, swaying side to side.

Oh my God, I think. *What have I done to this guy?*

What have we done to each other? Fucking idiots, the two of us, thinking we ever had a chance of making this work.

I don't remember walking down the hall and down the stairs to get him. The next thing I know I'm opening the front door and he's looking at me and it's like my heart falls five stories to land on the concrete between my feet.

His eyes—they're full. Sad.

"Hey," he breathes, taking the four front steps in a single leap.

"C'mon in," I say, and he follows me back up the stairs and down the hall.

He closes my door softly behind him.

"Hey," he says again. "How are you doing?"

I turn around to look at him. "I had no idea I'd be this upset."

"I'm so sorry you didn't get the internship. I know how much you wanted it."

"I'm sorry too," I say, lifting a shoulder to wipe my eye. "I guess I kinda thought it was in the bag. Landing the internship, I mean. I was confident after getting the one back home, you know? I also didn't want to consider the possibility of not getting it. And what that would mean for us."

My voice gets thin on that last sentence.

Fred's face falls. "Rachel—"

I fold my arms across my chest to keep him from approaching. I want him to take me in his arms. Jesus Christ, do I want to let him hold me. But if I do that, it's only going to hurt worse if I leave.

Has he touched me for the last time, I wonder? I don't even remember when I touched him last. Sometime this morning, probably. When we kissed goodbye, maybe? I had put my finger on his chin, just to see what he felt like there. His stubble poked my fingertip. He has a cute chin. Handsome, just like the rest of him.

Is that the last time I'm ever going to touch him?

I close my eyes against the burn of tears.

"I made some calls to the club on my way over here," he says.

"Yeah?"

"They won't budge. Not yet, anyway. I'm angry as hell, and they know that. But Antonio Gonzalez is a powerful bloke. Wants his nephew to have 'the best experience possible' or some rubbish like that. So they're not budging on creating another spot for you. Yet."

I shake my head. "Fred, it's over. I didn't get the internship."

"It's not over," he replies forcefully. "I still have calls to make. My manager won't be happy I'm upset. Neither will my sponsors . . ."

I open my eyes. Meet his.

"You're not going to outmaneuver a billionaire, Fred. He owns the club. He owns *you*. He couldn't care less about me."

"That's not true," Fred says. "He cares about me. Cares about keeping me happy, because I'm an asset to the squad. Which means he cares about you. Or he should."

"Maybe," I say. "But c'mon. We have to be real. The chances of me getting a place at the training facility are slim to none."

His face falls. He knows I'm right.

"So where does that leave us?" he asks, quietly.

I look away. Swallow. I wish things had worked out differently. I wish that more than anything.

I was so happy before, when things were perfect. But who am I when things are decidedly *not* perfect? What do I do when things don't work out like I want them to?

"I'm not sure," I say.

"I want you to stay, Rachel. I want to be with you."

"I want to be with you too. The past month has been . . . it's been wonderful, Fred."

It's been the happiest time of life.

But that doesn't mean staying in Madrid is the right choice for me right now.

"Maybe you can get an internship with one of the other football clubs in Madrid—there's three of them."

I shake my head. "Too late. And too uncertain. The internship back at Meryton—Fred, it will be a game changer for me. They help place you in the best grad schools, and they give you scholarships if your grades are good enough. It's an important step for my future. I've worked so freaking hard to get it."

Fred lets out a breath. "But what if your future is with me?"

"What if it's not?" I look at him. "What if we're just not meant to be, Fred? We've known each other for all of a month. You have to admit it'd be crazy for me to give up my dream job for a guy I've just met."

"Is that all I am to you?" he asks, stepping toward me. "A guy you've just met?"

I don't know how to answer that.

"What about trying long distance?" I ask. "I don't love the idea. But we could try it out, see if we can make it work?"

He shakes his head. "I'm on the road every week. I'm all over Spain with the club. And when I'm called up for international duty, the travel is even worse. Flying back and forth over an ocean—I'm not going to have the time to do that."

"Which means I'd have to come here all the time," I say. My heart sinks. "I have a full course load next semester. And then my internship starts in April . . . I mean. Yeah. I guess we'd just be prolonging the inevitable, wouldn't we?"

"Fuck," Fred says, tugging a hand through his hair.

"Yeah," I say.

Silence settles between us, heavy and unpleasant. We're hammering our coffin shut, one nail at a time.

"So it'd be your job or mine," he says. "One of them would have to go for us to be together."

I nod. My throat's closed up again. This is awful. My gut's twisted in knots. I don't know what it's telling me to do.

I do know the rational decision is to take the internship at Meryton. I have to focus on building my career. A career I'm crazy passionate about. It's the smart choice. The adult choice.

Maybe that means it's the right choice too.

"I can't give up the internship," I say. "Fred, I've busted

my ass for years to get good grades and build a solid résumé. I can't pass up this opportunity. I'm sorry."

Fred's eyes are wet. Dark.

I've hurt him. But what can I do? We have to be adults. There are important things at stake. Life changing things.

I just hate seeing him look at me like I'm a stranger. Like he doesn't know who I am anymore. The warmth in his eyes is gone. The happiness is gone.

The lonely boy underneath the stairs is back.

And it's all my fault.

Chapter Nineteen

FRED

I blink, hard, struggling against the sting in my eyes. I don't want to cry. I need to hold it together. Stay calm. Convince Rachel to fucking stay.

It's hard to stay calm, though, when I feel her slipping away from me.

The late afternoon gloom makes her dorm room feel dark and claustrophobic. The edge of a beat-up suitcase peeks out from underneath her bed. Has she already started packing?

Was this decision really so easy for her?

"You're sorry?" I shake my head. "For what? For leaving? Or for not even considering staying with me in Spain?"

Her black eyes flash with anger. "Would you consider leaving Spain for me?"

"How can I? I gave up loads to get where I am. My contract is being renegotiated. I'm making an impact here."

"But you see how unfair that is, Fred—you asking me to give up my career when you won't even consider making that sacrifice yourself. That's bullshit."

"It's just not done!" I blurt. "Footballers who play at my

level—they don't give up their careers. Not for family, not for girls. Not for anything."

Rachel holds up her hands. "God forbid the world stops revolving around you and your career. A career that's *clearly* so much more important than mine," she says, rolling her eyes. "Don't be an asshole, Fred. You're better than that."

I am being an asshole. I know it. But it's the truth.

"I can take care of you," I try. "You don't have to work at all if you don't want to."

Rachel spears me with a look.

"I'm going to pretend you didn't say that," she replies. "It's insulting for one thing, and patronizing for another. You, more than anyone else, know how important my career is to me. And it's never been about the money. If it were, I'd be heading home to take the MCAT and shadow some anesthe-siologists for the summer. It's about creating a happy life. A balanced life. And I think this internship is going to help me do that."

I look away. Look out the window. I feel like I'm going to be sick.

Rachel won't give up her internship. I won't give up my spot on the squad.

Which means we can't be together anymore. We're choosing our careers—our dreams—over each other.

"We have to be reasonable," she's saying. She's right, of course. "And who's to say our paths won't cross somewhere down the road? I don't know. Didn't David Beckham play football in California or whatever? If we're meant to be together, Fred, we'll be together. Eventually."

I meet her gaze. She's crying.

"You really believe that?" I ask.

"Yes," she says, firmly. But her eyes aren't quite so confident.

I wipe away a tear and look away again. The last time I

cried, I was leaving home to go to the academy in Munich. I felt such a keen sense of loss then.

It doesn't even compare to the loss I feel now.

But I've made my choice. I'd be mad to give up the career I've worked so hard to build.

And I know, deep down, that Rachel would be just as crazy to give up hers.

"That's it, then," I say. "You're going home."

She nods, her hair falling over her shoulder. "My flight's on Thursday. I've had it booked since the beginning of the semester. I didn't want to change or cancel it with things being up in the air, so . . ."

Thursday. The day after tomorrow.

"We have two more days," she offers, voice lilting with hope.

I shake my head. "I leave tonight for Valencia, remember? I'm not back until Friday morning."

"Right," she says, nodding. "So today's our last day together, then."

"Yeah." I toe an invisible mark on the carpet. "I suppose we won't get to watch the vampire show with all the boobs, then."

She sniffs. "You could watch it on your own."

"No," I say, meeting her eyes. "I don't want to watch it without you."

The thought of watching it without Rachel—knowing my flat is going to be empty when I leave here, that it will be empty for a long time to come—it fills me with so much sadness I can't breathe.

I cry instead, hanging my head.

Rachel's crying too. We're both crying.

"I fucking hate this," she says. Her voice this thick.

I lift my head to look at her. "I'm going to worry about you."

"Why?"

"I worry that when you go back to Dallas—alone—you'll end up doing what your mother pressures you to do. I think being away from her has given you courage. But when you're around her again . . . she's a bit of a bully, yeah?"

"She is." Rachel nods. "To be honest, I'm scared of that happening too. It's not so much being away from my mom that's given me courage. It's being with you. And once we're apart . . ."

I manage a tight grin. "You're not giving yourself enough credit. And you can always call me, Rachel."

"I know. But it's not going to be the same."

Of course it's not going to be the same. What can we do?

"Jesus, I'm going to miss you," she breathes.

She steps forward. Her arms are crossed protectively across her chest, but I can tell she wants me to hold her. I reach out and pull her to me. Without shoes on, she's even shorter than usual, her head barely comes up to my chest. I hold her against me, resting my cheek on the top of her head. I inhale her scent, the shampoo and the perfume. I lock it away in a far corner of my memory.

Her body is warm and soft. A flicker of heat ignites low in my belly. I've wondered if my raging desire for her would ever stop burning so hot.

Rachel looks up at me. Searches my eyes.

And then, before I know what I'm doing, I'm bending my neck and kissing her. I can't help it. I have to kiss her one last time.

It was less than three weeks ago that we were enjoying our firsts—first trip, first kiss, first fuck.

And now, all of the sudden, we're at our last kiss. How did it happen so quickly?

I had no idea it would hurt so much.

I open her lips with my tongue, tasting her, drinking her

in. She moans into my mouth, a sound I've grown to adore. Her palms move up my chest, fisting my shirt in her hands, and she goes up on her toes to deepen the kiss. Her breasts are firm against my chest.

This girl. My God, this girl.

Rachel breaks the kiss. She tugs at my shirt, pulling it, hard.

"You should go," she says.

"Okay," I say.

But she doesn't take her hands off me. I wait a beat, then another.

"How do we say goodbye?" she asks, looking up at me. Her lips waver in and out of a smile.

I shake my head. "I don't know."

"You should go," she says again.

But then she's pulling me to her, crushing her lips against mine. For a moment, I'm blinded by a bolt of lust. I kiss her back, breathing hard.

She reaches between my legs. Cups my erection in her hand. She thumbs the tip of my dick through my shorts.

I am so fucking attracted to this girl—I want her so badly —I can't see straight.

I take her waist in my hands. She moves into me, the muscles in the small of her back tightening as I firm my grip.

Rachel kisses me hard. Messy. It's desperate, this kiss.

It's desperate because it's our last one.

I put everything I can't say to her in this kiss. The regret. The longing.

The love.

She presses her hips into mine. I grunt.

And then I lift her up, holding her as I take one, two impatient steps across the room. I set her down on the edge of her desk. Pencils and notebooks spill everywhere, falling to the floor with a clatter. The lamp hits the wall.

Rachel doesn't stop kissing me as I stand between her legs.

I'm going to miss you like crazy, I tell her with my mouth. My lips move to her jaw, her chin, her throat. She pants, reaching inside the waistband of my shorts. Her fingers find my dick. They are warm. Sure.

I bite her, just beneath her ear lobe. She cries out.

My hands fall to the hem of her shirt.

"Yes," she whispers, holding up her arms. I peel it off her, tossing it aside. She reaches behind her and unhooks her bra. For a second I just stare. Her breasts are perfect, round and full. Her nipples are hardened to dark points, begging to be touched.

I duck my head and take one in my mouth. Her head falls back. Her whole torso falls back.

I can't. I can't. I *can't*.

I unbutton her jeans. Unzip the fly. She lifts her hips, and I tug her jeans and underwear to her knees. She kicks them off and wraps her legs around me, spreading them a bit. Inviting me in.

I reach down and run two fingers up her slit. It makes me want to cry again, how wet she is. How soft and hot and perfect.

I sink those two fingers inside her tight heat. Her hips surge to meet my fingers. I glide my thumb over her clit. She gasps, the girliest, wildest sound.

I don't wait. I can't.

I pull my fingers out of her and I pull down my shorts and I take my dick in my hand and guide it to her entrance.

I bend my head and dig my teeth into her neck. Then I grasp the back of her thighs and yank her onto me, bucking my hips so that I sink to the hilt inside her in one swift, smooth motion.

My eyes snap shut. She feels so sweet around me. Her

arms tighten around my neck, pulling me close. I begin to move, deep, gutting strokes that make the desk bang against the wall again and again and again. Everyone in the building will hear us.

I don't give a fuck.

I'm losing my girl. How could I care about such a thing when I'm losing the only girl I've ever loved?

I kiss her mouth. The scent of her perfume has me reeling. I slow my pace. I want to make this last as long as I possibly can. Because when we're done . . .

That's it.

Rachel won't be mine anymore to taste like this, to touch like this.

She won't be mine. And that fucking tears my heart out.

I kiss her gently. Deeply. She kisses me back. She's crying again, her tears falling on both our faces, onto my lips.

Her pussy clenches around me.

"Fred—Fred, I'm coming—" she gasps.

My orgasm is on me then too. It's coming, I'm coming, I'm coming apart.

"No," I grunt. Plead. "Not yet."

But Rachel comes, her impossibly tight pulses making me come too. I wrap an arm around her waist and clench her to me, burying my head in her neck as I'm hit by wave after wave of excruciating sensation. The hot seep of cum spreads between our bodies. I've made a mess of her desk.

She's made a mess of me.

Dear God, how am I going to leave her?

We're left panting and spent. I kiss her, one last, lingering kiss, and then I rest my forehead on hers, closing my eyes. I wrap my palm around the nape of her neck, holding her tightly. Both of us are breathing hard.

Both of us are crying.

"Jesus, you're good at this," Rachel says.

"Good at what?"

"Well, you're good at everything. But right now I'm talking about sex," she replies. "I don't know where you learned how—"

"I learned from you."

Rachel pulls back and looks me in the eye.

"You learned from me? Were the other girls you slept with not . . . you know, decent in bed?"

Shit, I can't breathe. I can't bloody breathe when she's looking at me like this.

"There were no other girls," I say. "You were my first. My only."

Rachel

My heart throbs, swells, breaks into a million pieces.

Not only did Fred like me enough to break all his rules. He also gave me this incredible gift—the gift of his trust, his virginity.

And now I'm leaving.

The girl he gave everything to is fucking leaving him.

How tragic is that?

"Fred," I stammer. "Why didn't you tell me?"

"Are you mad?" he asks.

"No!" I say. "No, of course I'm not mad. I mean, your sex life is your business. I just never would've guessed . . ."

He shrugs. "I didn't want to scare you away. I wanted to enjoy the time we had. I love how much you respect me, I love how you have respect for my rules. But all that went out the window in Salamanca. I wanted to be with you in every way I could. If I told you I was a virgin, I don't think you would have let things go as far as they did."

I look at him. "But you wanted them to go that far."

"Yes," he says. "I still do."

I look away. Hang my head. Start crying all over again, harder this time. My heart feels like a balloon inside my chest, squeezing all my other organs, making it difficult to breathe. I've never felt pain like this. Real, raw pain that has me clawing at Fred's chest.

"Thank you," I whisper. "For giving it to me. For trusting me like you did."

He kisses me on the top of my forehead.

"Thank you," he says. "For everything."

Fred

The intensity of my desire to stay here with Rachel terrifies me. What the hell am I going to do with myself for the rest of the afternoon? The rest of the week?

The rest of my life?

"Fred." Rachel puts her palms on my chest. My heart is hammering. "You should go."

I meet her eyes. It must be too much for her, the eye contact, because she closes hers. Tears leak out of them anyway.

I kiss each eyelid, smoothing back the tears. "All right," I say.

I clutch her to me one last time.

And then I let her go.

Chapter Twenty

RACHEL

Thursday

My carry-on slung over my shoulder, I look up at the aisle numbers as I make my way toward the back of the plane. It's gigantic, the kind of plane with about ten seats in each of its fifty rows. Maybe that's why this feels like a death march.

It won't freaking end.

My eyes start to burn and the numbers blur.

Oh, no, not again. I cried all day yesterday, packing up my shit. I cried all the way to the airport this morning. My eyes are practically open wounds, they're so sore and swollen from crying.

But I still managed to make it. I'm here, I'm getting on this plane, and I'm going home to pursue my sports medicine dreams. I have an exciting future to look forward to. This summer is going to be awesome.

At least that's what I keep telling myself.

Yeah, it hurts to leave Fred behind. It hurts more than I thought it would. I keep waiting to snap out of it. I'm making the right choice. The smart choice. I should be feeling good about that.

A part of me is. But then a large part of me really, really isn't. I mean, I took the guy's virginity. He gave it to me, freely, even though he's been saving it for someone—something—special for years now. How am I supposed to process that? How is that supposed to make me feel?

I find my seat—praise Jesus, I somehow managed to snag a window seat when I checked in yesterday online—and plop down. I dig my phone out of my bag and shoot Mom a text. *Boarded. See you on the ground.*

See you soon, she texts back. *Have a safe flight. Lots to talk about when you land.*

I let my head fall back into the headrest with a *thump*. I'm dreading that conversation. I have to stay strong and stick to my guns, but it's not going to be easy.

I called the Meryton Athletic Director this morning and officially accepted the internship. There's no going back now, not if I don't want to be blackballed by the athletic department for life.

Still. Fred's right. Mom is a bully. I totally expect her to put the full-court press on me when I get home to pick surgery over sports medicine. I just hope I'm strong enough on my own to make it through the holidays without breaking. I have two and a half weeks until classes start again at Meryton. I can make it two and a half weeks.

At least I hope I can.

While I wait for the boarding process to wrap up—on a plane this big it takes a while—I pull up my texts with Fred. I promised myself I wouldn't, because it's torture reading them, seeing how head over heels we were for each other. But I take a sick satisfaction in pretending I'm back in the thick of the excitement and the anticipation of being Fred's girlfriend, the two of us texting sweet nothings throughout the day just because we could.

I love closing my eyes and pretending today will go

exactly how the past three Thursdays have gone: I'm at Fred's apartment. We just woke up. We're about to have sex for the eighth time in as many hours. When we're done, we'll make French toast. Then I'll go to class, and he'll go to training, and when he's done he'll send me a shameless selfie of himself without a shirt on in. He'll invite me out that night for beers at our favorite bar. I'll spend the afternoon shopping for a smexy dress to wear—something I'll have to go commando for. I've never been fingered in public before, but there's a first time for everything . . .

I swallow the lump in my throat. It's agony, remembering how wonderful our time together was.

But we are not meant to be.

With a sigh, I put my phone away and grab the book I just bought at a kiosk by the airport food court. I tried to pick the driest, least romantic thing possible—*Don Quixote* in the original medieval Spanish—but two minutes in, and my eyes are already blurring with tears again.

I wish it'd stop hurting—the knowledge that I won't ever see Fred again. Well, except on TV. Which is horrible, because every time I'll see him, I know I'll wonder if he ever thinks of me. If he misses me.

And then there's the fact that there won't be any more Nutella French toast. No more Harry Potter musings. No more beers over a homemade dinner. No more naked mornings, no more happy, squinty green eyes.

It's the little things that get me the most. Like the way he drove—one enormous hand on the steering wheel, his grip confident—and how lit up he'd get when we talked football stats.

I miss how good he looked naked. I miss how good he looked in sweats on the sofa, the two of us curled up in front of a new episode of *Tournament of Kings*.

I miss him.

I squeeze my eyes shut. I take some deep breaths, try to focus on the fact that I nabbed my dream internship. I'm going to work in sports medicine! It's going to be awesome! I stood up to Mom and took ownership of my life! Yay!

Too bad I feel *not* so yay-exclamation-point. Don't get me wrong, I'm proud of how far I've come this semester and what I've accomplished.

But I wish I was on a plane to Germany right now, not Dallas. Fred would be beside me and we'd order beers from the flight attendant. He'd tell me a story about his mom, or maybe his sister, or maybe even a story about baby Lilli. He's told me so many stories, I feel like I already know his family.

I would really liked to have met the Ohrs.

Shit, I'm crying again. I dig my sunglasses out of my bag and shove them on my face.

This flight is going to suck.

Fred

That Night

I keep my head down as I follow the lads into the locker room. We slaughtered Valencia—it's our last match of the year before everyone heads home for the holidays—and the mood in the room is jubilant. Lads laugh and holler as they toe off their boots and roll down their socks and unwind the tape from their ankles, their wrists, their fingers.

No one says much to me. I've been avoiding human contact more than usual the past couple days. It never used to bother me, the fact that I didn't have much to do with the lads, and they didn't have much to do with me. But now, for some reason, it rankles.

It makes me feel lonelier than ever.

I am so bloody lonely since Rachel and I broke up. Lonely and bored and tired. I keep giving myself pep talks, and I spend a good deal of time on the phone with my agent, the two of us gloating over the extravagant numbers the club is throwing out to keep me in Madrid for another five years.

"You're at the top of your game, Fred," he'd said. "I'm not bullshitting you when I say I've never been this excited about a client. You're a fucking ten, mate, and you're only twenty-two! To think you're just starting your career. You're going places. Big places."

A month ago, this conversation would've excited me to the point that I couldn't sleep. And I am excited. My dreams are coming true. Never in a million years did I think I'd get this far, that I'd play this well, that I'd make this much money.

After I hang up, though, the loneliness returns, worse than before. It's almost like football isn't enough anymore. It's not enough to light me up the way it used to.

It's probably just a phase I'm going through, the worst of it right now, at least according to Sophie. These feelings of rawness and loneliness will pass. They have to. Right?

I mean, Rachel and I made our choice. We chose to chase our dreams. And my dreams are coming true. I'm winning matches. I'm winning at life, as awful and conceited as that sounds.

I just didn't think this victory would feel so . . . hollow, I guess.

I shove my dirty shit in my locker and slam the door.

Alexsandr, whose locker is beside mine, looks up from peeling off his shin guards.

"Want to talk about it?" he asks.

"No."

"I'm really sorry about what happened with you and Rachel."

I glare at him. "And what do you think happened with me and Rachel?"

He has the grace to look a little sheepish. "I heard a rumor or two from Rhys about you guys breaking up . . ."

"It's nothing," I snap, tugging a towel around my waist. "We had our fun. But she had to go home to the States, and I'm staying here . . . that's all there is to it."

"But last time we talked, you told me you were crazy about her—"

"I'm just anxious to get home for the holidays, that's all," I say. I don't want to talk about this. Not now. I'm worried if I do—well.

I won't be able to control myself.

"Right. Of course." Alexsandr offers me a tight smile. "But if you do want to talk about it, I'm here, yeah?"

"There's nothing to talk about," I say, and I turn and stalk toward the showers.

Chapter Twenty-One

RACHEL

Six Months Later—June
Durham, North Carolina
Meryton University

On paper, today should've been the best day ever.

I spent the morning in Mertyon's brand new, state-of-the-art weight room with the women's basketball team. They won the National Championship this year, and are heavy contenders to win it again. Being in the same room as these ladies—never mind working with them to improve their aerobic fitness or rehab low back injuries—blows my freaking mind. I chat stats with a starting forward for close to half an hour; I learn a few new exercises from a center who is back in the gym for the first time since her ACL surgery.

In the afternoon, Brendan, one of the best physiologists in the country who also happens to be my mentor, takes me to lunch with the athletic director. Our swimming program is in hot water following a scandal (the director laughs, hard, at his own pun), and he asks my opinion on how to bring it back from the brink. My answer must make an impression, because when lunch is over, he shakes my hand and tells me to email him directly for any recommendations I may need for graduate school applications.

"We're always looking for passionate, smart people like you," he says. "When you're ready to look for jobs, be sure to keep us in mind."

I smile at the compliment. A year ago, an exchange like this would've had me doing cartwheels, giddy with excitement. It *is* a wonderful feeling, knowing I'm appreciated, knowing I'm doing well enough here to merit such praise. I'm making my dreams come true. Everything I ever hoped would happen, career wise, is happening. It's a major victory.

But at the same time, that victory feels a little hollow. It doesn't change the fact that I'm lonely. Lost.

It doesn't change the fact that I still miss Fred like crazy. No amount of success or praise or 16-hour days spent doing what I love most seems to change that. It's like *I've* gone back to being the boy underneath the stairs after flying so high at Hogwarts. Terrible metaphor, I know. But it's true. This loneliness—it's worse now that I've experienced the joy of real companionship.

I knew Fred for all of *three weeks*. I should be over him by now. I should at least be feeling better—feeling like there's a light at the end of the tunnel.

But I'm only feeling worse. My unhappiness only seems to grow, no matter how well everything else in my life is going. And this internship is going really well. I'm learning a lot, I'm networking with awesome people. I get to live and breathe sports all day, every day.

But I'm unhappier than I've ever been—the kind of unhappiness that plagues me night and day, that ruins otherwise fun things or exciting things or things that would usually make me delirious with joy.

Even *Tournament of Kings* has lost its luster. I can't make it through a single episode without throwing the remote at my TV, too disgusted to watch Prince Jacoby make out with his fairy princess paramour (I kid you not) one. More. Time.

I'm doing everything I can to get over Fred. I'm throwing myself into my work, I'm hanging out with friends, I'm trying to meet new people.

None of it is helping.

I blink, swallowing the lump in my throat. Not again. Jesus, I don't want to cry at work *again*.

"Hey," Brendan says as we're pulling out of the restaurant parking lot. The air conditioning blasts directly into my face. I close the vent. "You okay?"

"Yeah," I reply, sniffling. "Sorry. My allergies have been crazy ever since I got back from Spain."

I think Brendan bought that excuse the first few times I cried at work. Now, though? Now I'm not sure what he makes of it. Frankly, I'm too tired to care. I haven't slept well in months.

Brendan offers me a tissue and takes me to one of the basketball gyms, where the men's team is running some drills. I may not be happy at the gym, but Brendan knows at least I won't cry there.

So, yeah. Today is supposed to be great. Every day is supposed to be great. I'm slaying my dream internship. I'm doing what I love. I even got Mom to come around to the idea of sports medicine—kinda—and while she's not thrilled, she's not pushing the surgery thing anymore. I'm surrounded by my Meryton friends, the few authentic ones I've managed to find.

But today is decidedly *not* great. I'm starting to think I may never have a great day again as long as Fred is gone.

I'm starting to think I made the wrong choice.

I crack open a can of my favorite beer—I can't find the good Bavarian stuff in Durham, so I've been drinking a sorry local substitute instead—and collapse onto the sofa. I'm exhausted, but sleep's still going to be hard to find. Might as well pass the time as painlessly as possible, and sports highlights should do the trick.

I turn on my favorite channel. Grateful for the chance to tune out and forget the painful numbness inside my chest, I settle into the cushions, draining my beer. God, this stuff is gross. I thought I was a beer snob before I met Fred, but now I'm a freaking purist. He's ruined me for even the best craft beers America has to offer.

God damn him.

I set the empty bottle on the coffee table. When I look up at the TV, my heart seizes.

It's Fred.

He's on the screen, dashing across the wide expanse of a green pitch as he makes an assist for the game-winning goal that nabbed Madrid its thirty-third league title last week. Sports shows can't get enough of this footage. Fred's assist is epic, as he outguns several rival forwards and keeps precise control of the ball meter after meter.

He is deliciously sweaty, his wet shirt plastered to his body as he dashes down the length of the field. His hair is stuck to his forehead, his eyes narrowed, intense with concentration. He looks so good out there. So ferocious and confident.

Seeing this clip kills me, every time.

Every time I'm plunged into a sadness so acute I can't breathe.

Does he ever think about me, I wonder? I haven't heard a word from him since the day he left my dorm room after we broke up. To be fair, football has kept him busy. Madrid went on a winning streak this spring, thanks in no small part to

Fred. He's dominating—he's had more assists and goals in the past four months than he has in the past two years combined.

Go figure. The second we break up, Fred starts playing his best football ever.

I also wonder who he talks sports with these days. He's not very close with his teammates, and I know his mom and sister aren't crazy about football. There's so much I want to tell him—so much I want to ask him, about his footwork and how his knee is doing and what he thinks about the current shake-up in British soccer. I'd love to know his opinion on this new rehab regimen I'm learning about.

I'd love to show him around Meryton's impressive sports complexes. I know he'd be as jazzed about it as I am.

God, I miss him.

I miss him so freaking much.

I pick up my cell phone from the cushion beside me. This part of the day—the part where I pull up his number and stare at—usually happens much later, when I'm lying in bed, aching with insomnia. Aching for him.

I've been so tempted to text him. *How have you been?* Something quick and casual. *Have you finished the last Harry Potter yet?*

Sometimes, on really bad nights, I'll even type the text out. But I have the good sense not to send it. There's no point. A text isn't going to change the fact that Fred is living his life—his best life—five thousand miles away.

I jump when my phone starts to ring. It's Mom. I don't smile, exactly, but I also don't start to sweat either. When it comes to our relationship, I consider that progress.

"Hey, Mom," I say with a sigh.

"You sound blue," she says. "Bluer than yesterday."

Her concern makes my throat swell. "I'm okay. I had a great day at work, so that's nice."

"That is nice. I'm not at all surprised the internship is

going well—I always knew you'd be fantastic at whatever you chose to do."

"Thanks," I say. "I appreciate that. I'm just . . . ugh, having a bad week I guess."

A bad week. Bad month. Bad year.

"It's Fred, isn't it?" Mom asks, gently. "You still miss him."

I suck in a breath. Fred is a sensitive subject between Mom and me. I know she was glad—relieved, maybe, is a better word—when I told her we broke up. I understand why. I mean, I was pretty much planning to run away with a foreign guy I'd known for all of a month. She was right to be concerned.

So imagine my surprise when she says, "You know, it may be time to start thinking about how the two of you can be together."

"What?" I blurt. "But I thought—you said—"

"I know what I said," she replies. "I'm sorry I was so . . . harsh. I wasn't aware how clearly attached you'd become to him. I mean, you're still thinking about this man how many months later? That says something."

I blink, hard, against the sting of tears. Mom's never referred to Fred as a *man* before. She always calls him "your European kidnapper" or "that foreign boy with the crooked nose."

"What do you mean, that says something?"

It's Mom's turn to sigh. "It means he must be special. You're a smart girl, Rachel. You make good decisions. I had assumed—wrongly, might I add—that because you're so young, you might fall for a guy who was bad for you. That you might bring home . . . I don't know, a bad boy with a motor-cycle and a mom tattoo."

"You really think I'd fall for a guy with a mom tattoo?" I ask, laughing. "Bad boys are so not my jam."

"I know," Mom says, and now she's laughing too. "Well,

now I know that. You don't like many guys, period. You've had, what, all of one boyfriend?"

"Psssh," I say. "I'd hardly call Eric a boyfriend. He was more of a—"

"Don't want to know," Mom says. "My point is, you don't fall for boys very often. You always said they were dumb, or superficial, or 'just friend material.' But the fact that you've clearly fallen so hard for Fred—that tells me he's different. Different enough to stand out in all the best ways."

Oh, God, now I'm going to cry for real.

"He is," I say, my voice thick. "That's exactly what he is— he's different. He's *my* kind of different. And I'm really struggling to get over him. I thought I made the right choice, coming home to do this internship. But now I'm not so sure."

"You made the *smart* choice, yes. I'm proud of you for that. Or rather, you should be proud of yourself for making such a difficult decision. But that doesn't mean you're married to it. That doesn't mean you can't go back and revise, maybe make some changes. Your personal life—Rachel, it's important. Look at me. I have barely any life outside of work . . ."

"And?"

She takes a deep breath. "And I wish I did. I like my work. It's important to me, the same way I want your work to be important to you. But it's not all it's cracked up to be. The money is great, sure. I get a lot of satisfaction from being good at what I do. At the end of the day, though, it's not my work that makes me happy. It's you. It's your dad."

My pulse hiccups.

"I make you happy?" I swipe the heel of my hand across my cheek. "Really?"

"Really. I know I don't always act like it. But you're my reason for everything, Rachel. I want the best of everything for you. And it seems like Fred is pretty freaking awesome. The best of the best."

She's right.

Holy shit, Mom is actually giving me good advice.

"He is," I say, sniffling. "But what am I supposed to do? I can't just uproot my life here—he can't just leave Spain—"

"Let's sleep on it," Mom says. "We'll figure something out, okay?"

I nod, smile, and thank her. I do feel better, if only because I feel like I'm truly turning a corner in my relationship with Mom. She's never been so real with me before. So honest. She's trying hard, and I appreciate that.

Deep down, though, I'm not so sure we'll find a happy solution to my problem. It's been six months, for God's sake. I haven't moved on, but there's a good chance Fred has. Plus my senior year starts in a month and a half and I'm taking important classes, classes I need if I want to get into graduate school.

Fred is the best of the best. But that doesn't mean we're meant to be together.

That doesn't guarantee us a happy ending.

Chapter Twenty-Two

FRED

June
Formentera, Spain

The pages of my book flutter and stick in the salty sea air. I read the last sentence once, twice, three times, willing myself to feel something. Anything. Grief or satisfaction or triumph. I mean, I just finished the seventh and final book in the series I've been working through for the past year.

Once upon a time, I loved the characters. I may or may not have dabbled in writing some especially awful fan fiction about Harry taking up football after he graduates from Hogwarts.

But when I set my copy of *Harry Potter and the Dealthy Hollows* on the sand beside my ice cold beer, all I feel is tired.

I glance at the line of beach chairs beside mine. Mama is lying back, eyes closed, her nose lathered in white zinc sunscreen. Sophie is digging sand out of Lilli's mouth under the shade of an umbrella while nearby, her husband scoops out a moat around their lopsided sandcastle.

Alexsandr may be wearing giant mirrored sunglasses, but even so, I can tell he's staring at the girls sunbathing topless down near the water. I asked him to join our family holiday on a whim, never expecting he'd accept the invitation. But three days into our two-week trip, and already Mama has adopted him as her second son. I suppose I've finally made a friend on the squad.

It's wonderful, being surrounded by family and friends like this. Especially after the squad's epic streak this spring that nabbed us the league title we've been chasing all year. My agent renegotiated my contract for an obscene amount of money—money that's paying for this extended holiday. I'm playing well. Exceptionally well. There are whispers I'm Madrid's next big breakout star.

My career is better than it's ever been. Everything I ever dreamed of—everything I ever hoped for—it's happening.

But the satisfaction this brings me doesn't compare to the desolation I feel at not having Rachel here with me to talk all things *Dealthy Hollows*.

I feel her absence like a paper cut that won't heal. Just when I think I'm okay, a fresh wave of pain reminds me I'm not.

No one can talk Harry Potter like Rachel. Mama doesn't get my obsession with it. Sophie is waiting to read the books until Lilli is old enough and they can do it together. And Alexsandr—I love the bloke, but I don't think he's read anything outside of *Maxim* in years.

There's so much I want to tell Rachel. Ask her. Does she think Hermoine and Ron make it in the long run? Is Ginny really the one for Harry? And what about this new book Rowling recently came out with—has Rachel read that one too? Is it worth my time? What should I read next?

I grab my beer and take a long, hard swallow. Rachel

would like this stuff. It's Spanish, refreshing, and malty, just a hint of hops. Perfect for the beach.

I wonder what she's drinking these days. Who she's drinking with.

I wonder if she's as miserable as I am.

When the fuck am I going to get over her? It's been six bloody months already. I should've moved on a while back.

But I haven't. And I don't know what to do about it.

I drain my beer and set it back on the sand. I look out over the crystal-clear sea, the blues of the water so bright they make my chest hurt. Christ, it's beautiful here. Beautiful and quiet. The arid hills of Ibiza are visible in the distance. Formentera is that flashy island's demure little sister, with restaurants and a few hotels and not much else. In other words, it's perfect for a bloke like me.

Perfect for Rachel too. She'd love it here. She'd love its quaintness, its small pleasures. The paella, the cold beer. The smell of the sea.

I wish she were with me.

I don't realize I'm clutching the plastic edges of my chair until Sophie is standing next to me, Lilli slung on her hip, her mouth twisted in concern.

"Let go," she says.

"What?"

"The chair—you hold it in the grip of death. Let go. And come walk with me by the water."

I relax my hands. "If it's okay, I'll just stay here. I'm knackered."

"You and Lilli, you nap together when we return. But now, we walk. Come." She holds out her free arm.

Lilli coos.

I sigh.

I let Sophie pull me to my feet. I take the baby from her, then we head toward the water.

Sophie and I walk in silence along the edge of the water. Lilli turns a seashell over in her hands, transfixed. My feet sink into the sand, the water lapping at my toes.

There's not a cloud in the sky, the sun is bright and hot on my shoulders. The heat feels good. Cleansing, almost.

"You are not okay," Sophie says, breaking the silence.

Lilli drops the seashell. I narrowly avoid impaling my foot on it.

"How do you know that?" I ask, quietly.

"You do not wash your hairs for many days," she says. "Also, you let the one love of your life go."

"Love of my life?" I cock a brow in an attempt to appear less rattled by this than I am. "Sophie, I'm twenty-two. There will be others. I mean, yeah, I miss Rachel. And I regret that we couldn't make it work. But it's been six months now. She has her life in the States, I have my life in Spain . . ."

Sophie slows her stride. Looks at me. "Fred, stop fooling yourself. You have no life at all without her."

I look away, slipping my thumb into Lilli's tiny fist. She squeezes it, hard, and I'm glad for the distraction from the pain gathering in the very center of my chest.

"I have a life," I say. "A very nice life."

"You have very nice *things*," she says. "A very nice job. Nice flat. Nice holidays. But they are just things. They have no meaning for you. Not without Rachel."

Sophie's words are like a well-aimed arrow, piercing my breastbone, slicing through my heart. She's right.

I don't have a life without Rachel. Yeah, I go through the motions, I do what I need to do. But none of it feels . . . I suppose none of it feels like it fucking matters anymore.

"You're right," I say, quietly. "But what the hell can I do

about it? I can't just pick up and leave Madrid after winning the title—"

"Yes, you most certainly can."

"No, I can't. Sophie, you've read the papers. You know how much money they're paying me. My future is here, in Spain."

"You don't need that money."

"What? Of course I need it! I've been working since I was fourteen bloody years old for that money. You'll get some of it too, you know."

"You're a sweet brother. But I don't need your monies. Neither do you."

"Pfsh! I've got to pay the bills somehow!"

"I know you, Fred. And I know you save much money these past years. You will be fine."

That is true. I've spent some money buying my car and my flat. Other than that, though, I haven't laid out much cash. I've been too busy working.

Still. The thought of leaving millions of euros on the table makes my stomach hurt.

I sigh. "I'll be fine, yeah. But I can't walk away from the club. Not now."

"Listen to me, Fred. You didn't leave home just to play football and make money." Sophie looks at me. "You left to be happy. You weren't going to be happy here, so you left. And you're not going to be happy in Madrid. Not without Rachel. So now you must leave there too."

This arrow's bite is worst than the one she hit me with before. It's so bad I suck in a breath.

It's true. Bloody hell, it's so true. Maybe that's why I haven't been sleeping. I'm scared to go back to Madrid after the summer holiday because I know football isn't going to be enough anymore. It's not going to keep me going the way it has all these years.

The money, the travel, the success—none of it means a damn thing without Rachel. Everything has its place when she's around, everything makes sense in a way it never has before. No wonder I feel so lost.

Maybe playing football for Madrid isn't my dream.

Maybe experiencing life with Rachel by my side is.

I thought the thing I couldn't live without was my football contract. I thought choosing my career was the smart choice.

But it's Rachel I can't live without. As long as I have her—as long as we're together—everything else will fall into place.

I hope.

Holy fuck, I need to leave Spain. I think I've known I'd have to do this all along, but I've just been so bloody scared. Scared to stay. Scared to go. But thinking about being with Rachel tomorrow, and the day after that, and the day after that . . .

It cuts the fear in half and replaces it with joy.

Rachel was right about David Beckham moving to Los Angeles to play for the football club there for several years. I know they're opening a new football—sorry, *soccer*—franchise in Charlotte, North Carolina. How far is Charlotte from Durham, I wonder?

My heart—well, what's left of it—skips around inside my chest.

Holy fuck. Holy *fuck*, this just might work. I'd be giving the club here the shaft, but I technically have the power to do that, if I wanted. Granted, the club is going to go bonkers and I may lose some money in the deal. I'll probably never play for another Spanish squad again. I'd also be taking a pretty significant pay cut. It's definitely not the smart move, not at this point in my career.

But it's the move I've got to make nonetheless. Plus, the summer transfer window opens up in a couple weeks.

I can't be with Rachel again soon enough.

The thought of holding her again, watching a show with boobs in it with her again, getting our French toast mojo back again—I can't breathe it makes me so fucking happy.

"Jesus Christ, Sophie," I scoff, even as my eyes blur with tears. "Why do you always have to be right?"

"I am your sister," she replies with a shrug. "Of course I am right. Also, I know you."

It's a gift, to be known like that. A gift my family gave me. A gift Rachel gave me too.

I wonder what other parts of life—parts of the world— Rachel and I can discover together. I've always wanted to go to Australia.

I've always wanted a family too. Of course, that's years down the road. But I hope to take that road one day with Rachel.

Lilli screams, happily, at a seagull that squawks overhead, punching out her arms and legs like a tiny lunatic. I have to hold on to her for dear life, tucking my pelvis away just before her little foot can nail me in the bollocks.

"So," Sophie says. "When do you go to Rachel?"

"I've got to call my agent first—he's certainly not going to be happy. After that . . . I haven't seen her for months. I'm bloody dying, but this could take a bit of time to work out. I don't want to go to her until all the details are in place. I'll put a call into Rhys. He'll know how to get to Rachel. Then, when everything is finalized, I'll fly to North Carolina . . ."

"Very good! I come with you," Sophie says.

I start. "What? No—"

"Lilli is very much wanting to meet Rachel, remember? So Lilli and me, we go with you to the Carolina."

"I think I should do the groveling part on my own, don't you?" I run a hand up the back of my head.

Sophie shakes her head. "I have the faith that Rachel will

take you back. But if she does not, a cute baby does not hurt your cause, yes?"

I look down at Lilli. She looks back at me and smiles.

"She *is* cute," I say, smiling because how could I not?

"The cutest. Yes! We go with you."

Chapter Twenty-Three

RACHEL

August—The Day Before Classes Start
Mertyon University, Durham, NC

I lean a little closer to the bathroom mirror, eyes focused on my bright red earlobe as I try for the tenth time to put on the dangliest, glitteriest earring I could find. Nothing like sparkles and a hell of a lot of champagne to cure a broken heart, right?

I suck in a breath when I finally manage to poke the earring through my ear. I remember having so much rough, delicious, physical sex with Fred that I couldn't wear earrings. I worried Fred and I would end up ripping them right out of my ears, so I didn't wear any. I continued the trend when I got back to Meryton, too depressed to eat, much less wear jewelry. I think the holes are partially closed up now.

Even as a pulse of heat moves between my legs, my heart curls in on itself. Classes start in two days. I'm a senior. A freaking *senior*. I thought I'd know my way around life by now.

I feel more lost than ever. Mom and I have talked, at

length, about how Fred and I could make it work. But so far, we've come up empty.

Besides, I'm wiped. What if I go back to Spain and Fred rejects me? That's the most likely scenario. It's been eight, nine months now since we broke up. He's probably moved on. I don't have the emotional wherewithal to go through all that again.

I don't think I could survive another heartbreak.

So here I am, treading water, hoping that one day I'll feel better.

I wonder what Fred's doing tonight. His season starts this week. Is he excited? Nervous?

As heartbroken and unhappy as I am? I doubt it. How could he be? He's absolutely killing it in a sport he loves. He's making his dreams come true.

Then again, so am I. And I'm still miserable.

I wonder what we would have done together over the summer if I'd gotten the internship and we were still together. Would we jet off to Italy, where we'd lie by a pool in Tuscany after eating pasta all day? Or would we head for the Maldives, where we'd sunbathe naked on the beach or have dirty floor sex for hours, never leaving our hotel room?

My eyes well. I aim my gaze at the ceiling and blink, fast. I just did my eye makeup and I don't want to ruin it. I've cried enough over the past months.

When am I ever going to stop crying over Fred?

Clearly the sparkles aren't working. Maybe the champagne will? My friends should be bringing some over soon. They insisted on taking me out tonight to celebrate our last "first day of classes." They know I still need a little, er, help readjusting to life without Fred.

There's a knock at my apartment door. Taking one last look in the mirror, I turn and scoot through the living room.

Paige, a mutual friend of mine and Laura's, smiles at me

when I open the door. She is barefoot in a robe, but her hair and makeup are done.

"Hey," she says, eyes glittering strangely. "You almost ready?"

"Yeah. What do you think of these jeans? I wasn't really in the mood to wear a dress—"

"You have to wear a dress," she says, pushing past me into my apartment. "What about that sexy beaded number you stole from me last semester? You should rock that."

I close the door and follow her into my bedroom, where she proceeds to start digging through the cluttered mess of my closet.

"Do you not like the jeans?" I ask. "I thought they'd look cute with a pair of strappy heels."

Emily waves me away. "Trust me. You want to wear a dress."

"Why?" I ask. "Paige, what's going on?"

"Nothing. It's just your first night back, and you need to look like the sexy, worldly woman that you are."

I plop onto my unmade bed with a sigh. "I'm really not in the mood tonight."

"Aha!" Paige pulls a short—very short—black dress out of the closet. "This is what you should wear. It's perfect."

It *is* the perfect going out dress. It's festive and sexy, embroidered with strands of tiny, glittery beads that sway when Em gives the hanger a shake.

Only I don't feel very festive or sexy at the moment, and I also haven't shaved my legs in about, oh, a week.

"I appreciate what you're trying to do, Paige, but I think I'm just going to stick to jeans," I say. "I want to be comfortable."

"Oh, come on, Rachel," she says, pouting. "Please wear it? For me? It's impossible not to have a good time in this dress."

I peer at her. It's not like Paige to be so pushy, especially about a dress.

"You're being weird," I say.

"No I'm not," she says, averting her eyes. "I just want you to have fun tonight, Rach. It's our first night out as seniors, it's the first time we've been together in, like, three months . . ."

I sigh again. "Fine," I say, holding out my hand. "I'll wear the dress, if only so you'll stop bugging me and finish getting dressed. I've been ready for a glass of champs for an hour now."

Paige jumps in excitement and hands me the dress. "I'm excited."

"Me too," I lie.

"All right. I'll be ready in five. What about you?"

"I just need to change."

She claps her hands. "Perfect! Everything is going to be perfect."

"Here, I'll let you out," I say, and we start walking back toward the front door.

"Oh!" She lunges for a box of tampons on the coffee table. "Put these away."

"Why?" I ask, watching her shove the box underneath the sink in the bathroom. "You really think I'm going to bring a dude home with me tonight?"

"You never know," she sniffs, making her way out of the bathroom.

She takes me by the arms, giving me a once over.

"You look gorgeous," she says. "Now go put on that dress!"

And then she lets herself out.

The door shuts. I blink.

What the *hell* was that? I mean, yeah, I haven't seen Paige since spring semester ended back in May. But she was . . . I don't know, jittery almost. Nervous. Excited.

We all love to go out, but not that much. Huh. Maybe she's excited to see the guy she's been crushing on tonight?

Whatever.

I put on the damn dress, but then I realize I need to wear a strapless bra with it. Damn it, I hate strapless bras with the fiery passion of a thousand burning suns. They slip, they hurt, they're a pain in the ass. But Paige insisted I wear this dress, so . . . ugh, a strapless bra it is. I just need to find one.

I'm tearing through my underwear drawer, trying to find a strapless bra that won't torment me all night, when there's another knock on my door.

Jesus mother, it's been two minutes. I love Paige, but she can really be needy sometimes.

"Come in!" I shout. "I'm in the bedroom."

I wait for the door to open, but it doesn't.

The knock comes again.

"Paige! For God's sake! You can come in. It's unlocked!"

She replies with another knock.

With a hiss of frustration, I quickly put on the least awful of all my strapless bra choices and stalk toward the door, pulling the straps of my dress over my shoulders.

"You're driving me crazy, you know that?" I say. "First, you make me put on a strapless bra. Do you know how uncomfortable this thing—"

The words stall in my throat when I open the door.

Fred looks up at me, his eyes—they're blue tonight— shimmering in the dim light from my living room. He looks at me like he always does. With honesty and heat.

My insides clench all at once. I freeze. Blink, to make sure it's really him. To make sure I'm awake and alive and this is really happening. Right here, right now, it's freaking happening.

I can't breathe, I can't breathe, *I can't breathe*.

"Hello, love," he says. The sound of his voice—familiar,

deep—sends a rush of warmth through me that settles behind my eyes. He holds up a tall brown bottle, wrapped in a green koozie with a donkey's butt on it. "Here. Drink this, and then you won't give a damn about how uncomfortable your bra is."

I reach out and take the bottle, wordlessly, staring at him.

"Fred," I say.

"Rachel," he says, grinning. His eyes get squinty.

"Fred," I say again, too stunned and happy and confused to actually think.

His gaze moves over my body. His eyes darken, just a little.

He clears his throat. "You look lovely."

"Fred," I say. He looks—he looks better than lovely. He's so fucking handsome. How did I forget how handsome he is? He's wearing jeans and a sharply cut blazer. His white collared shirt is pristine. His hair—I love it when it's still wet from the shower—is combed and neat. He's sweating a little, his forehead damp.

He smells good enough to eat, like sandalwood and soap.

Oh my God. *Fred is here*.

And he brought me a beer. In the koozie I gave him the night we met!

I have no idea what to think. Why is he here? Just to visit?

It's been such a long time since we spoke last. There's so much I want to ask him.

So much I want to say.

"Might I come in?" he asks. His British-German accent seems stronger now that I've been surrounded by Americans for so long.

"Yeah," I say, opening the door a bit more. "Of course."

He steps inside my apartment and I close the door behind him. I can't help but stare. He seems to take up the whole room, his head mere inches from the low ceiling. He's huge.

Longing strangles my heart and leaves me reeling.

I take a long, fast pull from the bottle. I recognize the malty, slightly bitter taste, one of his Bavarian beers. The kind we'd always drink together.

"God that's good," I manage.

"Glad you like it," I say.

"How did you—"

"Had it shipped overnight to your friend Paige's house. She said she'd bring it up when she drove from Charlotte."

"Paige? But you don't know her—"

"I got her number from Laura. I spoke to Rhys, who put me in touch with her."

"Oh."

Putting his hands in his pockets, he looks at me.

I look back. I want to touch him. Devour him for five days straight, then spend the next five days catching up on sports and Harry Potter and the new season of *Tournament of Kings*.

"Fred," I say. "I missed you. So freaking much. But what are you doing here? I thought we agreed to . . . you know. Not do this."

He takes a shaky breath. I'm so nervous I might vomit.

I try to drink the beer instead.

"I'm here because I can't bloody live without you," he says. "I thought I was doing the right thing, choosing my career. I thought football was enough, yeah? Because football's always been enough to keep me content. I thought I could go back to being the bloke I was before I met you. But I can't. I tried, but I can't fucking do it. No one can talk Quidditch quite like you."

I laugh, the pressure in my chest releasing, just the tiniest bit. "I wish I could say I'm not proud of that fact, but I am."

"You should be," he says. "My passions have never lined up with someone else's the way they line up with yours. We're not the same person, Rachel. But we love the same things.

We want the same things. Being with you—it made me fall in love with my life for the first time ever. And when you left— when you left, I got everything I thought I ever wanted. I got the contract—"

"I know," I say, shyly. "I've been following your career. Exciting times for you, Fred."

He spears a hand through his hair. A lump forms in my throat.

"That's just it. It wasn't exciting. It should've been. I should've been on cloud nine. The money, the awards, the praise I got for playing well—I had it all. And I've never been unhappier, because I don't have you. Rachel, I'm in love with you. I miss you so fucking badly, it"—he draws a sharp breath through his teeth as his voice wavers—"it's killing me."

Tears slip down my face, quiet and hot. My heart is beating hard, like it wants to be heard.

"Jesus, Fred, I'm in love with you too," I say. "But what can we do? We're miserable, yes, but that doesn't change the fact that we can't be together."

He takes a step toward me. I go still. "No, it doesn't. But me transferring to the new football franchise in Charlotte— that does, yeah?"

"What?" I blurt. "Wait, you're transferring? To a new team? *Here*, in the United States of America?"

"I am indeed." Fred nods, grinning again. "The news should be hitting the wires now. My agent brokered the whole thing. Granted, I almost gave him a heart attack when I told him what I wanted to do. But it's done. The papers are signed, the fees are paid, and I am the Charlotte Flight's fourth signing and first major acquisition."

I stare at him. "This is insane."

"You're insane if you think I'm going to spend another bloody day with you," he says. "So I need to find a flat. I was hoping you'd drive down there with me this weekend, perhaps help me pick something out? I hear Charlotte's only a two-hour drive from here. Which reminds me—I've also got to buy a new car . . ."

My heart beats louder, harder. Faster. Holy shit.

Holy shit, is this really happening? Is Fred giving up everything he's worked for to be with me?

"But what about your contract?" I ask. "The big one you just signed with the club in Madrid? You can't give all that money up, Fred. You're doing so well there."

He shrugs. "Madrid is going to hate me for a while, sure. They've a right to. But I convinced them this was a move I had to make. And the club in Charlotte is paying me more than I ever thought they would. Way more. I'll be their star player, so I'll have a chance to really make an impact. With things so new, I can help put together a solid squad, hone my leadership skills, maybe learn a bit about managing too. It really is an exciting opportunity, and I'm not just saying that to make you feel better."

"There's no way it's as exciting as playing for the best soccer team in the world," I say. "Fred, you don't have to do this. I want you to chase your dreams. I want you to be happy."

He's standing directly in front of me now, so close I have to crane my neck to meet his eyes. He takes my face in his hands, and I close my eyes, tears spilling out of them as I revel in the warmth of his touch, the confidence, the gentleness of it. He handles me like he knows what he's doing.

Maybe he knows what he's doing with all this soccer stuff too.

"Rachel. Look at me." His voice is gentle. I open my eyes. He searches them, his gaze earnest, intense. "The only way I'm going to be happy is if I'm with you."

The enormity of what he's saying—what he's willing to do

to keep us together—washes over me. It's so sweet, so unbearably sweet.

"Are you sure?" I ask, letting him thumb away my tears. "I mean, I don't want you to have any regrets. I don't want you to resent me. You mean too much to me for that to happen."

Fred grin broadens into a smile. "I've made my choice, love. And it's going to work out, all right? As long as we're together, everything will be fine. I asked you to be with me before, but I was a coward then. I was a child. I wasn't prepared to make a sacrifice to be with you. But now I am. So I ask you again, Rachel—be with me. For real this time. I'm putting everything I have on the line so I can finally, genuinely promise you forever." Keeping his eyes open, he kisses my lips, quickly and softly. "Be with me."

I'm glad Fred is holding me. I'm dizzy, dizzy with happiness. So much freaking happiness. I get to chase my dreams *and* have my dream guy by my side while I do it. I wonder what I did in my past life to deserve such goodness in this one.

"Yes," I say. "Holy God, *yes*. If only so I can *finally* watch the new season of *Tournament of Kings*."

"Wait," he says. "You haven't watched it either?"

I shake my head. "I couldn't. Didn't feel right to do it without you. I know how much you like your vampire boobs."

He laughs and so do I, and then he kisses me hard and well, so hard I have to hold on to his arms to remain upright. The feel of his lips on mine—it's better than I remembered. It's better because I know I'll get to feel it every day from now on, hopefully for a long time to come.

Behind me, the door opens, and there's a strange cooing noise. Fred and I come up for air, and I stand on my tiptoes to look over his shoulder.

A gorgeous blonde woman—early thirties, I'd say—steps carefully into my apartment. She's got a baby slung on her hip with dark hair and big blue eyes. They both smile at me, a familiar smile that makes their eyes get all squinty.

My stomach flips.

"Sophie!" I breathe. "And Lilli! Oh my God, you came all this way!"

I launch myself into Sophie's arms—well, the one arm she has available—and start crying all over again.

"Rachel! My goodness! How eager we are to meet this lady love of my brother's. Lilli has been impatient all of the day for this moment! So you say yes?"

I laugh. "Of course I said yes! Fred is . . . well, he's the one. Thank you for helping to raise such an excellent human being."

"We do our best," she says, laughing.

Fred looks at me sheepishly. "Thought you might like to meet some of the family, yeah? I hope you don't mind that they're here . . ."

"Not at all," I say. "I couldn't be happier. Or more grateful. Should we all grab dinner together? We have so much to talk about . . ."

"No talking tonight. At least not about anything serious." Fred says, looping an arm around my shoulders. "We're going to celebrate instead. I have a case of beer and some koozies I bought at the petrol station waiting in our suite at the hotel. Perhaps we might grab a bite there, then watch *Tournament*?"

Lilli coos her approval.

I tuck my head into Fred's shoulder. I don't think I'll ever get over how solid he is. How big.

How wonderful.

"Beer and koozies—sounds like the perfect way to our begin happily ever after, no?"

"I've got a thing or two I'd like to add to that list," Fred says, wagging his eyebrows. "But beer and koozies sounds like a brilliant place to start."

EPILOGUE

Fred

December—Four Months Later
Madrid

It's close to nine P.M., but the city is alive and bustling, people high on holiday spirit crowding the sidewalks. Rachel navigates the throngs with ease. I follow her into a wide alley lined with bars and restaurants on either side. A ceiling of white Christmas lights illuminates the people bundled up on the cobblestones below. The air is tinged with the scent of cigarette smoke and roasted garlic.

I take a deep breath, let it out. A smile tugs at my mouth. It's good to be back. I don't miss Spain, not really. What I loved most about it was being there with Rachel. And now that Rachel and I are together pretty much all the time, I don't have occasion to get nostalgic about the years I spent in Madrid.

Still, I'm glad we made the trip. Spain is a beautiful place, especially around the holidays; Madrid is all dolled up with lights and markets, and people seem to be in a jolly mood. I'm also excited to revisit the food. An hour ago, Rachel and

I tucked into a pretty incredible pan of paella. We sampled some shrimp and peppers too, washed down with—what else —a handful of beers.

I give Rachel's gloved hand a squeeze. She looks at me and smiles.

"Happy?" I ask.

"I am," she says. "You?"

I bend down to give her a kiss. "What do you think?" I tease.

"I think we made the right call, doing a quick layover. I'm so excited to see the girls!"

We originally planned a trip to Germany to spend Christmas with my family. But all of Rachel's friends from studying abroad—the Madrileñas—are in Spain, and she's missed them. At the last minute, we decided to pop into Madrid overnight on our way to Munich. Now Rachel gets to catch up with her friends, and I get to see some of the lads from the squad.

I'm a bit nervous, to be honest. I took the world of football by surprise last summer when I transferred from what is arguably the best club in Europe to a team in the States that doesn't even have a stadium yet. William Wallace lost his bloody mind and swore never to forgive or forget. I'm not sure the lads have forgiven me yet either. They're doing well enough without me this season—top of the league tables, as usual—but that doesn't mean they don't hold a grudge.

"This is it," Rachel says, nodding at one of the bigger bars in the middle of the alley. A line of people snakes out of the door and out into the street ahead.

"Holy shit," I say. "I didn't know Javier was so famous. I thought you said this show was a surprise?"

Rachel grins. "It is. I've been under strict instructions from Maddie not to tell a soul. You know his band, The Gods of the Desert, is going on tour, right? Something crazy, thirty or forty cities. They're on the verge of blowing up."

"Judging by this line, they already have."

"Don't worry—Maddie said she'd look out for us so we don't have to wait. Oh—oh, look, there she is!"

Rachel waves at a pretty brunette girl waiting just inside the door. Maddie's face lights up when she sees Rachel. They make a mad dash into each other's arms and start squealing like they haven't seen each other in decades.

"Fred!" she says when they're done hugging and kissing and generally obsessing over each other. Ignoring the dark looks she gets from the people freezing their asses off waiting in line, Maddie yanks me inside the bar and wraps me in a bear hug. "It's so great to see you. How are you? How are things? I hear you're crushing it with the team in Charlotte. Rach told me you're the captain?"

I grin. Is it wrong that I sort of adore being adored by Rachel's friends? I worked hard to win them over after we got back together. I guess I'm doing a bang-up job of it.

"I am," I say. "Never thought I was cut out to lead, but I'm actually enjoying it. Jury's still out if I'm any good at it—"

"That's not true," Rachel cuts in with a smile. "His team-mates freaking *love* him. I mean, how could you not?"

While the squad in Charlotte is still young, and we're still working on bringing in talent to flesh out our roster, we *have* won some big matches this year, and attendance has been growing steadily. I'm enjoying my new leadership role more than I thought I would. Makes me think I'd like to be a manager—or coach as they say here in the States—when I retire as a player.

Maddie beams at us. "Look at you two. You're practically glowing with happiness. They should make a *Lifetime* movie out of your story. Boy meets girl, boy falls in love with girl, boy loses girl but then moves across the world to get her back. Seriously, it's, like, the most romantic thing I've ever heard."

"Being chased by a hot Spanish rockstar—I think that actually might be the most romantic thing *I've* ever heard," Rachel says, winking at Maddie.

Rachel told me the whole story about Maddie and Javier —how Maddie resisted him for a while because she was a mess over her parents' divorce, how he eventually won her over by playing sexy flamenco tunes on his guitar and helping her with her thesis. It sounds a bit dramatic for my taste, but then again, I suppose our story—mine and Rachel's—is a tad dramatic too.

I wouldn't have it any other way.

"So are you going to go on tour with Javier or what?" Rachel asks.

Maddie shrugs, a coy gesture. "Maybe. I finished my thesis, but I'm already thinking about doing another one for grad school. If I go with Javier, I'll get to study architecture all over Europe. How cool would that be?"

"Very cool. We might have to crash your party," I say, glancing at Rachel. "What do you think—should we go see Javier and his band play in Barcelona? Paris?"

Rachel bites her lip. "Yes and *hell* yes."

Maddie grabs both our hands and bounces on her toes. "I was hoping you'd come visit. C'mon, let's grab a spot by the stage. It's going to be a mob scene in a bit here."

"Rachel said this show was supposed to be a surprise," I say as we move toward the stage.

"Yeah," Maddie says over her shoulder. "But Javier's lead guitarist—this guy Leo, he's really great, but . . . ugh, kind of a mess too. Anyway, he was trying to impress this girl, so he posts an Instagram about the show tonight, thinking she's the only one who could see it. The post ends up going viral, and —well—here we are." She gestures to the crowd around us.

My heart skips a beat when a small knot of people just to the left of the stage comes into view. I recognize Rhys Maddox's white hat right away. Olivier Seydoux, the team captain of my former squad, stands next to him, sipping what can only be top shelf vodka.

It's Rachel's turn to give my hand a squeeze.

"You're going to be fine," she says. "Trust me, Rhys is way too into Laura these days to care about your football career. No offense."

I hold up my hands, my grin deepening. "None taken."

We run into Rachel's friend Vivian, and her boyfriend, Rafa, before we get to the stage. Rachel and I both freak out because Viv just landed a job working on the Spanish set of *Tournament of Kings* (it's filmed in several locations around Europe, most notably Iceland, Northern Ireland, and Spain).

"Is the actor who plays Prince Jacoby really a prick in real life?" Rachel asks.

"How awkward are the naked scenes to film?" I smart at a pointed glance Rachel shoots me. "I'm, um. Asking for a friend, clearly."

Vivian laughs. "The guy who plays Jacoby is actually a nice guy. A bit of a diva, but very nice. And I haven't been in the room when—um—you know, the naked stuff happens. But I imagine it is pretty awkward."

"We're obsessed with that show," I say.

"I can tell," she says.

Rachel nods at Rafa. "I bet you're thrilled Viv got this job. Probably means she's sticking around Spain for a while."

"That's the plan." Rafa grins at Viv. "I'd love to keep her here forever . . ."

"Don't worry, love, I have no plans to leave," Viv says, grinning back.

Never mind making a *Lifetime* movie out of my story. I feel like I'm in a Lifetime movie right now. All of Rachel's friends are so in love. Like, alarmingly in love. If I didn't know any better, I'd think they were all drugged.

Is that what people see when they look at Rachel and me? Genuine, sickening, joyful happiness? Because, honestly, that's the sort of happiness I feel when I'm with her.

I take a deep breath, and together Rachel and I head for the lads. Relief washes through me when Rhys smiles and holds out his arm, the other draped around Laura's shoulders. We weren't sure if the two of them would make it—Rhys has always struggled with demons from his past—but tonight, they look just as blissed out as everyone else. Rhys was photographed coming out of a jeweler's shop on his last visit to London. I heard a rumor he has plans to propose after the holidays.

"Cabbage!" I say, taking his hand. I know he hates that nickname, but I can't resist.

"Look at this, an American soccer star, come back to say hello to his old squad!" He tugs me into a hug. "How the hell have you been? We miss you, you know."

I glance at Olivier. "You do?"

"You 'ave no idea, how much we missez our awkward German friend," Olivier replies, and then he hugs me too. "Iz there any chances, any chance at all, zat we could lure you back to Spain? Surely this squad in America, it iz good, but not as good as our squad 'ere? I work somezing out for you. And ze squad, we very much regrets not giving Rachel ze internship she wanted. Perhaps we get it for her zis time, non?"

Rachel and I exchange a glance. A beat passes between us.

Then we both break out into shy smiles.

"We appreciate your offer," I say.

"Really, we do," Rachel adds. "But I'm already set up with a sweet internship back at Meryton. I'm applying to grad schools in the States too . . ."

"And I'm excited about starting a new chapter," I say. "I love my new squad. I love the role I'm playing. I'm learning a lot—learning about management, about building a team. Learning about myself."

"Ah." Olivier's eyes cut to Rachel. A knowing grin plays at his lips. "Your life together, it make you both very 'appy."

"Exactly," I say. "I'm happy."

"Me too," Rachel says.

"And it's nice to be happy," I reply.

Rachel looks at me. "It really is."

Rhys and Laura nod, like they know exactly what we're talking about.

"All zis love," Olivier says, shaking his head with a sigh. "It make my 'eart burst. Lovers, let zem love!"

The crowd erupts in cheers as the band takes the stage. I recognize Javier, tall and scruffy in a hipster-rock-star way. I pick out the kind-of-a-mess guitarist. Not twelve seconds on stage and he's already winking at a girl in the front row, tossing his guitar pick in her general direction.

Javier says a few words—words mostly about his "lovely girlfriend Maddie"—and then The Gods of the Desert launch into the catchy single that's catapulting them into stardom. The bar goes nuts.

So do we.

Rachel and I are both terrible dancers—we discovered that fact not long after I moved to North Carolina at one of Rachel's formals—but that's never stopped us before. We start dancing like the awkward people we are, not caring a fig what anyone else thinks.

On stage, Leo thrusts his hips. Some of the girls up front step back, just a little. I feel the thump of the beat in the floor, in my breastbone.

Rachel shimmies her hips against me. I grin, and try to shimmy back. Only I end up knocking her to the side because my shimmies are more like lethal boomerangs. I grab her by the arm, just before she launches headfirst into the speakers.

For a moment I'm worried I hurt her. But then she starts laughing, laughing so hard tears leak out of her eyes. It's contagious, her laugh, and I start laughing too, my ribs aching as I curl her body into mine. God, she smells good.

She smells familiar.

She smells like home.

Thank you so much for reading the STUDY ABROAD series! **In the mood for more sexy Europeans? Be sure to check out my bestselling Thorne Monarchs Series. I kick off the series with ROYAL RUIN, a second chance, fake relationship romance. Turn the page for an exclusive excerpt!**

ROYAL RUIN EXCERPT

Prince Kit

"Nice place," Emily said, glancing at the room around us.

"Nice dress," I said.

Her mouth twitched. "Thank you."

I ordered a bottle of Château Lafite Rothschild and waited until we were through our first glass to start feeling Emily out.

"So tell me about you," I said. "What you've been up to since university."

Emily tilted her head and peered at me from the corner of her eye. "Why do I get the feeling I'm being interviewed again?"

I'd forgotten how smart she was. Of course she'd see through this whole charade.

Still. I wasn't ready to show her my cards just yet.

"You're not." I cleared my throat for the hundredth time. "It's just been a while, that's all. I read your résumé and went through your portfolio. Incredible work. You started your own firm?"

She looked at me for another beat. Then she leaned forward and settled her forearms on the table. She slid the stem of her glass between her first and middle fingers, giving it a quick twirl. I got the feeling she didn't want to talk about her business. Why? She'd been so excited about it in class. So hungry for the chance to get out in the world and *do* something.

Emily sighed. "I did. I started it right after I graduated, as a matter of fact. Well, I started with a blog, really. And as luck would have it, 2007 turned out to be the beginning of a golden age for blogging. I got small projects at first. You know, readers hiring me to give their apartments some personality. But I worked hard to get my name out there—"

"Using the marketing strategies you learned in my class, obviously."

"Obviously," she said, the edges of her mouth curling upward. "And a few years later, business started to boom. I hired my first assistant, Aly. We got so busy I had to hire three more. Running your own business is hard, don't get me wrong. But I loved every minute of it."

I sipped my wine, meeting Emily's eyes. "You said 'loved'—past tense."

She shifted in her seat, clearly uncomfortable. The weariness I'd seen in her eyes earlier was back. No, it wasn't weariness—it was sadness.

It was a broken heart.

"My husband and I got divorced last year. Because we were married when I'd started EP Designs, he owned a fifty percent stake in the business."

I already saw where this was going. "That's a shit rule."

"No kidding. But it's the law, so..." Emily took a big gulp of wine. "Anyway. I tried to buy him out of his fifty percent— buy back his stake in the business. Luke wanted more, though."

My heart throbbed, once, sending an almost audible rush of blood through my skin. "Is this the same Luke—"

"Yes." She nodded, falling back into the booth. "He said he wouldn't sell me his stake for less than one hundred and fifty percent of its value. Which of course was just the amount that would put us, as a business, on life support. But I had no choice. I wanted Luke out of the picture for good. So I paid his price. It broke me, and he knew it. He wanted EP Designs to limp and die a slow, painful death. And that is exactly what's happened."

I set down my glass and looked at her. I felt terribly for her. I did, truly. But that didn't stop the triumph from blooming inside my chest.

I'd just found out how to get Emily to agree to my insane proposition. Knowing I'd help revive the firm she clearly loved also made me feel like slightly less of a dickwad for what I was about to ask. I wanted Emily to find success. She deserved it.

"EP Designs is going bankrupt?" I asked carefully.

"Yes, unfortunately." She nodded again, blinking hard. "This trip is our last hurrah before our doors close for good. I tried everything I could to dig us out of the hole Luke put us in, but..." Her eyes flicked to meet mine. "It wasn't enough."

The waiter returned. I ordered some oysters and another bottle of wine.

"I'm curious," I said when he left. "What would you need to get EP Designs back on its feet?"

Emily puckered her lips to the side side, shrugging. She looked down at her wine. "Right now? Probably close to two hundred grand. Something ridiculous like that."

"Done."

Her gaze darted to my face. "What?"

"I said it's done." I dabbed at my mouth with my napkin. "I'll give you the two hundred k, plus the School for the Arts commission."

Emily was staring at me like I'd just told her I was pregnant.

"That's not very funny, Kit."

I put my hands on the table. "I wasn't joking, Emily."

Her lips moved, like she was practicing what she was about to say in her head.

"So you're just...you're just going to swoop in and save my company. Just like that." She snapped her fingers.

"That's what I hope to do, yes."

I watched the long, elegant lines of her throat move as she swallowed. "What do you want in return?"

"I want you to marry me."

Emily's eyes bulged. "You're still not joking, are you?"

"Not in the slightest."

"Oh my God," she replied. She reached for her glass and drained it. Her cheeks had gone a vibrant shade of pink. "But...Jesus, where do I even start? I'm not princess material. I'm divorced. I have a job. Princesses don't have jobs, Kit. How can you give me money so I can keep my business open—"

"We're not talking about a real marriage, of course," I said. That seemed to relax her. I leaned in and lowered my voice. "This engagement would be fake. A show. My family is in a bit of a bind. I don't know if you've seen the headlines about my sister—"

"I've seen them."

"So you know that Jane's behavior is turning public opinion against us. And public opinion matters because it's where we get our power, Emily. Our influence. My parents taught me to use that power and influence for good. I'd like to think I've done a lot of good over the years."

"You have," Emily said quietly. "Everyone I know loves you. Although that could have something to do with...well..." She shook her palm in my general direction.

I smirked. "With what?"

She smirked right back. "Your personality, of course."

She was doing it again. Talking to me like I was a friend, not a future monarch. I felt my lips pulling into a grin.

"My personality? But I haven't got one of those," I teased. "At least according to the press. They call me the Ice Prince."

Emily's smirk faded. "It's your eyes. I noticed they can be a little...cold sometimes. Closed off."

Of course she'd noticed. But I wasn't here to have that conversation. I was here to convince Emily Kilpatrick to be my fake fiancée.

Focus. I was focusing on the right thing.

So far, so good.

"We need a distraction. Something that will get us back in the public's good graces so we can keep doing our work. We've learned from experience that a royal engagement does just the trick."

Emily blinked. "That still doesn't answer my question about having a job and being divorced. I'd make a terrible princess."

"You're looking at those things as weaknesses, Emily, when really they're your strengths in this situation. So you work. You have a past. You're lovely, but you're not perfect. People can relate to that. And that's exactly what we need—someone relatable and down to earth."

Emily studied my face. "How are people supposed to feel about you, then?"

The waiter arrived with our wine. The air between Emily and I tightened as we watched him uncork the bottle and sample it. He seemed to be moving especially slow this evening. At last—thank Jesus—he left us alone.

I dove right back in. "What do you mean?"

"You seem to be pretty damn near perfect," she replied. "Perfect, hardworking prince. Perfect brother. Perfect heir."

I looked down as I swirled the wine in my glass. "Believe me, I'm far from it." I took a sip. "As to your question about the job situation—you are correct. If you and I were actually going to get married, you would need to give up your career. There's not enough hours in the day to work a civilian job while also fulfilling your duties as a member of the royal family. People have tried to do both. But in the end, you'd need to be one-hundred-percent committed to the monarchy for this family to function and maintain our ability to do good work. We're a fighting force, Emily. It's all hands on deck, all the time."

Emily nodded thoughtfully. "I get it. I could never give up my career, but I get why someone would do it." She looked at me. "I can't imagine what the pressure must be like."

"You get used to it," I replied. Another rote answer. Another half-lie.

"Do you ever get scared you'll fuck it up? Not to imply you ever would. But sounds like you walk a thin line."

I met her eyes. *All the time*, I wanted to say. I was scared out of my mind all the time I'd fuck up. I was up on a pedestal, all by myself. I dealt with competing objectives every day. Put on a smile while doing important but often tedious, dull work. Make my siblings happy while keeping them in line. Always put the prince above the person.

One wrong step, and the whole house of cards could tumble down.

"It is difficult," I said. What a rubbish reply. But opening up to Emily—telling her how I really felt—seemed like a dangerous precedence to set. "So. What do you say? Will you play the part?"

Emily stared at me. "I don't get any time to think it over?"

"You'll get time if you want it." I folded my napkin and set it back down on my lap. "But you know this is a good trade for you. Three months in exchange for your entire future. I'll be by your side every step of the way. I'll do everything in my power to protect you. I'll make it worth your while, Emily. I promise."

Her eyes, darker now, narrowed. I'd forgotten just how lovely she looked when she was thinking. It'd been an admittedly bold move to imply she already had her answer. But I knew Emily. At least I'd known her a while ago. Some things about her had changed. But that ambitious streak of hers—the one I'd known so well—I was betting that hadn't.

Emily put a hand to her neck. "Will I have to live with you?"

"Yes." She winced. "I know. It's weird. But Primrose Palace is a fortress. You'll be safe there. Part of the contract—"

"There's a contract?"

"Of course. That way you know what to expect. I'll email it to you when we're done with dinner. Even if you verbally agree tonight, you won't be legally bound to anything until you sign the contract. Fair enough?"

After a beat, Emily tipped her head. "Fair enough."

"Is that a yes?"

Another beat passed. Then another. For half a second I worried I'd made a mistake. Maybe she'd burst into laughter and tell me to stick my inane proposal up my ass.

I didn't want to do this any more than she did. But we both had our reasons. Good reasons. Reasons that mattered.

"It is." She nodded. "Yes. Subject to review of the contract, I'll be your pretend princess."

I nearly choked on my mine. Holy *fuck*. This was actually happening.

I put the glass down. "Brilliant. Thank you."

Was that relief I felt? Or anxiety? You'd think I'd be able to tell, considering the two were complete opposites.

"When do we start?" Emily asked.

Swallowing the thump of my heart, I reached across the table and covered her hand with mine.

"Right now."

Read the rest of Kit + Emily's story here, or wherever books are sold!

THANK YOU

Thank you very much for reading LESSONS IN LOSING IT! I hope you laughed, you cried, you got turned on by the sassy bits. If you got *especially* turned on, please consider leaving a review. Reviews help readers find new authors like me, and every little bit helps. Don't forget to help spread the word by telling your friends about Fred and Rachel.

Be sure to check out my bestselling Thorne Monarchs Series next!

I'd love to stay in touch—here are a few ways to reach me:

- Check out Jessica Peterson's City Girls, my reader group on Facebook
- Follow my not-so-glamorous life as a romance author on Instagram @JessicaPAuthor
- Follow me on Goodreads
- Follow me on Bookbub
- Like my Facebook Author Page

- Drop me a line at
  jessicapauthor@jessicapeterson.com

DEAR READER

Dear Reader,

Thank you very much for reading LESSONS IN LOSING IT. This book almost killed me to write—it's pretty much my MO these days to rewrite all of my books a couple of times before they're ready to be published—but I am very, very proud of the end result, and I sincerely hoped you enjoyed reading Fred and Rachel's story.

I didn't set out to write a book that explores the choice between chasing love and chasing your dreams, but I'm glad LESSONS IN LOSING IT turned out that way. I think it's a great conflict, and a common one, especially with people moving all over the globe these days to go to school, to work, or just to travel and experience the world. I also liked exploring the idea of destiny. There's something incredibly romantic about believing such a thing exists—believing we are destined to end up somewhere or with some*one*. That love is pre-ordained and it just happens to us, without our help.

But what if love isn't so easy? What if we need to be active participants in making that love last? I've always been a big believer in the power of action—I'd like to think we have significant control over where we end up in life. But I'm also a romantic (obviously—I write romance for a living), and I love the idea that some things are truly *meant* to be.

I knew I'd hit on something good when the conflict between these ideas started to swirl in my head as I wrote. I kept writing and rewriting the black moment, digging deeper, wondering how I could work one last sex scene in (sex scenes are, after all, my favorite to write). I honestly didn't know which side of the fence I'd end up on—is love meant to be or *made* to be—but I'm happy with how the book ended. I mean, Fred may be an even bigger romantic than I am, but ultimately he was the one who made his happily ever after happen. Not fate. Not destiny. Just holy-hell-amazing-in-bed, squinty-eyed Fred. I hope you enjoyed the ending as much as I did!

This is the fourth and final book in my STUDY ABROAD series. It's bittersweet to end it here. I loved revisiting my own study abroad days in Madrid, and I've learned so much in the past year about craft, about the business side of books, and about myself. I'm not sure where I'll go next—maybe a spinoff series set in London with Kit the Prince and Emily—but wherever I end up, I hope you'll follow me there. Thanks again for reading my books—knowing you enjoy them brings me some pretty major joy. Take care, and happy reading!

XO,
  Jessica

ALSO BY JESSICA PETERSON

ABOUT THE AUTHOR

Jessica Peterson writes romance with heat, humor, and heart. Heroes with hot accents are her specialty. When she's not writing, she can be found bellying up to a bar in the south's best restaurants with her husband Ben, reading books with her adorable daughter Gracie, or snuggling up with her 70-pound lap dog, Martha.

A Carolina girl at heart, she fantasizes about splitting her time between Charleston and Asheville, but currently lives in Charlotte, NC. You can check out her books at www.jessicapeterson.com.